THE
PING-PONG
QUEEN OF
CHINATOWN

ALSO BY ANDREW YANG
I'm Not Here to Make Friends

THE
PING-PONG
QUEEN OF
CHINATOWN

ANDREW YANG

Quill Tree Books
An Imprint of HarperCollinsPublishers

Quill Tree Books is an imprint of HarperCollins Publishers.

The Ping-Pong Queen of Chinatown
Copyright © 2024 by Andrew Yang
All rights reserved. Printed in the United States of America.
No part of this book may be used or reproduced in any manner
whatsoever without written permission except in the case of
brief quotations embodied in critical articles and reviews. For
information address HarperCollins Children's Books, a division of
HarperCollins Publishers, 195 Broadway, New York, NY 10007.
www.harpercollinschildrens.com

Library of Congress Control Number: 2023944259
ISBN 978-0-06-334041-1

Typography by Kathy H. Lam
24 25 26 27 28 LBC 5 4 3 2 1
First Edition

FOR MY PARENTS

PART ONE

ONE

"YOU AGAIN?"

Even though I'm in the middle of an absolutely epic run on Pyramid Chase—literal seconds away from hitting my high score, with enough power-ups and saves in the bank to easily blow past it—my head snaps up by instinct. Because of my locked-in, LeBron-like focus on my game, it takes me a second to recognize the girl who's leaning over me, staring daggers into my eyes.

"Pardon?" I mutter weakly.

"It *is* you. I recognize you for sure now, so don't act like you forgot. You're Felix Ma. You even have the same glasses you had back then."

She's right, of course. Even though it's been three years since we've last seen each other, and I've grown three inches and started dressing in *much* cooler clothes since then, I'm still wearing the same glasses. Shout-out to my mom, who upon buying me this pair of glasses (my first) told me that I had to "make them count," then canceled our cable subscription, changed the passwords on our streaming accounts, and now makes me spend fifteen minutes per day wearing medicinal eye patches that are supposed to nourish my retinas.

"And you're Cassie Chow," I mumble back. "Nice to see you again too."

I glance back down at my phone and see that I have died. The zone I got into will go down in history as one of the great what-ifs, like the 2016 Warriors blowing a 3–1 lead. Now that I'm no longer absorbed in the game, the chaos of our surroundings rushes back into my senses. The bouncing Ping-Pong balls, the squeak of rubber soles on vinyl, the shouts in English, Cantonese, Mandarin, and Fujianese.

Cassie grins. "I knew you'd remember me. I guess losing in piano wasn't enough for you. Now you've come to get beaten in Ping-Pong too?"

Cassie is referring to the Rubenstein Center piano competition, where she finished first, and I finished second. I remember our awkward handshake on the podium, the commemorative photo we took together that still hangs in the lobby. And now I'm remembering that she's a big trash- talker.

"You don't know that you can beat me," I shoot back, my voice cracking a little. "Who's your coach, anyway? Is he a former Olympian, like Coach Fang?"

Cassie looks down at me contemptuously. "I don't care if your coach won every gold medal in table tennis for the last thirty years. When you're playing against me, he won't be in there to save you.

And I know you, Felix Ma. I know you can't handle the pressure."

She winks at me, then whirls around and strides away, leaving me sitting speechless in my chair.

Good going, Felix. You could have at least stood up to her, I think to myself. Although, as she walks away, I realize that she's very tall, possibly taller than I am. It would have been worse to stand up straight and still have her look down at me.

The truth is, she probably *can* beat me at Ping-Pong. While I was actually quite the prodigy in piano—Cassie got totally lucky to win at Rubenstein, where I may or may not have choked on my sonata—I'm not even the best Ping-Pong player at the Flushing Community Center. That would be Dan Piao, who spent the last two summers training at an über-intense sports academy in Shanghai.

I used to be almost on the same level as he is, but my skills have seriously declined ever since I quit playing on the national circuit. Even at a casual tournament like this, there should be plenty of kids who are better than I am.

On a hunch, I check the bracket posted on the wall. Sure enough, my first match is against Cassie. She must have seen it, recognized my name, and then come up to me to get in my head. Great. And all I wanted was to make it to the second round.

My phone buzzes.

What time should I pick you up again?

It's my mom. Now that we've moved out of Flushing and into the suburbs, she uses my Chinese-school days to do her grocery shopping, go to her favorite beauty salon, and catch up with the other moms over tea and dim sum.

> Depends when I get eliminated
>
> 3 pm at the latest
>
> I'll keep you posted

With my match against Cassie looming, I'm too nervous to sit still and play Pyramid Chase. I ask Coach Fang to hit with me so I can warm up.

"You okay? Look tense. You need to go to bathroom?"

I shake my head. "I'm fine."

Coach Fang slaps me on the back, and I flinch. "Shape up! This is a competition!"

I've always felt that for Coach Fang, the Cold War never ended. He still yells instructions and doles out criticism like Ping-Pong isn't just a game, but rather a metaphor for the struggle between ideologies, between Eastern and Western civilization.

We start to hit, first forehand, then backhand, and the rhythm of our exchange helps settle my nerves. *I've got this.* I may not be as good as Dan Piao, but I'm no slouch. Unless Cassie Chow is a Ping-Pong god, I should be able to hold my own.

"Remember, Felix, lěng jìng. Even if you are losing, stick to fundamentals! Don't get fancy. Consistency always wins!" Coach Fang reminds me.

"Yes, Coach," I say.

When my match with Cassie is announced, I shuffle to the assigned table and unzip my game paddle from my case. Across the table, Cassie smirks at me. But right away, I notice the glaring red flags with her setup. First of all, she's using some off-brand paddle, with thin, flimsy rubber that's starting to peel at the edges. It looks like a rec center paddle, the kind that comes in a pack of three at Target. It can't compare to my beautiful Stiga Pro Carbon, with its microscopic sub-surface air capsules and custom anti-spin rubber. Second of all, her grip is all wrong. Never mind that she doesn't use a penhold; she doesn't even have her index finger on the back of the paddle for a normal shakehand. Instead, she's gripping the handle all fist, like she's holding an ice-cream cone, like she's playing tennis. Has she even played Ping-Pong before? Or is this some kind of hustle, meant to make me let my guard down?

"Do your worst, Felix!" she mouths at me as I crouch down for my serve. She raises an eyebrow provocatively. God, I better not lose to her after all this.

But very quickly, I can tell that she's overmatched. She practically lobs my first serve back to me, and I easily smash it for the opening point. During the second point, I play a forehand with lots of topspin, and she doesn't even try to counterspin. When she hits the ball back, it dives straight down, landing well short of the net. Easy.

I take the first game, 11–5. In the second, I get into a zone with my serve and win even more convincingly, 11–3.

"Feeling the pressure?" I ask as the third game is about to start.

Cassie raises an eyebrow. "Pressure? There's no pressure. You're supposed to win now. All the pressure's on you."

At the beginning of the third game, I serve the ball into the net. This is something I used to do very often, and although I've mostly practiced it out of my system, it does still happen occasionally. Nothing to worry about.

Until it happens again.

Now I've given her a 2–0 lead. Cassie smirks—clearly she thinks the trash talk is getting to me. I take a deep breath, try to relax. I dominated the first two games. Coming back should be no problem.

But I'm still struggling to find my serve again. It's kind of like tying shoelaces—usually it comes naturally to me, but every once in a while I suddenly have to focus very hard to get it right. Meanwhile, Cassie starts playing better too. She gets aggressive, hitting hard shots toward the corners of the table. Sometimes she misses altogether, but she lands enough of them to cling to a thin lead for the entire game and take it, 11–9.

In the fourth game, I manage to find some footing. My serve is coming back to me, and I'm targeting her forehand, which I finally notice is weaker than her backhand. At 4–1, I'm feeling good. The third game was just a brief hiccup. I've got this.

That's when Cassie goes on a run.

Those fast, wild shots from the third game are back, only this time, she can't miss. Even as I spray the ball to different areas, trying to throw her off her rhythm, she keeps coming back at me with powerful smashes that paint the edges of the table. When I put in some spin to try to slow her down, she reads it just well enough to counter, or hits the ball so hard that her shots still clear the net. By the time she gets to 10–7, I'm starting to feel sick.

It's my serve, game point. I put the ball to the far left side of the table, targeting her forehand. Cassie lunges and mishits it, sending it sailing high into the air. A sure miss. I relax and watch the ball's trajectory. Only after it comes out of its apex, and starts hurtling back down to the earth, do I realize with horror what's about to happen.

The ball hits off the edge of the table and bounces completely sideways. A miracle shot.

We're tied at two games apiece.

I'm really about to blow a two-game lead against a girl who doesn't even hold the paddle right. Who trash-talked me and told me that I can't handle the pressure. The same girl who beat me at the piano competition three years ago.

Even Coach Fang seems resigned. "She play good. You just stay tight. Give your best effort. One point at a time."

In the third game, it's all I can do just to stave off a nervous breakdown. I go into each point terrified of what Cassie is going to do. There's something magical about her game, some combination of boldness, brashness, and sheer force of will that seems to defy the logic of unequal skill. I can't help but be impressed—I've watched enough sports to recognize a winner when I see one.

But somehow, things finally start breaking my way. I heat up a little bit and play my way out to a 5–3 lead. Then Cassie's invincibility star wears off, and she starts missing smashes. Late in the game, she tries to mount a comeback, abandoning technique and throwing herself wildly around the table to play back my shots, but it's not enough. I take the game and the match. I don't feel like a winner so much as a survivor.

After the match, we shake hands.

"Good game," I say.

"Yeah, you too." Cassie flashes a devilish grin. "I almost had you there, didn't I? I thought I was going to win. You managed to hold it together, though, Felix. Didn't know you had it in you!"

"You too. The fact that you were able to figure out how to win points off me, even with your—well, anyways, you played a good game."

Cassie glares at me. "I know what you were about to say. 'Even with your janky paddle and your weird grip.' A backhanded compliment. Admit it!"

Cassie is absolutely right, and I have to fight to keep from smiling. "No, I'm serious! I was genuinely impressed."

"Yeah, yeah. Just remember, Felix. At my house, in a frame on my wall, is the document certifying that I, Cassandra Chow, won first place at the Rubenstein piano competition. Me, not you." She winks. "And no one can ever take that away from me."

I chuckle. I should have known that she wouldn't stop talking trash just because I beat her.

"Anyways, you got your revenge. I play the saxophone now, so my glory days on the keys are over." She points to the saxophone case on the chair behind her. "I have rehearsal later today, so in a way you did me a favor. Now I have plenty of time to get over there."

"You keep telling yourself that, Cassie."

"Whatever. Enjoy your win, Felix. It was nice bumping into you again. I'll see you around."

She turns and whisks herself away, leaving me dazed by how quickly, how strangely, our latest encounter has unfolded. I haven't thought about Cassie in years. She's gotten taller, but she still has the same impudent quality about her. It's amazing how effortless these competitions seem to be for her—the opposite of me. I wonder what she's up to now. One thing is for sure: it's been a long time since I had so much fun playing Ping-Pong.

I end up making it into the semifinals, where I play Dan Piao. We know each other's games so well that our match feels like just another practice; as usual, he beats me, although I manage to take one game off of him. With that, my day is over. I text my mom.

Okay I'm done

I consider staying to watch the final, but it's getting late, and I want to make it back home in time to watch football. I find a seat away from the noise and the cheering and whip out my phone for another round of Pyramid Chase. That's when I see it.

On the floor under one of the fold-out chairs is a white folder with a picture of a saxophone on it. Written across the bottom, in florid cursive, is the name Cassandra Chow.

I pick it up and flip it open. Inside are a few pages of sheet music. Across the folder flaps are pasted a series of sticky notes, covered in doodles of chubby cartoon animals with captions like *My little dumpling* and *The ultimate fuzzball!*; there are some games of tic-tac-toe too, all stalemates. These sticky notes are oddly intimate in a way that makes me uncomfortable, so I quickly shut the folder.

I cast a glance back toward the Ping-Pong tournament, but I know Cassie is already gone. I could easily put the folder back under the chair and walk away, put her out of my mind forever.

But I don't.

When my mom arrives, I slip the folder into my bag along with my paddle and my Chinese textbook. I get into the car, she asks how the tournament went, and I tell her that I lost to Dan Piao, as expected. I don't mention Cassie. We drive out of the city, the rows of apartment buildings melt away into the trees, and we head farther and farther into Long Island, toward home.

TWO

YOU COULD SAY THAT CASSIE CHOW AND I HAVE
a history of chance encounters. The first one was the Rubenstein
piano competition.

The funny thing about the competition was that I almost
didn't go. I was nearing the end of a tumultuous career on the
piano bench, and for months I'd been needling my mom to let
me quit. It wasn't that I hated playing, I just didn't want to keep
taking lessons, or have to practice every week knowing that my
teacher would yell at me if I didn't. So my mom and I made a deal.
I'd enter Rubenstein, and if I made it to the final round, she'd
let me retire, go out on top. I think she was hoping that all the
practice for the competition, plus the thrill of victory, would make
me fall in love with the instrument again. Ironically, the chance of
quitting *did* make me practice harder than I ever had before, and
in the first round, I completely nailed my concerto; I'm talking
standing ovation, perfect score from the judges. Before the final
round, as I sat in the waiting area with the other finalists, I noticed

that the girl sitting next to me kept giving me dirty looks. I tried to ignore her, but then she accidentally-on-purpose elbowed me.

"Can I help you?" I asked.

She smiled innocently. "Why yes, you can. You can mess up your sonata so I can beat you. Not the whole thing, mind you, maybe just the very beginning and the very end, and once or twice in the middle. What do you say?"

Needless to say, she got her wish. I was flustered, and I did mess up, just like she asked me to. During the awards ceremony, when she got first place and I got runner-up, she had the nerve to shake my hand, smile at me, and say, "Good job, Felix."

Just a couple of weeks later, my parents wanted to go to the Met museum to see a special exhibition with treasures from a Han Dynasty imperial tomb. I didn't want to go—at that age, museums were tied with dental cleanings as my least favorite weekend activity—but my parents bribed me with the promise of post-art cheeseburgers.

As we were going into the exhibit, we saw Cassie, coming out of it alone. Our eyes met, and she smiled at me. By instinct, I smiled back. Then she pointed at me, gave me a cheeky wink, and held up two fingers. At first I thought she was making a peace sign. By the time I realized that she was taunting me for finishing in second place, she was gone. I soothed myself with the knowledge that I got to quit, while she was probably still click-clacking away, sucker that she was.

The third, of course, was the Ping-Pong tournament. And now, as I look at Cassie's social media profile, I see a fourth crossing of our stars that almost came to be.

Before my freshman year of high school, my family moved out of Flushing and into the Long Island suburbs. But before the move was final, I applied to some city schools and got into Van Der Donck, in Tribeca. In Cassie's bio, I see that she's there now. We almost went to the same high school. Funny how life works.

I send her a follow request, then try to busy myself with homework and readings. After a few minutes, there's a knock on the door. It's my dad, reminding me that I have a video call with Mr. Qin in ten minutes.

"Yeah, got it. Thanks, Dad," I say.

"Make sure to listen carefully to what he says. Mr. Qin knows a lot. If you have a positive attitude about the call, you'll get a lot out of it."

"Yup. Positive attitude. I got you, Dad."

Mr. Qin is the college admissions coach that my parents hired for me near the end of my sophomore year. Now that I'm starting off my junior year, he's having me write my essays. Today I'm supposed to get his feedback on my first draft.

When we connect on the call, Mr. Qin's face takes up the whole screen, like he's trying to peer through the lens to see if a tiny Felix is stuck inside the camera. I can practically count his nose hairs.

"Hey, Mr. Qin. Can you see me?" I say politely, trying not to laugh.

"Oh hey, Felix. Yup, there you are. So how are things going?

How are your mother and father doing?"

Behind Mr. Qin on the wall are a Harvard pennant and an NYU pennant, and below them, the Harvard College and NYU Law degrees to match. I can't blame him for including his credentials in the video frame—those flags are catnip to people like my parents, and they probably get a lot of clients to hire him on the spot—but there's something garish about it. I always thought that people who went to fancy colleges said things like, "I went to school near Boston," to show that they're too classy to name-drop.

"Listen, Felix. I read the first draft of your essay. It was a nice essay, had some good sentences. A solid first attempt."

I can feel Mr. Qin winding up for the but. To be fair to Mr. Qin, he seems like a cheerful, friendly guy. But he has a way of talking to me about my college apps that makes him sound like a sports fan, yelling at his hapless team on the TV, as it once again chokes away a huge fourth-quarter lead. Every statement carries in it the whiff of a question, and the question is, 'What the hell is wrong with you?"

"The thing is, Felix, the topic you choose for your essay is very important. You have to remember that this essay is your *personal* statement. If you were to die today, God forbid, this essay should be the thing you'd want written on your tombstone. Now, I think your passion for this subject comes through very clearly. But Felix, you just can't write your college essay about Jeremy Lin."

I was expecting this. I knew it was pointless to try to convince Mr. Qin about the cultural and moral significance of Jeremy

Lin, aka Linsansity, aka Super Lintendo, aka the greatest male Chinese-American athlete of all time. Maybe if I'd thought things through, I would have picked another topic. But I had my reasons.

"He saved our season, and he brought hope back to a legendary franchise," I protest. "He showed a whole generation of kids that anything is possible. That the hero of the story can be someone who looks like him. Also, I think that the statistical analysis that I put together showing why he's been systematically underrated by sports writers and pundits demonstrates my intellectual curiosity and analytical—"

"Felix, do you even play basketball?" Mr. Qin cuts in.

"I play," I say quickly, feeling a little offended. "I used to play one-on-one all the time back when we lived in Flushing. Besides, what does that have to do with it?"

"Think about it from the perspective of an admissions officer. You're the twelfth Asian kid in a row with good grades and solid extracurriculars. How are you going to stand out? Maybe if Jeremy Lin had inspired you to play basketball, and you'd won the state championship, then you'd have something. But otherwise, all you're showing the officer is that you like to watch sports. Reject!"

Whenever Mr. Qin asks me to think from the perspective of an admissions officer, I end up feeling inadequate. There's nothing like pouring your heart into an essay designed to make you sound talented and unique to remind you that you're nothing special after all.

"Anyways, this was a good warm-up," Mr. Qin goes on,

suddenly cheerful again. "Your first couple essays are bound to be bad. This is just an exercise to get your engines going. What you really need to figure out is this—what is something that we can build a story around? To make yourself seem passionate on your college app, it's going to take three things. First, you have to pick something original. The weirder the better. For example, I had a student last year who was big into crossword puzzles. Did the *New York Times* crossword every single day.

"Once you've got that picked out, the next thing you need is some kind of achievement. Ideally you'd win an award, or a contest. Something concrete to put on your résumé. That'll show how serious you are about it. The crossword kid? Got a crossword published in the *Los Angeles Times*. No kidding. You'd be surprised how easy it is to do that, by the way. Doesn't matter. Point is, it sounds impressive.

"The last thing you need is the cherry on top. The little bit of tugging on the heartstrings that'll tie it all together. Let's go back to the crossword kid. That crossword in the *LA Times*? Turns out one of the clues had some personal significance. Oh? What was it? Read the essay. Twenty-three across, 'Bollywood star Shah Rukh _____.' Answer is Khan. And who's Khan? That's the last name of the kid's grandfather. Who loves crosswords, by the way, and lives in a nursing home because of his dementia. Yeah, that's right. That crossword? Tribute to the grandfather. Hello!? All of a sudden, that kid isn't just some Asian with a good SAT score anymore. That kid is the crossword kid who loves Grandpa. If I'm an admissions officer, that's all I need to hear. Welcome to Harvard. As a matter of fact, take a scholarship. Here's a hoodie and a free pen."

Mr. Qin is so worked up that I half expect him to start pounding the table with his fist. He makes it sound so easy too. My problem is, my grandfather is perfectly healthy. And instead of crossword puzzles, I like to watch old highlights of Jeremy Lin shredding the Toronto Raptors. I don't think there's an award for that.

Mr. Qin gives me a homework assignment, which is to think about all of my interests and come up with potential achievements and essay concepts for each. I hang up on the call feeling exhausted.

At dinner, I tell my parents about Mr. Qin's unusual essay tactics. Big mistake. They eat it up immediately, and I can tell my mom is weighing whether or not to send me upstairs with my plate so I can start working on it right away. They love Mr. Qin. I swear, there should be government regulations on hanging up Harvard flags.

"See? I told you he was worth every penny. In this country, things are expensive, but you always get what you pay for," my mom says triumphantly.

"I don't know, Mom."

"Don't know? What don't you know?"

"Doesn't this all feel a bit fake to you? College applications are supposed to be more . . . organic."

"Organic? Why are you using that word? Organic is what the

grocery store says so they can sell apples for five dollars a pound. What does it have to do with your college?"

"I think the point is, you should give Mr. Qin a chance, Felix," my dad says. "Don't turn his advice down right away. He knows what he's doing. He's gotten a lot of kids into good schools."

Well, of course he has, I want to protest. *The man is manufacturing college essays in the most cynical, formulaic way possible.*

Back upstairs, I try to list out my interests.

- *Reading books*
- *Ping-Pong*
- *World War II history*
- *Video games*
- *Old movies*

The last one seems the most promising. It all started when I was home alone from school for a professional development day, free to watch whatever I wanted. *Taxi Driver* was playing on one of the classic movie channels, and despite the incongruous censorship ("Who the *heck* do you think you're talking to?") and grossly mature themes—most of which went over my head—I was into it. I liked the scene where Robert De Niro talks into the mirror, acting tough, all because he's so painfully alone.

After that, I started looking for more movies like it. I picked titles off AFI and *Sight & Sound* and the TIME 100, starting with big classics like *The Godfather* and *Pulp Fiction*, then moving on to the harder stuff—*Tokyo Story, La Règle du Jeu, Citizen Kane.* Some of them were snoozefests, but some of them I liked.

My favorite director was Wong Kar-wai. When my parents took me to Manhattan Chinatown, I'd pretend I was walking through the crowded streets of Hong Kong in *Chungking Express*, coming within inches of strangers whose lives I would never truly know.

I haven't done anything résumé-worthy with it. Watching movies has always been a private interest for me; no one is going to give me an award for knowing who François Truffaut is. But at least it's unique. That's a start.

My phone buzzes with a notification.

Cassie Chow has accepted your follow request.

It's so surreal to be back in touch again, after I hadn't thought about her in so long. With the utmost care, I take a photo of Cassie's music folder, then crop it so nothing from my room ends up in the background. After I send the photo, I write, with equal care, an opening message. After double-checking it to make sure I haven't accidentally written "I miss you" or something weird like that, I send it out.

Hey Cassie I think you left your music folder at the Ping-Pong tournament. I picked it up, is there a way I can get it back to you?

Is it weird that I picked it up? She's not going to think I'm stalking her, right? Or worse, that I stole it from her?

By the grace of the heavens, she responds quickly.

Cassie:

omg THANK YOU

Literal lifesaver

I was freaking out I thought I lost it

The teacher gave me so much crap when I showed
up without it

I read the texts in her voice: forward, breathless, the words coming a mile a minute. She seems like a person who isn't self-conscious, simply because her brain runs too quickly to ever stop and second-guess itself.

I live in Great Neck now, but I'm in Flushing
every weekend

Can I give it back to you next Sunday?

Cassie:

You're telling me I have to go all the way to Flushing?

Dude I live in Chinatown that's like 3 hours round trip
T_T

Hmm yeah, I get it. Do you have a better idea?

Cassie:

. . .

Ugh FINE

It's my fault anyways

You better buy me bubble tea or something for my troubles

Is 1 pm okay?

We agree on a time and place. After Cassie logs off, I feel oddly satisfied with myself, like I've just pulled off a tricky shot in Ping-Pong, or narrowly dodged death in Pyramid Chase. Which is silly of me. It's not like getting her to meet up is some big accomplishment. I'm just returning some sheet music to a girl I barely know. I'll probably see her one last time next weekend, she'll crack a couple of jokes about the piano competition, and then we'll both be on our way. I've got more important things to worry about. Like how to convince college admissions officers that my hours and hours of film watching are sufficient criteria for them to let me into their schools.

THREE

TO BE FAIR TO MY PARENTS AND MR. QIN, I GET why junior year makes them so uptight. After hearing so much hype from teachers and upperclassmen about how this is the most important year for college apps, I'm rather on edge myself. One week in, nothing remarkable has happened, aside from an increased workload in my classes, but that doesn't remove my feeling of dread. I have this sense that at some point, the other shoe is going to drop. I'm going to have a test in my AP Chemistry class that I didn't know about or study for, or I'm going to get a letter from a college preemptively rejecting me to save both sides from the bother of my application.

After I send Mr. Qin my list of interests, he seems on board with the film idea. I don't have any aging relatives to whom to dedicate my love of cinema, but that's okay—baby steps.

All of that is why I'm staying behind after school to meet with my guidance counselor, Ms. Haverchak, with a most unusual proposal.

"You want to start your own student club?" she asks with an incredulity that I find reasonable, but a little rude. "But you've never participated in after-school activities before."

"Because none of them interested me. That's why I'm starting this one. The classic film club. I think it will be a great addition to the already diverse and appealing slate of offerings at our school," I reply.

"Do you have any classmates in mind to join the club with you?"

Ms. Haverchak is asking a lot of questions. If someone popular like Dana Rothberg or Mark Caruso wanted to start a club, would she level these implicit accusations of friendlessness? But maybe I'm just salty because she's sniffed out the truth so quickly, which is that—

"No. Well, not yet. I'm planning to put up flyers and invite people to the first screening. That's how I'll get members. Assuming you can help me incorporate the club."

Ms. Haverchak nods slowly. I'm forced to question whether I shouldn't have cultivated this relationship more. For the past two years I've mostly floated through our meetings together; now that I'm realizing that she has this life-altering power over my college application process and thus my future, I wonder if I should have gotten her a Starbucks gift card or two somewhere along the way.

"Well, unfortunately I can't get your club into the registry until you've got at least two members. Also, if you're going to be screening movies, then they have to be rated PG-13 or lower, unless you have your faculty sponsor collect signed permission slips from everyone in attendance."

My heart sinks. I was banking on drawing people in with a samurai series, starting with *Kill Bill* and working backward through *Lone Wolf and Cub* and Akira Kurosawa. But all the dismemberment and geysering blood are probably going to rule that out.

"Can I at least get a room and a TV for starters?" I ask.

"I'm sorry, Felix, but first you'll need to have a faculty sponsor and another club member. Come on, it shouldn't be too hard to find one more movie lover. Put up that flyer, and I'm sure they'll come out of the woodwork."

I nod, feeling dejected, and slink out of the room.

"I'm glad you're taking the initiative!" Ms. Haverchak calls out as I go.

Sigh. The first step on my journey toward club-trepreneurship has been met with rejection. On my walk home, I reflect on the fundamental arrogance of extracurricular leadership. Seriously, what kind of egomaniac has enough self-confidence to say, "I'm building a rocket ship to the Ivy League, and you're all going to help me build it at little to no benefit to yourself," and expect people to fall into line?

Still, mama didn't raise no quitter. If Kobe had given up his dreams when his guidance counselor first told him that he needed one more student in his club, then the world would never have seen an eighty-one-point game.

Back at home, I put together a flyer. The hardest part is choosing the main image; I need something that conveys the potential old-ness and weirdness of the movies I want to watch in the classic film club, while still keeping it approachable. I consider, then scrap Vito Corleone, stroking his cat over the caption "An offer you can't refuse" (too obvious); and Clint Eastwood, snarling over "Go ahead, make my day" (too aggressive). Finally I settle on Rick Blaine and Captain Renault, with "The beginning of a beautiful film club."

Underneath it, I write:

Calling all cinephiles!
Are you interested in being a part of
Edmund J. Cooper High's first-ever film club?
Inaugural meeting on Friday
at 2:30 p.m. in the cafeteria!

I print out the first poster and examine my handiwork. But right away, I have doubts. Calling all cinephiles? I sound like a dweeb. I picture myself sitting alone in the cafeteria, with a flimsy sign that says FILM CLUB, getting totally ignored.

The truth is, Ms. Haverchak was right to be skeptical. I've never been particularly involved with anything at my school. I don't do any clubs or sports, mostly because I've always made a point of trying to spend as little time on campus as possible. This late attempt to get involved feels too nakedly like what it is, which is a desperate push to nail down something I can use to get into college.

I can't help but blame my parents a little. I get why they wanted us to move to Great Neck: great schools, a foothold in the suburbs, a house they could own and pass on to me. But it also meant that I had to start my life over. I had to leave behind all my friends and take on high school, the most critical juncture of my life, alone. The rules for how to dress, how to fit in, how to not get made fun of, were completely different. At the very least, that made it hard to hit the ground running in terms of impressive activities.

In the end, I decide to put up the poster anyhow. I've already told Mr. Qin about the film club, and if I back out now, he's just going to yell at me. After I staple it to the billboard by the school entrance, I do my best not to think about it. On Friday, if no one shows, I'll take the poster down, and by next week everyone will have forgotten the whole thing.

Thursday night, I accidentally spill to my parents about the film club at dinner. This turns out to be a big mistake. On Friday morning, my mom greets me in the kitchen with a tray of supermarket cupcakes.

"For you to give to whoever comes," she explains.

"I don't need to give out anything," I say hastily. "It's just an informational meeting. It'll be weird to try to bribe people with treats."

She shakes her head. "This film club is important. You have to put your best foot forward, like you mean it."

"Mom, there are *twelve* of these. They're not going to fit in my locker. I'm going to have to carry them all day."

"Don't always think about yourself. It's good to offer something to people if they come. But don't make them feel obligated. Try to have a spirit of generosity." She speaks with a tone of finality, and I know better than to argue.

Over the course of the day, hungry hey-can-I-have-one vultures pick off my cupcakes one by one. More than one person asks me sarcastically if it's my birthday. By the time the final bell rings, I'm down to seven. In the cafeteria, with half a tray of cupcakes, I look like I've been snacking on my own supply.

I set up at a table in the corner, with the open tray of cupcakes and a sheet of paper for sign-ups. I wonder if a single person even noticed my flyer. Maybe I should have gone with Vito Corleone. He's probably a lot more recognizable than an old black-and-white photo of Humphrey Bogart.

People are bustling around in the after-school rush. Band kids lug their instruments; football players lounge around before practice; the yearbook committee waits for the printer room to open. In one corner, a kid has plugged in his boombox and is break dancing by himself.

In the middle of the cafeteria, in clear view of my table, I see a familiar group of skater kids assembling. Black hoodies, ripped jeans, and colorful beanies. I forgot that they'd be here; they always meet up at the cafeteria so they can head to the skate park together. At the edge of the group, fidgeting with a lighter, is Henry Wijaya.

29

Seeing him brings up a swell of anger, as it always does. We haven't spoken since the end of freshman year, when we stopped being friends. I watch him flicking the lighter on and off, laughing at the jokes his friends are making.

Then, as if he feels my eyes on him, he turns to look at me. I stare at the wall behind him like I don't notice him, like I'm just staring into space. But I can clearly see that he's studying me, looking at the tray of cupcakes, the blank sign-up sheet. For a moment it looks like he might walk over to me, and I'm seized by panic. I don't know what I'd say to him. I imagine him coming up to my table, looking at my corny setup and mocking me, like "So this is what you've come to now."

The arrival of the final member of their group snaps Henry's attention away. There's an exchange of bro hugs, and then the group is off. I watch Henry as he pockets the lighter and exits. Only now do I realize how fast my heart is beating.

Gradually the cafeteria empties out, as everyone moves on to where they're supposed to be. As expected, the film club is a bust, and I'm not sure whether to be disappointed or relieved. Mr. Qin won't be thrilled, that's for sure.

I close the lid on the cupcakes and prepare to make the long walk back home.

"Am I too late?"

I look up from my bag and see Gaspard Pierre-Duluc. *Not* who I was expecting.

Gaspard is a late arrival to Great Neck, like me. He joined

our graduating class as a sophomore. We've never spoken before, except for one time when I accidentally got graphite dust on his sleeve and he glared at me and said, "Ugh."

"You're interested in the film club?" I ask.

"Potentially," he says, sliding into the seat across from me. He points at the tray of cupcakes, and I lift the lid so he can take one. "It depends on what kinds of cinema we'll be viewing."

He says "cinema," as if to call attention to the fact that he doesn't just watch "movies" or even "films." I've heard a rumor that he lived in France for a year; maybe he picked up an interest in French film while he was there.

Perhaps because Gaspard wasn't here for freshman year, and because of his distinctive way of dressing (lots of collared shirts, preppy sweaters, dazzlingly white sneakers, and never, ever shorts), I've always thought of him as being kind of separate from the student body. Gaspard's isolation is defined by a certain haughtiness, an immunity to embarrassment, like moving to Great Neck was a step down for him.

But maybe that's exactly what the film club needs.

With someone just as pretentious as me in the mix, we'll be able to dive right into the good stuff. I'm talking surrealist historical dramas like *Aguirre, the Wrath of God*; French New Wave; silent films from the 1920s.

"We can watch anything. This is a brand-new club, so we can take it any direction you like. I thought we could start with a Kurosawa series. But we could also go era by era, so we can compare

31

different directors. Or explore the evolution of genre films. How does Western Wednesdays sound?"

"Is that what the first meeting is for? To decide?" he asks. He takes a careful bite of a cupcake, chewing slowly and regarding me with a raised eyebrow that says, "Your move."

"Well, it could be. To be honest, we're not quite there yet. Technically the club doesn't even exist, because it's just me. And now you. Potentially. If you're on board, the two of us have to register the club with Ms. Haverchak. And then we have to get a faculty sponsor, book an empty room, and get set up with a TV. After that, we can pick some movies to watch."

Gaspard takes another bite of the cupcake, looking thoughtful. Now that I've shown my hand, he must realize that it all depends on him. Unless there's another late arrival, he's the film club's only hope.

"So what are some of your favorite films?" he asks me. It's clear in his voice that everything hinges on my answer. This is no time to be talking about obvious choices like *The Shawshank Redemption* or *Citizen Kane*. To win this man over, I'm going to need a real deep cut.

"Well, it's probably a tie between *Lost in Translation* and *Chungking Express*. But depending on the day, I might say *Cinema Paradiso*."

"And how do you rate movies? Do you go out of four, or out of ten?"

"Gaspard, I'm glad you asked. I use a four-axis rating system— performances, narrative, filmmaking, and emotional impact. For each category I add zero to two stars, and the final rating is out of five."

After cultivating this system in my head for years, this is the first time I've talked about it out loud. It's slightly embarrassing to reveal my inner monologue to a total stranger like this, even though I've always been convinced of the superior accuracy of my four-axis ratings over your standard IMDB or Rotten Tomatoes score.

"That's not bad," Gaspard agrees. "Take *Forrest Gump*, for instance. It's hard to give more than one star in any of those categories. But it's also hard to give less. Four stars. But then look at *Princess Mononoke*. The performances are nothing special, but it's easily two stars in every other category. That gets you to six stars: hence, five out of five."

I nod as hope blooms in my chest. Somehow I'm passing haughty, Frenchy Gaspard's test. It's a plot twist worthy of M. Night Shyamalan. He seems like he'd have good taste, and he gets extra credit for watching anime.

"So what's my title?" he asks. "Vice president? Head of programming?"

"Either. Both. You can even be president, if you want. We'll be copresidents."

"So we'll both be president of a club with zero members?" he scoffs.

I shrug. "If we do a good job, we might not have zero members for long."

Gaspard finally breaks into a smile. "Zero members is fine with me. As long as I have a say in what we watch. You had me at Kuro-sawa."

He sticks out a hand for me to shake. Internally, I breathe a sigh of relief. Negotiations may have come right down to the wire, but for now, the film club lives.

FOUR

IT'S SUNDAY, AND I'M DITCHING THE END OF
Ping-Pong practice to return Cassie's music folder. Coach Fang
gives me a dirty look as I pack up my paddle, but it can't be helped.

I shuffle my way down a packed Roosevelt Avenue toward Ten
Ren Tea, where Cassie and I are supposed to meet. When the
shop comes into view, I start to feel nervous. It occurs to me that
I might have overstepped by taking something that belonged to
Cassie and holding on to it, forcing her to come all the way out
here. She could ask, "Why didn't you just give it to one of my
teammates to bring back?" A totally reasonable question. And that
could lead her, step by step, to the same conclusion that I'm starting to reach now: that I picked up the music folder because deep
down, I wanted to see her again.

I shake my head. I was leaving the tournament; I saw the folder
at the last minute; it's forgivable that I didn't think of the most
efficient way of returning it to her. No reason to get worked up.
She'll get here, we'll chitchat for like fifteen minutes tops, and

then she'll be back on her way to Manhattan.

Suddenly the crowd parts, and I see her standing in front of the store. She's wearing jeans and a hoodie, and she looks totally different than she did at the Ping-Pong tournament, in her track pants and team T-shirt, with her hair tied back.

"Hi, Felix!" She waves. I stagger toward her and thrust the music folder out in front of me.

"Thanks so much again!" she says, taking it back. "These are for you."

She holds out a pink cardboard box with oil stains on the sides. It smells good.

"They're egg tarts from my mom's bakery. Do you like egg tarts? Well anyways, I'm sure you can find someone to eat them. I brought those all the way here, so the usual expression of gratitude is in order."

"Thanks," I say hoarsely. I clear my throat. "Hey, I'll buy you a bubble tea. Since you came this far out."

Cassie waves a hand in front of her face. "There's no need! I was kidding when I said that."

"I insist. I'm getting one for myself, so I need the second one to hit the credit card minimum."

"Oh. Okay!" Cassie says cheerfully. "I was just being polite. I want that boba."

As I wait in line, Cassie examines the many varieties of tea on the wall; jars of dried leaves in shades from pale green to black, thick cakes of pu-er wrapped in fancy paper. Every so often she calls out the prices—"This one's a hundred and twenty dollars! This one is one fifty-nine!"—like she's looking for the most expensive one. When it's my turn, I take her order—green milk tea, regular sugar, regular ice. I've always thought that one's bubble tea order is a mini personality quiz: not as deep as Myers-Briggs, but it does say a little something about your priorities in this world. Cassie's order is respectable, though I always opt for less ice myself.

We get our drinks and snag two high chairs by the window, where we can lean against the bar and peer out at the people on the sidewalk.

"Not bad," Cassie says after her first sip.

"Not bad? This is the best bubble tea shop in New York City! And therefore New York State, most likely."

"No way, dude. The Kung Fu Tea on Chrystie Street is better. I know you've never been there, so don't try to argue. My friend used to work there. They run it like a sports team, with drills and timers and stuff. Their shaker machine even has a name. It's Jyut Gwai Fei. What do they call the machine here?"

I don't have a comeback for that. It's hard to argue with a name straight out of a C-drama.

"So how's piano going for you these days?" Cassie asks.

"It's not. I quit. Right after Rubenstein, actually."

"Wait, what? *The* Felix Ma quit piano?"

"Why are you acting so surprised? You quit too!"

"Yeah, but that's different," Cassie says, shaking her head. "I was doing group classes at the Chinatown Piano Academy. You had that private teacher, the one who lived in Forest Hills. What was her name?"

"Yin Laoshi," I said. "The bane of my existence."

I used to hate going to that house every week. Yin Laoshi would sit on the bench next to me, hovering over my shoulder as I played my piece. Every time I messed up, she'd raise her hand, then play the passage herself, the way she wanted it. I'd have to run the passage over and over until I'd gotten it right at least twice in a row; she never let me progress otherwise. After one lesson, when we spent practically the whole hour on the same two measures, I cried in the car on the way home.

"But you were so good," Cassie continues. "That piece you played at Rubenstein was so much harder than mine. When I heard you practicing, I knew I had no chance. You were perfect. I only won because you choked."

I wince. "That competition was supposed to be my last hurrah. My mom promised she'd let me quit after Rubenstein. But on the drive home, I told her that I was done for good, and she pulled the car over to the side of the road to tell me that she wanted me to keep playing. She went on and on, until I eventually opened the car door and told her I was going to walk home. That's how I got her to back down."

"Jeez. That's bold. You would have felt bad if she'd just driven off."

"I wasn't thinking about that. I just knew I had to take her all the way to the edge."

She pats me on the shoulder. "Hey, I'm sorry it was like that for you. I won't make fun of you for beating you anymore. Although I am glad I got my gloating in before you told me all that."

"Do you remember what you said to me? Right before I went on, you asked me to do you a favor and mess up my sonata."

Cassie laughs. "That sounds like something I would do. Sorry, Felix. I always go into those things with the biggest chip on my shoulder. I'm going up against all these people with fancy piano teachers or Ping-Pong coaches who played in the Olympics, so I have to do *something* to give myself an edge. Nothing personal."

The shop is filling up, and the line is almost out the door. A pair of girls holding tall, sugary slushies eye our seats impatiently, but I ignore them.

"I almost went to Van Der Donck, you know. I got in, anyways. I would have gone if we hadn't moved to Great Neck."

"Oh, no way! Maybe we would have been friends. Although I guess we probably wouldn't have met."

"Why not?"

Cassie shrugs. "There's like three thousand students."

For a moment, I feel disappointed by the frankness of this statement. But then a thought occurs to me. "Wait, we would have recognized each other from piano, though. You'd have at least trash-talked me a little more."

"Oh yeah, duh," Cassie says. "Well, in that case, we probably would have been rivals. It's pretty clear by now that we're natural enemies. If we went to the same school, there'd be so much more stuff to compete over. It would have been hard for you to have to lose to me over and over."

"Pssh, if you say so. You're just lucky I left."

The idea of being rivals with Cassie puts a smile on my face. It would be stressful, but it would certainly never be boring.

Cassie leans back, looks at me appraisingly, then squints, as if searching for some hidden detail.

"What?" I ask.

"I'm trying to decide what group you would have joined at Vandie. Based on your vibe, I would have said debate kid, one hundred percent. But now that I'm talking to you, I'm not sure."

"Debate? I'm offended."

"Hey, it's a compliment. Debate kids are cool. They can talk super, super fast, don't hate." She scratches her chin. "I can't see you doing math team, or student government. You don't really strike me as a dance kid or an a cappella kid either."

"Van Der Donck has a table-tennis team, right? I probably would have just done that."

"Oh, true. Big-time jock, then. Top of the food chain, zero doubt."

"Now that's more like it."

I've thought about what my life at Van Der Donck might have been like before, but this is the first time I've actually pictured it, spoken to someone who's there. Even though we're joking around, it feels tantalizing.

"So how do you like the suburbs?" Cassie asks.

"It's fine," I sigh.

"It's fine," she repeats flatly, mimicking my voice. "That's it?"

"I mean, I don't like it, to be honest. Is that surprising?"

"Yeah, a little. I'm not saying it's paradise out there, but I always thought of the suburbs as an upgrade. You get a bigger house, a driveway, your own yard. Climbing that ladder."

"That's why my parents moved us," I say. "They always say stuff like, 'One day, you can raise your kids in this house too.'"

"So what don't you like about it?"

My mind goes to my early memories in Great Neck, when I got made fun of for my bad haircut, my cheap running shoes, my old track pants that were so small on me that they only went to my shins, like they were capris. In Flushing, I never thought much about my appearance. But once I moved to a town full of rich kids, all these attributes about myself that were totally normal to me, that I never cared about before, suddenly became things to be ashamed of.

But that was just a surface-level issue. Once I harried my parents into buying new clothes and shoes for me, the problem was solved, even if they grumbled about the expense. It was still hard to make friends, and there was that terrible episode with Henry, but the real problem was something else. Something that developed slowly, that couldn't be solved so easily.

"It's like you said—we were climbing the ladder. Moving to the suburbs was supposed to set me up for some big success, or whatever. But instead I've let my parents down. I don't play piano anymore, I stopped being serious about Ping-Pong . . . basically all the stuff that I was supposed to be good at hasn't gone right."

"Oh, but that's everywhere. When are you ever going to be good enough for your parents?"

"It was different when we still lived here, though," I say. "There wasn't so much pressure. Or there was, but it wasn't as big of a deal. Maybe it was easier because there was more going on. In Flushing, I had a lot more friends, and we were always going out, bumping into people that we knew. That made it bearable."

Cassie nods. "I know what you mean. You have a community. Whatever you're going through, your friends that you've known forever are too. And when the adults ask how you're doing, it's like they're following along and rooting for you."

"Yeah! It's like you're a plant, and everyone is coming by to check up, make sure you're growing. Then you get pulled up and replanted in new soil, where the environment is harder, but you're still expected to thrive even more than before."

"Dang, nice metaphor," Cassie says with a cheeky wink. "Felix the plant. I like that. What kind of plant would you be?"

"I don't know," I say, feeling discouraged. I was hoping she'd take what I said more seriously. "Maybe a cactus. Dry and covered in spines."

"Hey, don't sell yourself short! You'd definitely be a flower of some kind. Something that stands out." Sensing my mood, her smile drops. "Sorry to joke around so much. That's just what I'm like. I see how it could be rough to start over. Especially since you moved so late.

"If it makes you feel better, I think going to high school feels bad no matter what. Nobody warns you how different it's going to be," Cassie continues, shaking her head. "Especially at a place like Van Der Donck, where they draw from the whole city. It's like growing up in your own little district, then turning fourteen and suddenly getting tossed into the Hunger Games with kids from all over Panem."

"Maybe you're right."

There's a break in the conversation as we both work on our drinks. I feel better, but now it occurs to me that we've been talking almost exclusively about me. I hope I'm not coming off as self-centered.

"So your mom runs a bakery?" I ask.

"Yup. It's called Golden Promises. It's a cafe too. The specialty is the waffle sundae. If you ever come by, I'll give you the friends and family discount."

"What about your dad?"

Cassie's face darkens. "He's not around. It's just me and my mom."

"Oh. Sorry," I say quickly.

She shakes her head. "It's fine."

After that, though, it's like a spell is broken. As we finish up our bubble tea, Cassie looks distant. I can't guess what she's thinking about. It's like the real world is pulling her back. When she says it's time for her to head to the train station, I try one more time to apologize.

"Don't worry, Felix. You didn't do anything wrong. I'm fine, by the way. It's not like talking about it changes anything."

By "it," I assume she means her dad. Why did I have to bring that up? We were having such a good afternoon. From the way she said "my mom's bakery," I should have guessed that her dad might be a sore subject. All I would have to do was ask a different question.

"Anyways, thanks again for saving my sheet music. And buying me bubble tea. I'll see you around, Felix."

She waves, and I wave back. Just like that, she's gone.

For the rest of the day, I can't stop thinking about our conversation in the tea shop. It's the first time I've talked to someone about what it felt like to leave Flushing. My brain is still crackling with new realizations—above all, how different things could have been. Cassie grew up in a neighborhood like mine, only she's still there, and whatever feelings of self-doubt I've developed since moving don't seem to affect her.

I want to hear more about Cassie's life, what it's like for her to be at Van Der Donck, what answers she might have. Talking to her feels like going back to my old self, getting a window into what could have been. It's fun to visit that reality. I wish I got to stay in it for a bit longer.

FIVE

GASPARD AND I GET OUR CLUB REGISTERED WITH
Ms. Haverchak, who seems just as surprised as I was to see the two
of us together. We must seem like an odd pairing to her, two loner
types from opposite sides of the school social map who somehow
ended up in the same boat.

After our club is officially instituted, Gaspard and I agree to
meet every Monday and Thursday. On Mondays we'll plan—that
is, talk about movies, rate and debate them, and after a half hour
or so, settle on a title that we're both willing to watch. On Thursdays, we'll have screenings. The idea is to pull people in while
they're getting ready to check out for the weekend, but not keep
them at school for extra time on a Friday.

For our first screening, we watch *Spellbound*. Our hope is that
people will recognize the name Alfred Hitchcock, come for the
old-timey dream sequences, and stay for the cinematography. But
no one shows, so it's just the two of us, watching on an overhead
projector in an empty French classroom.

"I'm still glad you agreed to do this," I tell Gaspard after it's over. "If I'd known that the school would hook us up like this, I would have started the film club years ago."

"Next time we can do something more crowd-pleasing. I was thinking a classic high school movie, like *Heathers*."

"*Heathers* is your favorite eighties high school movie? Gaspard, Gaspard, we need to have a little talk."

"Oh please, what's yours? Don't tell me it's *The Breakfast Club*, or *Ferris Bueller*. God forbid a movie has a message other than 'Live life to the fullest' or 'We're not so different after all.'"

"So the message should be, 'If your classmates are bullies it's okay to murder them'?"

It feels surprising we didn't meet earlier. Gaspard is easy to talk to, so much so that I question whether I didn't previously just have unfair biases about people who wear collared shirts. We can riff on movies all day—especially if we're ripping on movies we think are overrated. Our partnership has made me wonder whether there aren't more people out there with solitary, burning passions like mine. Maybe we just have to keep throwing posters into the void until they finally appear.

At my next meeting with Mr. Qin, I'm amped to tell him the good news. I tell him that the film club is now officially established; Gaspard and I will even show up in a picture together at the back of our yearbook. In other words, I'm well on my way to knocking out step two of the three-step plan. And it isn't even October yet.

"Listen, that's good to hear, Felix," Mr. Qin says, looking rather bored. "Sounds like you're making a start. Keep it up, and remember to think big. A film club with two people isn't much to write home about. Get ten people, maybe put on some kind of event for your whole town or something, and then we'll be talking. Or you could, say, start writing articles and publishing them online. If you get enough attention, maybe you can arrange a real screening for an indie filmmaker. Something that sounds impressive. Got it?"

I feel a little deflated. Finding a copresident and getting the club registered had felt like pretty awesome progress while it was happening. I was hoping Mr. Qin would have a stronger reaction.

"Now, I want to focus on the essay. I told you about Sheela Abbas, right? Crossword girl, got into Northwestern and Amherst? Well, listen, I know you don't have a sick relative you can just dig out of the closet. Wait, do you? Doesn't matter. This isn't about cheap tearjerker tactics. That's last year's story.

"Felix, the essay is all about finding out who you are. Now, you're over there thinking, 'What do you mean, Mr. Qin? I'm me.' Let me explain. If you ask most people who they are, they'll say, 'Oh yeah, I'm from Long Island, I like to paint, and play volleyball, and I'm intellectually curious.' Boring! If you want to stand out, you have to find that deep story, the one that no one else is telling. That one-liner that hooks you, right away. 'Do you know what it's like to kill a man?' Something like that. But nothing illegal, obviously. Once you've done that, the essay writes itself."

By the time Mr. Qin finishes his speech, he's a little out of breath. He holds out a hand, and a second later, someone—maybe his assistant, or his kid—hands him a water bottle from offscreen. I watch in silence as Mr. Qin takes a long swig, then hands the water bottle back. Clearly he's running a tight ship over there.

My next homework assignment is to come up with five one-sentence hooks for my essay. Then the two of us are going to pick the best one, and I'm going to go out and bring it into existence. It's like reverse engineering my own life. The example he uses is "To honor her grandfather, one honors math student must dive into the world of words." It sounds like the tagline of a movie.

I'm left feeling dismayed by Mr. Qin's way of always moving the goalposts out just a bit farther. I wonder if he's following some kind of script, if there's a spreadsheet where he's just updated me from "3-step process" to "who u r."

Still, I should have known that just getting the film club started wouldn't be enough. Clubs at my school are a dime a dozen, a landscape littered with crumbling monuments to Common Apps past.

In times like these, I turn to a reliable pastime for taking my mind off of my troubles—social media.

At the top of my feed are the usual NBA Top 75 Plays of the Decade, Table Tennis Shots—If They Weren't Filmed, Nobody Would Believe It, and UNREAL 81 KILLSTREAK—Starfall Deathmatch. After my meeting with Mr. Qin, though, all of this just feels like evidence of my mediocrity.

Below that, though, is a post from Cassie. She asks,

IS THERE ANYBODY ALIVE OUT THERE?

The time stamp says it was posted just fifteen seconds ago. Which means that at this very moment she's probably sitting at her keyboard at home, waiting for the reacts to come in. I bet she'd have a good retort for Mr. Qin's bummer of a speech. Since our meeting at Ten Ren, I've been dwelling on her Hunger Games quip. In a weird way, it comforts me. Not because I identify with Katniss or something—I know I'm not the hero of whatever story I'm part of in Great Neck—but because it reassures me that there was a certain inevitability to what happened at my high school. There was always going to be that kid from District Nine Point Five, who popped in for a quick cameo and then disappeared into obscurity.

I wonder what she means with that cryptic post. I picture her in the middle of a barren wasteland, throwing her head back and crying out to the heavens. Everything I've heard about Van Der Donck suggests that it's a difficult place: narrow hallways stuffed to the gills with New York's finest standardized-test takers, all struggling to secure a coveted seat at an elite college. Cassie seems to love competition, but even she must get tired sometimes.

I try to go back to my one-sentence hooks, but I can't focus. I keep thinking about Cassie's post, what it's like for her at Van Der Donck, whether or not I could have handled going there.

Before I know it, I'm typing a new message.

I'm alive out here

I hesitate over whether to send it. Messaging Cassie out of the blue like this would be an admission that I want to talk to her more. I'd be opening myself up to the possibility of being ignored.

But then again, it's not a crime to be friendly. Besides, it still bothers me a little how abruptly our conversation at Ten Ren ended. Maybe this is a good chance to smooth things over, leave off in a better place.

I hit send.

I watch in slow motion as the message goes to read, and then the typing bubble pops up above her profile picture.

Cassie:

Lol

It's a song

But I'm glad to hear it!

Boy, do I feel silly. Why didn't I think to look up her post before replying? Too late, I search "Is there anybody alive out there" and see videos of Bruce Springsteen concerts. Between this and bringing up Cassie's dad, I clearly have some kind of inborn tendency that predisposes me toward making a complete fool out of myself.

But then Cassie goes on.

Cassie:

I on the other hand am on the brink of death

I've been working on my college apps for six hours straight

Lol seriously? How come?

Cassie:

My thoughts exactly

Why do they need me to tell them how great I am

I think my record speaks for itself

Cassie's response doesn't really answer my question, which is "Why are you working so much on your actual college apps a year before you apply?" After a moment of confusion, I understand.

Wait, are you a senior this year?

Cassie:

Yeah, dude

Aren't you?

I'm a junior

Cassie:

Awww a baby

Doesn't this mean you were already in high school during Rubenstein

Cassie:

Yup. I was born like three hours after the age cutoff so they let me in anyways

Ohhhh

What are you writing your essay about

Cassie:

Ugh great question

My mom wants me to write about saxophone

Show off my creativity and passion for art

But it's hard to write about so it sounds gross

"As I play a run of sixteenth notes, I reflect on the value of hard work and the importance of art to human civilization."

Haha I feel you

My parents have me working with a college admissions coach

It's the most depressing thing ever

He's basically teaching me how to fake having this incredibly inspiring life

Cassie:

You have an admissions coach?!?

I know right

It's a new level of overintense parenting, even for them

Cassie:

Dude I would LOVE to have an admissions coach

Some kids at my school have them but they're so expensive

You have one now and you're only a junior?

Well, that's the point I think

There's still time for him to fix me

I have one year to turn myself from a faceless nerd into a unique hook

If you don't start until senior year it's basically too late already

Or so he'd have you believe

Cassie:

Harrumph. I am indignant!!! Indignant, I tell you!!!

Haha

Cassie:

What is he telling you to do?

Well, there's a whole three-step plan

First I had to start a film club at school

The next step is to win an award of some kind. By having the best film club of the year or something

And then for the essay I have to come up with some kind of emotional story to tie it all together. Like, I don't just watch movies for fun, I'm a deep and complicated person, and movies are what saved me

I tell her Mr. Qin's story about the crossword girl and her grandpa.

Cassie:

That . . . actually sounds really smart

If you can pull it off, then you're in. What's a couple Bs on your transcript next to a story like that?

Well, easier said than done

It's hard to see how watching movies translates into a deeply affecting narrative about myself

I feel like after a few months of no dice, Mr. Qin is just going to tell me to straight-up lie

Cassie:

Might as well go all in

You know what you should do? You should make a movie. About your life. An autobiographical film. *Felix Ma: The Movie.*

That would be the worst movie ever

Cassie:

How come?

Because my life is completely uninteresting

What would it be about? And who would be in it? And why would anyone watch it?

Cassie:

Everyone who's ever made a movie faced those same questions and they still made it happen

Idk it just seemed like the natural idea

My other suggestion was that you could start an online conspiracy theory

If it gets REAL big, I bet you could put it in your extracurriculars

But what do I know? You're the one with the admissions coach

Okay, I gotta go. Thanks again for getting my music!
I hope you liked the egg tarts!

After she's gone, I feel an echo of the sense of loss that I felt after she left Flushing. Cassie *gets* it; she's been through a lot of the same things I have. We both grew up in the city, we competed in the same competitions, and we were supposed to go to the same school. It's like our lives were on parallel tracks, and just before they were supposed to meet, I got pulled away and thrown in somewhere else.

Maybe this conversation is only a brief coda to our string of coincidental contacts, but I'm still happy that we got to talk one last time. It's enough to buoy me through the rest of the evening, which I spend scrawling out one ridiculous idea after another for how to get some achievements for the film club slash find out who I really am.

At our second film club meeting, I tell Gaspard that we need to start thinking bigger.

"Bigger?" he replies, blinking blankly back at me. "Bigger how? We're still working on getting a third person to show up. How much bigger are we supposed to be?"

"I'm just thinking we should get a couple of irons in the fire. Maybe start reaching out to film professionals, see if we can get them to come give a talk, or do a screening with us. By the time we get it all arranged, we'll have more members."

"Feels a little premature. What if we put together a big screening and only the two of us show up?"

I'm not sure how to respond. So far, both of us have left unacknowledged that the club is a thinly veiled résumé booster. I have to assume Gaspard is in on the scheme, but it seems crass to come out and say it.

"I just think it would be cool. Imagine if we get a real filmmaker into the building to talk to us, and later on they make it big. We'd be way ahead of the curve!"

"We can try, I guess," he says. But he sounds unconvinced.

"The other idea is for us to make our own movie," I say weakly, mostly as an afterthought.

Gaspard chuckles. "You're a pretty ambitious guy, aren't you?"

"No, it's just . . . it was Cassie's idea. Forget it."

"Whoa, whoa, hold up. Who's Cassie?"

"She's this girl I used to know from like, middle school."

"*In-teresting.* So a girl asked you to make a movie for her. That's what this is about?" A smirk spreads across Gaspard's face.

"Hey, chill, it's not like that," I say. I tell him about our brief run-ins at the piano contest, at the Ping-Pong tournament. When I try to explain what happened after that, though—that I picked up her music folder, that I treated her for bubble tea, that I wish we could have talked longer—Gaspard's grin grows wider and wider.

"So you met this girl a while ago, and you missed your chance to talk to her. And now you're meeting her again, you realize you like her, and you're not gonna miss your chance again," he says, wiggling his eyebrows suggestively.

"Okay, yes, that's technically true. But it's not as simple as you're making it sound," I protest.

I can't blame Gaspard for teasing me. The summary I've given basically makes it sound like I have a garden-variety crush. But I want to believe that there's something deeper. Even at the very first moment, when I picked up Cassie's music folder and realized that our story would continue, I felt like something big was happening. I don't want to have that feeling explained away as mere infatuation.

"Forget that I brought it up," I say. "You're right, this is all premature. We should focus on getting some more members."

"I think we should make the movie."

"What?"

Suddenly Gaspard isn't smirking anymore. Instead there's a gleam in his eye. "You heard me. Let's do it. You love movies, I love movies, let's show your girl what we can do."

"I told you, she's not—"

"I know, I know." Gaspard waves me off and pulls out his phone.

"Check this out," he says. He opens an app called FiltroPro. "I've used this for class projects before. You can edit everything on your phone; it's easy. There's even filters and special effects."

He shows me a video that he made for his Spanish class. It's a short film called *Los Padres Descubren un Tesoro*. In it, Gaspard and a girl are dressed as eighteenth-century Spanish missionaries, aka they're wearing brown hoodies, plastic rosaries, and fake mustaches. I can't understand most of the dialogue, so I focus on the grainy quality and sepia tint of the footage.

"It looks like an old silent film," I say.

Gaspard nods. "That's the *Great Train Robbery* filter. There are dozens of them."

The two padres happen upon a small cross in the middle of the woods, and there's a flash of lightning. The girl padre disappears, leaving her disembodied mustache and rosary suspended in the air for a moment before they drop to the ground.

"Dios mío!" Padre Gaspard cries.

"How did you get it to look like that?" I ask. The special effects are cheesy, but they're passable.

"That's a secret I can't reveal," Gaspard says, with a wink. "All I'll say is, we used a tape measure and it took many, many takes."

There's another flash of lightning, and Gaspard too is transported away. The padres find themselves in a boat in the middle of a pond. Brilliant light shines down from above, and a voice tests them with a series of questions. Some of them, like "Dónde está el aeropuerto?" sound less like a religious trial and more like a later chapter in Gaspard's Spanish textbook. When the padres pass the test, they're transported back to the woods and gifted with a priceless treasure: El Santo Grial. Gracias a Dios! Fin. Gaspard is a lot goofier than I thought he was.

"This is pretty sweet," I say.

"It was easy to make. There are plenty of free apps for editing movies."

Afterward, Gaspard shows me more filters. There's one that looks like a 1940s newsreel, one that is gritty and lo-fi like 16mm film, and one that's a perfect imitation of grainy 2000s camcorder footage, right down to the digital time stamp in the corner.

"But what's our movie supposed to be about?" I ask.

He shrugs. "I say we film first, ask questions later. That's what Lexie and I did for this Spanish video. Sometimes all you need to get started are some fake mustaches and a list of prompts. We got an A, by the way. Well, technically it was an A minus."

"I don't know. Do you really think we can make something good with a couple of filters? For this to work, it has to be—well . . ."

I trail off. In my head is Mr. Qin's voice, finishing my sentence: it has to be *good*, it has to be *award-winning*. If he saw me and Gaspard with these cheap costumes and janky special effects, he'd probably return my parents' money and tell them that their son is a lost cause.

Gaspard shrugs. "Hey, bro, this was your idea. We don't have to do it if you don't want to. But there's no harm in giving it a shot, right? Why don't you ask Cassie if she wants to be in it?"

I blink, lost for words. Cassie, of course, is the reason that I'm excited about this idea in the first place. It would be cool to tell her that my friend and I are using her movie suggestion. And it would be even cooler if she was in it too. If the idea didn't occur to me earlier, it's only because I didn't have the audacity to admit to myself what I really wanted. Gaspard must sense this, because he snaps his fingers and points at me like "Gotcha!"

"Aha! So you'll do it?"

"I'll ask her," I murmur.

"My man!" He reaches out for a handshake. "Can't wait to meet this Cassie. You must like her a lot."

"Yeah, yeah."

I tell myself that I'm doing this because of Mr. Qin. I can't keep having this defeatist attitude about fulfilling his directives; I have to at least put in an honest effort. Even if this movie is destined to fail, I have to actually let it fail before giving up. But truthfully, I'm not worried about how the movie is going to turn out. Instead I feel optimistic, light. Because now there's a chance that I might see Cassie again after all.

SIX

IN THE EVENING, I SPEND A GOOD HOUR TRYING
to think of a funny opening message to Cassie. Something way
cleverer than last time, when I didn't realize that she was post-
ing Bruce Springsteen lyrics. Since she made that quip at the
end about conspiracy theories, I start researching some, and fall
down a deep internet rabbit hole—the government is hiding the
existence of aliens, the entire universe is a giant computer simu-
lation, dinosaurs never existed. Only when I find myself scrolling
through old posts on a blog called TheDinoLie do I finally snap
out of it. I need to just suck it up and message her.

> My friend Gaspard and I are going with your idea

> We're going to make a movie!

Cassie:

> Nice nice, does this mean if this idea gets you into a
> college, they have to let me in as well?

Wow maybe I should become a college admissions counselor

I was wondering if you wanted to be in it

Cassie:
Lol me?

Hahaha why

That's so random

She doesn't seem that into it, and my courage falters. Yesterday I spent about an hour coming up with a concept for the movie, and even a cool title. At the time, I thought it might help make the project seem more real to Cassie, so that she'd want to be a part of it. Now, though, it's occurring to me that all that effort will just make it even more sad when she decides to say no.

Still, I press on.

So the movie is about this star Ping-Pong player who's feared throughout New York

It's called The Ping-Pong Queen of Chinatown

Gaspard and I are directing, so we need someone else to be the star

Cassie:
Oh dang so the queen is me?

I have always dreamed of inspiring fear in others, it's true

Just to be clear, I'm assuming I'm the queen of MANHATTAN Chinatown. Because if I have to drag myself out to Flushing again, then we're gonna need to discuss my contract

Gaspard and I are totally down to come to Manhattan

The movie will look better if we have all of the skyscrapers and stuff in the background anyways

Technically, that's a lie, since Gaspard and I never discussed this. But I'm sure a little trip isn't going to stop him once our lead actor is on board.

Cassie:
Wow, the dedication

You really ran with this idea haha

Do you think you'd be up for it?

Cassie:
I'm worried about getting too busy and letting you guys down

I still have college apps and stuff always comes up at the bakery, especially for the holidays

This honestly does sound pretty fun though

I like this idea more than Felix Ma: The Movie. Respectfully. And I'm not just saying that cause I'd be in it

Do you wanna try it? We can do one shoot in Manhattan and see how it goes

Cassie:

Lol I admire the persistence

Yeah, why not! Especially if you're coming here

Ok gotta go but lemme know when you're thinking about coming

I'm lowkey kind of excited about this haha, I've never acted before

I type out, then delete, a few different responses: **YAY!!!** and **OMG THANK YOU** and **DLFJSLDKFEFK!!!** Before I can send anything, Cassie goes offline again. I sit in my chair, staring at the messages, my hands still vibrating.

A wide, dopey grin spreads across my face.

There's no reason for me to be so happy, at least not one that I can put into words. Cassie and I met a couple of times back before my move, yes, but it's not like we got to know each other in any meaningful way. So why does she feel so much like an old friend?

I feel embarrassed to be smiling so hard, but since I'm alone in my room where no one can see me, I don't bother trying to hold it back. Instead, I sit back and embrace the fact that there's something coming up that I'm really, really looking forward to.

Gaspard:

You never mentioned the part where Cassie lives in Manhattan

I told you I knew her from middle school! You know that I moved, right?

Gaspard:

Yeah, but I thought you moved from like Bethpage or something

Need I remind you that you were the one who suggested I ask Cassie to be in the movie?

This is what you get for teasing me about her with zero context

Gaspard:

After some convincing, Gaspard gets on board. Now, for the hard part: convincing my parents to let me make a trip to Manhattan.

"But why do you need to go all the way out there?" my mom asks.

"Gaspard and I are making a movie for the film club. Mr. Qin says I need to have a concrete achievement for my essay, and this movie could be it."

"You're making a movie for Mr. Qin?"

"Sure. He thinks we could enter it into a contest, maybe win a prize. Or we can find a local organization and screen it there. Then I'll have something meaningful to write about for my essay."

"What kind of movie is it?"

"It's about Ping-Pong. It's called *The Ping-Pong Queen of Chinatown*."

My mom raises an eyebrow. "Oh, so you like Ping-Pong again?"

"Mom, it's just a movie."

"I know. I just think, if you like Ping-Pong again, then why did you have to quit in the first place?"

"Mom, please."

Are we really doing this right now? Other than the weekend practices in Flushing, my mom and I have had a tacit agreement not to talk about Ping-Pong. It's been a touchy subject ever since I stopped competing seriously.

"The point is, Mr. Qin thinks this is a good idea," I continue.

"Gaspard and I can take the LIRR to the city together. So I just need a ride to the station.

"Sure, that's fine," she says. "I can always give you a ride. Just hope you take it seriously. If Mr. Qin thinks it's a good idea, then you better put your best effort in. Not give up and quit, like before."

My mom never backs down without getting her digs in.

On Saturday, Gaspard and I take the Long Island Railroad to Penn Station. The ride takes us about half an hour, and we spend most of it discussing the most famous LIRR scene in cinema—Joel and Clementine's meet-cute in *Eternal Sunshine of the Spotless Mind.*

"You wouldn't expect Jim Carrey and Kate Winslet to have so much chemistry," I say. "Rose from *Titanic* and Bruce Almighty? On paper it makes no sense."

"It's underrated how close to not-that-good that movie is," Gaspard adds sagely. "The script is doing just a little too much. If Kate Winslet doesn't nail the Clementine role, the 'I'm just a fucked-up girl who's looking for my own peace of mind' line veers corny, and the whole ending falls flat."

Whenever we talk like this, there's a part of me that loves it and a part of me that wants to cringe. I sometimes think we should record our conversations so we can listen back in a few years and see how pretentious we sounded.

From Penn Station, we take the C train down to Canal Street. When we emerge from the subway station, the air is unexpectedly cold. It's early October, but today feels like mid-November at least.

"This could be good for filming," Gaspard says, rubbing his hands together. "You can see the puffs of steam coming out of your mouth. That'll be atmospheric. Especially if we drink something hot right before we film."

As we get closer to Chinatown proper, the throngs of people on the sidewalk thicken. Gaspard and I shuffle behind a line of senior citizens wheeling dollies full of groceries, parents leading their kids by the hand. Near Mott Street, the flow of people bends around a street cart selling roasted chestnuts.

"Dude, I have to pee so bad," Gaspard says.

"We're almost there."

We turn up Elizabeth Street and I spot Cassie, waiting outside Golden Promises. When she spots us, I raise both of my arms and jump up and down. In response, she gives us a half-hearted wave. She looks decidedly unenthused, which feels discouraging.

Gaspard quickly introduces himself and then rushes inside to use the bathroom.

"Hey, Cassie, what's up?" I ask.

Cassie works out a smile but doesn't reply. She closes her eyes, and her lip quivers for a moment. Then a tear shoots down her cheek, leaving a long, straight trail down to her chin. She lifts an arm to cover her eyes.

"Sorry, sorry. This is embarrassing. I'm okay. I'm fine," she whispers.

"What's wrong?"

"Nothing! I'm sorry, I was super happy and excited for this all morning. I just had a fight with my mom. Not even a fight. She just says things sometimes. And she doesn't know when to stop. I guess I don't know when to stop either, so we fight. So now I'm in a bad mood."

I don't have much experience with people crying, especially girls, so I'm frozen still and basically at a loss.

"Oh. I'm sorry," I manage to say.

"I'll be over it in a minute or two. It always hits me all at once, and then I bounce back."

"Okay. That's good," I say, looking down at my feet. "Thanks for being in our movie."

"It's nice to be hanging out again. I mean, it's kind of weird. But nice."

"Weird how?"

"Okay, not weird like, 'Why is this guy talking to me?'" she says.

I let out a nervous chuckle.

"Just surprising," Cassie continues. "I always figured that you were meant to make that one appearance in my life, for this one very specific purpose. Felix Ma, intense piano guy who I managed to steal a competition win from. I didn't think we'd get to know each other. And I especially didn't think we'd end up working together on a movie."

"Yeah, it feels like we should still be competing, right? Like you should be making your own movie that ends up being way better than mine."

Gaspard comes out of the shop. I introduce the two of them, and they shake hands.

"Nice to meet you, Gaspard. I like the way you dress. More high school boys should wear button-down shirts," Cassie says. Gaspard looks immensely pleased.

"Should we go inside?" I ask.

Cassie purses her lips. "Can we start out here? I've been inside all day. I want to get some air."

It's a reasonable request, but between this and the way she was crying, I start to feel like Gaspard and I are intruding. Maybe that was the real reason she hesitated over being in this movie.

"Good idea! Let's warm up with some establishing shots of you walking down the street," Gaspard suggests. "Felix, you can direct. In the meantime, I'll get some B-roll of buildings and signs."

It's awkward at first, telling Cassie how to act in front of the camera. After I call out "Action!" and hit record, she starts moseying down the sidewalk looking unsure of herself.

"Come on, guys, step it up," Gaspard says when he sees us. "Cassie, you gotta carry yourself like you run this city. You're the Ping-Pong Queen! Everybody wants a piece of you on the tables! At least take your hands out of your pockets."

"But they'll get cold."

"Great! You like pain! Your tough-as-nails persona was molded by the mean streets of Manhattan Chinatown!"

Cassie lets out a small chuckle. She pulls her hands out of her pockets and waves them above her head, wiggling her fingers like she's trying to get them as cold as possible.

Gradually, Gaspard's positive energy rubs off on me and Cassie. Once I get used to giving instructions, the two of us get into a groove—eyes up! Too fast! Longer strides! Not that long! Meanwhile, Gaspard runs circles around us to grab shots from different heights and angles.

Once we've gotten a few clips, Cassie takes us to the rec center so we can shoot some game footage. The tables are in the basement, and the lighting is stark, which gives the place a dark, gritty atmosphere.

"Do I need to adjust my grip?" Cassie asks, holding her paddle like a turkey leg. I hadn't thought about that part.

"No, you should keep it," I say. "It gives your character an iconoclastic vibe. Especially in contrast to people with a flawless penhold, like me."

We get a table, and Cassie and I hit to warm up. Even though we're just sending easy forehands back and forth, Gaspard's eyes bulge as he films us.

"Wait, you're like, really good," he says. "Is this real? How long can you keep going for? You're both machines!"

"Oh, I can end this any time I want," I say cockily.

"Sneak attack!" Cassie cries as she sends a looping shot at my body. I snap into my backhand and manage to get my paddle on the ball, but I send back a meatball that Cassie easily smashes out of my reach.

"This is why I'm the Ping-Pong Queen. I'm ruthless. I'm merciless. I'm willing to use every dirty trick in the book." Cassie looks straight into the camera as she monologues, and finishes with a toothy sneer.

Gaspard gives her a thumbs-up. We gather around him to watch the footage back. Cassie is a good performer—her delivery is natural, and her competitive swagger shows up on camera.

"So what is this movie about, exactly?" she asks.

"It's about Ping-Pong. Specifically you, playing Ping-Pong," I answer.

"But what's my motivation? And what's my conflict? Did my teacher force me to play, causing me to question whether this game is what I really want? Or was I adopted across the ocean, and now I'm trying to play my way into the Olympics as a way to reunite with my biological parents?"

Gaspard and I exchange looks. So far we haven't thought about much beyond the title.

"We were thinking of you as kind of an enigma," Gaspard says tentatively.

Cassie raises an eyebrow. "An enigma?"

"Yeah, you're too mysterious to have a serious backstory like that," I chime in. "You're more of a philosophical type. Inside, you burn with hunger and confusion. Ping-Pong just happens to be the way you express yourself. But what truly drives you is something deeper."

"Something deeper, eh?" Cassie says slowly, like she's trying the idea on for size. "Okay, I can roll with that. Sounds like you want me to immerse myself in the role, figure out what she's about. That, or you were just too lazy to write a script."

"That's about right. Maybe if you were more supportive, you wouldn't use a word like 'lazy,'" Gaspard says.

"Gaspard and I follow the, um, naturalistic school of filmmaking. We like to let things develop organically, so that the whole evolution is caught on camera."

"Oho, *naturalistic* is it?"

We spend another half hour or so getting various Ping-Pong action shots. Some of them are standard filler—Cassie crouching in front of the table, eyes narrowed in focus, passing the paddle back and forth between her hands. But one clip in particular gets Gaspard really excited. He shows us—the camera is zoomed in so close that Cassie's face is all you can see. The focus is on her eyes, darting around, following the movements of an unseen opponent. Then the blurry, out-of-focus Ping-Pong ball zings across the bottom of the frame like a lunar eclipse, and you can see Cassie's eyes following it off camera. Finally, the camera slowly pans out to an explosion of coiled tension, a blur of movement, as Cassie returns the ball. With some intense orchestral music, and maybe the 16mm filter, it's going to look epic.

"You're both seriously mad good at Ping-Pong," Gaspard gushes. "What's the secret? Is it easier than it looks?"

Cassie and I exchange a glance.

"Nope, it's very hard," I say.

"Arguably impossible," Cassie adds.

"You're right to be impressed. Sometimes you're just friends with exceptional people. No need to feel inadequate."

Gaspard's eyes are filled with confusion, like he's not sure whether we're joking or we're just *that* good at Ping-Pong. This is the benefit of having an unusual side talent. Most people have never seen high-level Ping-Pong, only played it amateurishly themselves, so they're easy to impress.

Cassie seems more relaxed now. For the first time, the movie idea doesn't feel forced. It feels like we're just three friends, doing a fun project together.

After we finish up in the rec center, we're all hungry. Cassie takes us to a new place that she's been wanting to try, a Korean chicken spot.

Inside, we sit at a glossy white table. There are only two items on the menu—spicy fried chicken and soy-garlic fried chicken. On the wall next to us is an array of instant camera photos, featuring sweaty and dazed-looking people giving the thumbs-up over a plate of bones. Each photo has a name and date written across the bottom.

"This place has a spicy wing challenge," Cassie explains. "If you can eat six of their hottest wings in under thirty minutes, then they'll put you on the wall."

Gaspard scoffs. "That sounds easy. Only six? If all these chumps can get themselves on the wall, then it's light work for me."

I, uninterested in the prospect of intense suffering for little reward, say that I'll pass. Cassie, though, has a gleam in her eye—the same one she had at the Ping-Pong tournament, right before she went on her improbable comeback run.

"Are you good at eating spicy food, Gaspard?"

"Good? My face is on restaurant walls all over Long Island. Spicy ramen, spicy curry, it doesn't matter. I don't feel it."

This is news to me. I haven't seen this side of Gaspard before. Knowing Cassie, this is music to her ears.

"If you think this is going to be easy, then how about we make it a little more interesting? Let's see who can eat more spicy wings. You versus me," Cassie says.

Gaspard raises an eyebrow in a way that says, "Do you know who you're talking to?"

"I'm just worried they don't have enough wings for that," Gaspard says. "We might be here all day."

"I'm sure that once we explain what a big, strong boy you are, they can quadruple their spice-per-wing ratio and get us out of here before sunset."

We go up to the counter and explain what we want. The cashier, who looks to be about our age, chuckles at our request but says she'll talk to her manager. After a minute or two, she comes back out.

"You can take your seats. We'll bring the wings out for you, six at a time. You can pay at the end."

I feel a little bit soft as I order my no-heat soy-garlic wings.

Back at the table, Cassie kicks the bravado into high gear.

"I was built for this. I've been eating má là ever since my teeth came in. I put Sriracha in my cereal. But forget all that. The reason I'm going to win, Gaspard, is because this isn't a contest of skill. It's a battle of will. And I'm willing to *die*, right here in this restaurant, before I give up against you."

"You're all talk," Gaspard replies.

On the eve of battle, I'm not sure what to expect. Both Cassie and Gaspard have absolute confidence. It's like going into the NBA Finals—both teams look unbeatable, the analysts chirp and chatter and predict away, but you never know how the contest is going to shape up until it goes down for real.

The first plates of wings arrive.

Each piece of chicken has a toothpick flag planted on top that says *Ganghan salam challenge! Atomic spice relieves stress and fortifies constitution!*

It's on.

Cassie takes her first bite and starts coughing and sputtering. I don't even want to imagine how peppery and hot the wings are. From the brief look of surprise in her eyes, I can tell she's in over her head. Meanwhile, Gaspard tears through his first wing and hardly reacts. There's a reason he was so confident. This is going to be over quickly.

By the time Cassie finishes her first wing, Gaspard is already halfway done with his plate. Cassie is sweating profusely. She looks like she might cry.

"You sure you're gonna be okay?" I ask her.

Cassie just shakes her head in reply. I'm not sure if she means, "No, I'm not," or "Don't ask so many questions." Whatever the case, she bites into another wing.

Gaspard finishes his first plate and arranges the toothpicks into a neat pile. The cashier asks if he wants another round, but he tells her to hold off. Cassie is just starting on her third wing, and it's not clear that she'll finish the plate. As she painfully makes her way through it, Gaspard watches calmly, with only a slight twitch in the corner of his mouth that asks, "Are you sure you haven't had enough?"

But bite by bite, Cassie finds a way to pull through. When she finally finishes, a splotchy red rash has sprung up on her face, like she's having a terrible allergic reaction. She tosses the last toothpick down and pounds the table, waving her finger in a circle to signal for more.

At the very least, two new pictures are going up on the wall.

"Not bad, Cassie. I'm impressed," Gaspard says mildly.

His voice is genuine, but Cassie just glares at him. To her, the compliment is nothing more than a premature celebration. He's trying to tell her "Good game, you've made your point." But I can see in her eyes that she isn't nearly done yet.

The second round of wings arrives.

For this round, Cassie adopts a new strategy—she starts eating the wings as quickly as she can, inhaling the meat off the bones and choking it down before her mouth has time to feel pain. Her fingers and cheeks are quickly splattered with bright red sauce.

With each bite, she grimaces as the fiery heat burns its way down her esophagus. Gaspard, going slow and steady, looks just as unbothered as before.

For the second time today, tears stream in neat rows down Cassie's cheeks. I remember her taunts about never giving up, and I'm afraid she's actually going to put herself in the hospital. I want to stop her—I put a hand on her shoulder, but she shrugs it off and looks at me with iron in her eyes.

"The body protests, but the mind holds firm," she says. Or at least, I think that's what she's saying; her lips are swollen, so it sounds more like, "Na motty potess mut na mine hole firrrr."

Cassie finishes her second plate quickly and puts her head down. Her hair is a tangled mess, and her back is heaving up and down from the deep, spicy breaths she's taking. Gaspard, meanwhile, seems to be slowing, almost imperceptibly. After the fifth wing, he has to take a quick break. There's no trace of a smile on his face anymore. If anything, his haughty brow is creasing into a slight frown. When he bites into the final wing of his second plate, I can see surprise flicker across his eyes. A single bead of sweat slides down his brow.

That's when I realize.

Amazing moments in sports start like this. A familiar situation—a routine regular season game against the Toronto Raptors, say—gradually opens into an unfamiliar result. Kobe scores twenty-six in the first half, meaning he's headed for another big game.

Only it's not just another big game. Bucket by bucket, that

exciting point total marches onward into the realm of the extraordinary. The crowd on TV moves from excitement, to disbelief, and finally to the dawning realization of what's really happening. Before you know it, a singular moment in history has unfolded right before your eyes . . . eighty-one points.

The third plate comes, but I already know what's going to happen. Sooner or later, Gaspard is going to wear down, and Cassie isn't. She decided, before this contest, that she was going to keep eating until Gaspard gave up, or she blacked out. And that's why she's going to win.

Gaspard knows it too. I can see the fear in his eyes as he starts on his third plate. It's the same fear that I felt as Cassie came back against me in Ping-Pong. Only in this contest, skill can't save him.

Cassie stares Gaspard down as she matches him wing for wing. She can smell blood. Gaspard is sweating heavily now, and his brow is bent into a deep frown. Each bite leaves him panting, falling deeper into the well of pain. He recognizes it now too—that Cassie isn't going to lose. Whatever she's experiencing, whether she's hiding her suffering or has stopped feeling altogether, she isn't going to stop eating those damn chicken wings.

With two wings left on the third plate, Gaspard taps out. He looks utterly broken, with nothing to do but wait for the fires in his mouth to subside. Cassie eats her fifth wing, then her sixth. Then she reaches across the table, takes Gaspard's plate, and finishes *his* last two wings.

"TWUNNY!" she roars, thumping her chest like King Kong.

My head is spinning. I'm caught between deep pity and utter awe for the trials that Cassie and Gaspard have just put themselves through, the agonizing wait for their mouths to return to normal, and the second burning reckoning that is surely coming back for them in the next day or two, the one that they'll each have to suffer privately.

And Cassie. There's something so familiar about the way she acts. She reminds me of the kids I grew up with Flushing, back when we were all collectively living through an era of irrational self-confidence mixed with zero self-consciousness. I remember my own moments of glory—hitting a game-winning three-pointer on the playground and deciding that I was going to the NBA; finding a shiny Deoxys card in a booster pack and feeling destined for greatness, like I was Ash Ketchum himself.

She and I both grew up with those kids. We were both at the exact same place once, playing piano even though we didn't want to. Except she stayed, and as far as I can tell, she kept taking that feeling to the next level, and the next. Maybe I could have ended up like that too, if I hadn't moved to a new town, where I learned that if I didn't dress the right way and I was different and loud about it, then people would treat me like absolute dirt.

We pay for all the wings we ate, and then we leave the store. Both Cassie and Gaspard are suffering, and I practically have to carry them back toward Golden Promises. Each of them puts an arm around my shoulder, and we limp off like soldiers on a battlefield.

"How do you do it, Cassie?" I ask.

"What? Eat chicken wings?" She winks. "Simple. One wing at a time."

What I mean is, how do you not feel pressure? How are you so sure of yourself? How do you decide you're going to do something impossible and then *actually go and do it?*

Cassie seems to read what I'm thinking. "Don't be so dramatic, Felix," she says. "It's not like I defied the laws of physics or something. If you think of something funny to do, you give it a shot. Maybe you fail. But maybe you succeed. The important part is to always act as overconfident as possible. It's more fun that way."

This strikes me as the kind of it's-really-that-easy advice that Michael Jordan might give ("If you work hard and want it bad enough, you too can become a six-foot-six NBA superstar with off-the-charts athleticism and an unshakable killer instinct"). There has to be something more. When she gets that look in her eye, when that grin starts to spread across her face, there must be some kind of magic behind it.

As we're passing through Roosevelt Park, Gaspard stops to sit on a bench.

"Go on without me," he says. "I need to chill for a bit. Chill and reflect on my choices. Plus, I don't want Cassie's mom to see me like this."

"My mom?" Cassie raises an eyebrow.

"I met her when I went inside the bakery. Nice lady. I think she was disappointed I didn't buy anything though."

Cassie and I exchange a look. I open my mouth to speak, but Gaspard waves me off. "Go! Trust me, I can't talk to anybody right now. My body is here, but my brain is deep in the Shadow Realm. Felix, just come get me when you're ready."

I shrug, and Cassie and I move on. As we're turning the corner onto Elizabeth Street, Cassie grabs my arm. I freeze.

"Hold on," she says. "I think I need a minute too. Can we take the long way around the block?"

"Everything okay?" I ask.

"It's just my mom. She was taking my head off earlier. I want to hang out for a little bit longer before I talk to her."

"Fine with me."

We slowly walk past Elizabeth Street and turn up at the next block. Cassie's handprint is burned into my arm. I sneak a glance at her, try to glean what's going through her head.

"Sorry you had to see me cry today. Twice," Cassie says.

"It happens. Besides, the second time was because of the spicy food, so that doesn't count."

"It arguably counts more. Now you've seen me at my lowest point."

The streets are less crowded than when Gaspard and I arrived. Cassie's eyes scan the signs overhead, the fluorescent lights that are just now turning on. Her expression is thoughtful, but distant.

"I can try to make myself cry right now, to even it out," I offer.

"Do you cry?"

"Not that often. It happens sometimes."

Cassie nods. "No need to force it, then. I cry a lot. My mom says that for me, crying is like blowing my nose. My body needs to do it just to flush itself out."

We've reached the end of the street. We turn onto Canal, which is now busy with cars, and already the other end of Elizabeth Street is in view. Our time together is coming to an end, and I can't shake my heightened awareness of the moment, my desire to say something meaningful. I don't want this awe that I'm feeling to fade away; I want to hold on to it, to use it.

"The last time I cried was in freshman year of high school. It was after my best friend said that he didn't want to hang out with me anymore."

Cassie's eyebrows shoot up.

"He did what?"

She stops in her tracks. We're standing right on the corner. Golden Promises is in sight.

I wish I had something happier to talk about than my past with Henry Wijaya. But now I'm thinking about him, and the emotions are bubbling back up, and I *want* to show them to Cassie. So I do.

I tell Cassie about how we met on the school bus, how we used to watch basketball and play video games at his house. I'd been stressed about making friends in Great Neck, and I was so relieved to have found someone—someone wonderful, whose house always smelled like good cooking, who did cool stuff like ride a skateboard.

But our friendship was doomed from the start.

"I didn't realize how different we were. Henry's other friends were the kids from the skate park. He brought me there a couple times, but I didn't skate, so I just kind of hung out and watched. One time I did try to ride his board, but I fell off and landed on my butt. It hurt.

"At school, I used to sit with him and his skater friends at lunch. At first they just ignored me, but eventually they started making fun of me. It got to the point where I just stayed quiet all through lunch, because I knew if I opened my mouth, everyone else would jump down my throat.

"And then one day Henry just told me it was better if I didn't sit with them at lunch anymore. So I said okay. And that was it, we weren't friends anymore."

"What the hell? That's so messed up!" Cassie says. For me, this all happened long enough ago that it doesn't hurt anymore, but Cassie seems furious on my behalf.

"I'm not mad at him," I add. "He wasn't mean about it. He even said he was sorry. I get that he was in a tough position. I didn't expect him to stand up for me in front of all his other friends just because we'd hung out at his house a couple of times."

Cassie shakes her head. "You don't get to just dump people like that. You don't get to make someone care about you and then get buyer's remorse. If I were you, I wouldn't have let him leave so cleanly. You're worth more than that. I would have made a scene, or forced him to fight me, or something."

I nod, but I know I never could have done that. Once I realized what Henry was telling me, I just wanted to get away, let the whole thing end and be forgotten as quickly as possible.

"So after that, I went home. My parents could tell that something was up. So I tried to explain, but then I just started crying. Ugly crying too. Like, my whole face went numb, I was covered with snot, and my mouth shriveled up like a dead bug. I just couldn't stop."

"Probably because you don't cry regularly. So it comes out all at once. See, that's what I mean by your body flushing things out," Cassie says. "What did your parents say?"

"My mom offered to buy gifts for the skater kids, to win them over. That's her solution to everything. My dad said that I should join the math team, so I could make more friends that way." I let out a chuckle. "He got mad when I said there was no way I would ever join the math team."

"I'm sorry that happened to you, Felix." Cassie pats me on the back. "No wonder you seem so lukewarm about your town. That's a terrible memory to have so early on."

We start walking toward the bakery again, and the world beyond the shop front becomes a planetary force, pushing me away, pulling Cassie back in. The day will end, Cassie will turn back into a name and a picture behind a screen. I brace myself for another goodbye.

"Anyways, thanks for letting me tell you all of that. Sorry to be such a downer." I take a breath and work up a smile. "The important thing is to remember that this date, October fifth, will always mark the anniversary of that time you smoked Gaspard in a spicy-food-eating challenge."

Cassie smiles. "Today was fun. Let's do it again."

She waves and disappears behind the bakery door.

Back at the park, Gaspard is still sitting on a bench, staring up at the sky with a dazed look in his eyes, as if asking the heavens why they allowed this fate to befall him.

"You good, dude?" I ask.

When Gaspard sees me, his mouth twitches into a half-smile, half-grimace. "I've been better. Don't worry about me, though. I just thought you and Cassie might want some alone time."

I roll my eyes. "Not this again."

He elbows me in the ribs. "C'mon, don't be embarrassed. Nothing wrong with young love."

"I know. That's not what this is, though."

On the train ride home, I try to explain further.

"I like thinking about Cassie, and I get excited about seeing her, but not in a romantic way. That kind of thing must happen, right?"

"Yeah, I guess you're right. In a world so big, it must happen," Gaspard admits. "How do you know it's not a crush, though?"

"The word 'crush' sounds so superficial, like I don't really know Cassie, and I just want to be around her because I think she's pretty or something. It's more than that. The thing that gets me so much is that are our lives were so similar, but then I moved away and she stayed, and now we're so different."

A thought occurs to me. "You moved too," I say. "What was that like for you? Do you like Great Neck?"

"It's fine," Gaspard says. He looks unsure as to what I'm getting at.

"You like our school?"

"Yeah. The teachers are great. Way better than my old school. Plus they have every AP, and lots of clubs. And for some club stuff, the school even gives money."

"Oh," I say. "I guess that's true."

Gaspard cocks his head. "You don't think so?"

"No, you're right," I say, impressed by his positive attitude.

"But you still don't like it," Gaspard says, smiling gently. "And that has something to do with why you like Cassie."

I try to explain what I've realized about myself since meeting her. That after I moved to Great Neck, the person that I used to be was slowly eaten up by pressure and loneliness, by self-doubt. Without realizing it, I slipped into a malaise, like I was hypnotized. But then I met someone from before, someone who shook me out of it, made me remember my old life, my real life. If I can understand everything that's gone differently for her since we first met at the piano competition, then maybe they'll add up to something like an answer.

"Does that make sense?" I ask when I'm finished.

Gaspard is still smiling gently, perhaps even fondly, at me. "I think so," he says after considering me for a moment. "I may not fully understand what leaving Flushing was like, but I can see why it'd be something that you still think about. How do you know Cassie has all the answers, though?"

"I don't. I'm sure she doesn't have all of the answers. But before we met, I didn't even know how to put this into words."

"I see. You're a man of multitudes, Felix." He winks at me. "Anyway, if you say it's not a crush, then I believe you."

I'm glad to have won this small concession, but my mind is still in disorder. Today I felt something that I've never felt before: a yearning to be closer to Cassie, learn more about her. Why was she crying when we showed up at the bakery? And why did she get so mad when I told her about Henry, like she was personally offended by him? It felt so good to tell her about that, to unload some of that weight and have her be on my side.

No, it's not romantic. But it's not how I normally feel about my friends, either. What do you call it when you know you don't want to date someone, but you do want their approval, their secrets, their everything else?

PART TWO

SEVEN

AFTER RUBENSTEIN, WHEN I TOLD MY MOM THAT I was holding firm in wanting to quit piano, she bit her tongue. I could tell that she was disappointed, but perhaps because of our agreement, she decided not to give me a hard time about it.

In my sophomore year of high school, when I told her that I wanted to quit Ping-Pong, I wasn't so lucky.

I didn't see what the big deal was. Ping-Pong was always meant to be something that I did for fun. After we moved to Great Neck, it was a way to spend some extra time at the Chinese school so that my mom would have time to go to the nail salon or get a facial. But things changed when I started to get good at it.

In the fall of my freshman year, Coach Fang took me and Dan Piao to play in a regional Ping-Pong tournament. It was my first time playing in an ITTF-regulation tournament, and I was impressed by how official and organized it felt. I played really well, and I ended up beating someone who had a few points in the U15 mens' singles rankings. Suddenly I was a Ping-Pong prodigy.

93

Coach Fang asked me to register for the US Open. So I did.

It's funny how much a single weekend can change the trajectory of your whole high school life. The US Open was in Las Vegas, and I was still excited by the novelty of traveling, staying at a hotel on the Strip, and playing in a convention center instead of a basement. I won two out of my five matches, which was enough to get me my own spot in the U15 rankings. Sure, I was on the eighteenth page, and sure, it was short-lived (my fifteenth birthday was a week after the tournament), but it still counted for a lot. Especially to my mom.

Now that I was achieving meaningful, résumé-boosting success, she decided that I was going to be the Ping-Pong kid. Henceforth, my life was to be dedicated to practices, tournaments, and the slow climb up the rankings. I was still excited by my newfound powers, and tantalized by the beautiful new Ping-Pong paddle she bought me, so I went along with it.

I got better, and a part of me enjoyed becoming a beast at Ping-Pong, someone that the other kids at the Chinese school would talk about in hushed tones or point out in the halls. It was nice to make my mom happy, hear her say that she was proud of me and speculate on my bright future. But it was also exhausting.

The practices were endless, and I got sick of the repetitive drills, the pressure to keep improving. The worst part was the tournaments. Now that I was a ranked player, Coach Fang would point out the kids that I needed to beat when we spotted them at the hotels or on the tables. Looking at them, I'd get a horrible sick feeling in my stomach. I'd lose sleep the night before my match, and on the big day itself I'd be a nervous wreck; after one or two bad points I'd be in shambles.

My sophomore year, I was scheduled to play in the US Open in Fort Worth. I didn't tell anyone, but I was thinking of it like Rubenstein—I'd train hard for it, make my final push, and after it was over, I'd give it up. I didn't like playing anymore.

At the US Open, I played miserably. I lost all five of my matches, and it felt like a bad dream. Coach Fang kept up a steady stream of advice, trying to snap me out of it. But no matter what he said, I couldn't turn it around. When it was over, he shook my hand with this sad, solemn look in his eyes, like he'd failed me. After it was over, my mom could see how upset I was. She took me to Torchy's Tacos to cheer me up, and she tried to give me a pep talk about how much she still believed in me, how proud she was that I'd spent the last year working so hard.

"I want to quit," I said softly.

"What?"

"I don't want to play Ping-Pong anymore."

She was dead silent. I could see her face change from sympathy to surprise, even a brief moment of what looked like revulsion. Then she cleared her throat and spoke in a clear, steely voice.

"When did you decide this?"

"I just can't do it. It's too hard. It's not fun anymore."

"Do you understand how important it is? This isn't just a game, Felix. It's for your future. It's going to open up a lot of opportunities for you. If you just stick with it for a few more years, it could change the rest of your life."

I knew she was right, but that only made it worse. I told her I wouldn't change my mind. She shook her head in disbelief, but just like with piano, she didn't try to force me.

"Zhème ruǎnruò," she muttered. So weak.

I knew right away what she meant. Just like with piano, I was on a good trajectory, but I gave up when things got hard. Whatever it took to be really great at something, I didn't have it, and that shortcoming was the defining characteristic of my existence.

For the first few weeks after I quit Ping-Pong, I'd get this empty feeling during the times when I normally would have been at practice. It was like I'd turned myself in for a crime, and only now that I was home in a quiet house did I realize how the world would judge me for it. I knew that if I was at the community center, I'd feel even more unhappy, but that didn't make it better. It took me a long time to get over that.

Eventually, I even started going to Ping-Pong after Chinese school again, playing for fun. Coach Fang taught me without pressuring me, the way he had before that first fateful tournament. But he also sometimes looked at me with this faraway, sad expression, like I was a forgotten cause that he'd once fought for with all his might.

As for my mom, she didn't hold it against me that I quit. She had her moment of shocked anger, when she said some words that hurt, but then she got right back to scheming. In the meantime, she still asked how school was going, celebrated when I got a good grade on a big test, took me for bubble tea or ice cream after Chinese school if I wanted. At the end of my sophomore year, she told me that I was to start speaking with a college admissions coach. She'd found him through her network of WeChat friends, and he came highly recommended from a parent who had one kid at Dartmouth and another about to start at Pomona. His name, of course, was Mr. Qin.

"So the idea is that this movie is giving you some kind of redemption arc?" Mr. Qin asks. In his voice is another question, something along the lines of "Is this your idea of a sick joke?"

Two days earlier, I'd sent him another potential college essay draft, in which I talked about quitting piano and Ping-Pong. I wrote that in looking back, I could see some areas where I went wrong—trying to play pieces that I wasn't ready for, or trying to overpower opponents instead of reading their spin and countering it. I wrote about how painful it was to disappoint my parents. How I wanted to find a way to prove myself to them, to show them that I did have what it takes to follow through on an activity.

"Listen, Felix. You've got a nice essay here. These are some slick-sounding sentences, for sure. I can feel what you went through with these two activities. You're making yourself vulnerable, which takes a lot of courage. If you were writing a newspaper article or a memoir or something, I'd say you were on the right track."

Even though I can tell Mr. Qin is loading up for a "but," I try to enjoy his compliments. I do think that I showed a lot of courage in making myself vulnerable, thank you very much.

"But this is a college essay," Mr. Qin continues. "In a college essay, it's risky to talk about your failures unless they're leading to some big success. Without the success part, your failures are just failures. And for an admissions committee, that's death."

Hearing Mr. Qin say "your failures" so bluntly stings a little. I mean, I guess that's what they are, but it would be nice if he were more encouraging about it.

"Keep your focus on this movie. It's your best shot. We're going whale hunting here. If you can get it into an independent film festival, or better yet, sell it to a production company, then we'll have our whale. If we pull that off, then you can write about failure as much as you want. Otherwise, I'd say lose the sad stuff and try to sound more sure of yourself."

"Yup. I got you, Mr. Qin," I say numbly.

After we hang up on the call, I sit in my room in silence. I have plenty of homework and studying left to do, but I can't find the energy. As the numbness from the conversation fades, my brain starts to fall into a familiar disarray.

I never asked to play piano or Ping-Pong. I didn't ask to be good at them, and it isn't my fault that I don't love those things the way other people do. But because I couldn't learn to love them, couldn't devote my whole life to them in the way that everyone else wanted, I'm a failure.

On Monday, Gaspard and I use our film club meeting to do some editing. We spend our allotted hour in the French classroom bent over our phones, cutting and dragging video clips with our fingers. Cassie has sent us her recordings of some hokey monologues about Ping-Pong, which we overlay on top of our footage.

"When I was little, I always knew that I was destined to do something spectacular. It wasn't just the simple daydreaming of a child who doesn't know any better. I could tell that I had abilities that no one else had. In preschool, I was always the leader. I'd come up with some story—if all of us stand in a line in the center of the playground, then together we can stop the sun from setting, and we won't have to go home. And the other kids would listen to me and do as I said," she says, in a voice burning with quiet intensity.

Gaspard puts this over the close-up shot of Cassie's face as she gets ready to receive the serve. He adds a little bit of Philip Glass music (the main theme from *Mishima: A Life in Four Chapters*) to crank up the intensity. At the end of this first part of the monologue, he cuts to black.

"I knew that I had a voice. I just had to find the right thing to say. When I was ten years old, I started to play the game of Ping-Pong."

We time the end of this line with an explosive crescendo of strings. The screen goes back to Cassie. In slow motion, the ball crosses the frame and Cassie springs into action. She goes into a fast-paced sequence of shots, the speed jarring in contrast to the slow motion. The ball zips back and forth across the table, until finally Cassie wins the point. Then the camera zooms into her face, ending on a blurred freeze-frame of her with her fist pumped, her mouth open in a cry of celebration.

Gaspard thumps his own chest. "I'm an incredibly humble person, but the situation requires me to say this: I filmed the crap out of this scene. I might just be a cinematic genius."

"Yeah, it's pretty sweet," I say.

"Pretty sweet? Straight fuego, is what it is. Show some enthusiasm, dude! We're making a movie here!"

"It's cool. You're a good editor," I say. I want to match Gaspard's energy, but it's not coming out right. "Sorry, I'm just in a weird mood right now."

"Something on your mind, Felix?" he asks.

"It's nothing."

"Come on, spit it out."

"It's a long story."

"So let's hear it." Gaspard puts the phone down and turns his chair toward me, crossing his arms expectantly.

I take a deep breath and begin to tell Gaspard about how I quit first piano, then Ping-Pong. How disappointed my mom was, how I want to prove to her that I'm not just a quitter.

"I thought it might make for a good college essay. But when I told my admissions coach about it, he lit into me. Thinks it'll just make me look bad."

"You have a college admissions coach?"

"Yeah."

"Sheesh. Your parents go all out, huh?" He smiles. "So is the movie supposed to be for college apps too?"

"This whole film club is supposed to be for college apps," I say weakly. "Wasn't that obvious?"

It occurs to me that if Gaspard didn't realize this, he might feel used. Which, to be honest, would be completely fair.

"Well, not really. I mean, I figured you had ulterior motives, but I always thought you were trying to get the taxpayers to pay for your subscription to the Criterion Collection." He smirks. "No offense, but being copresident of a two-person club is a little underwhelming. If you're trying to boost your résumé, shouldn't you be trying to become president of something that already exists? Something bigger?"

I explain Mr. Qin's patented three-step plan. Saying it out loud in front of Gaspard makes it sound more ridiculous than it did when Mr. Qin first explained it to me. In the end, though, Gaspard nods.

"Very devious. I guess this is why your admissions coach gets paid the big bucks."

"My parents want this movie to finally be the thing that works out for me. And I do too. But I've been through this part before, so I'm trying not to get my hopes up."

"Geez, dude, I didn't know it was like that. That's a lot of pressure. You're still having fun with this, right? You do know that this

101

is supposed to be fun?"

"I am having fun. What we have so far is awesome, Gaspard. Don't worry about me. I'll feel better soon."

"Glad to hear it, Felix. And try not to stress too much about your coach. I'm going to take good care of you. With me on the team, this movie is guaranteed to be good." Gaspard pats me on the back.

I'm a little surprised by this sudden show of affection, but it feels nice. There's a key difference between this situation and my last two failed activities—unlike piano and Ping-Pong, filmmaking is a team sport. It's nice that I'm not out on an island, working on my future alone.

"Just do me a favor, Felix," Gaspard adds, his face turning suddenly grave. "Never, ever let my parents find out about college admissions coaches. If they ever catch wind of this, they'll hire, like, three of them. In fact, I think it's better if your parents and my parents don't meet until graduation. I'm afraid of what they'd cook up together."

Gaspard extracts a solemn promise out of me that if I ever meet Mr. and Mrs. Pierre-Duluc, I'm to tell him that I'm one of those parachute kids, sent overseas by his rich Chinese parents to get an education in Měi guó, with my seat in the Ivy League already secured by a generous donation to the school's endowment fund.

EIGHT

WITH THE WEEKEND APPROACHING, I'M DYING to get back onto the LIRR with Gaspard to head into the city for another day of shooting. But on Friday, Gaspard shatters my dreams.

Gaspard:

Duuude I totally forgot we have family in town this weekend

Won't be able to shoot

I can't get out of it, sorry

Nooooo

Damn dude that sucks

Gaspard:

You should still go without me though

On the bright side, more alone time for you and your girl 😌

I thought this wasn't going to be a thing anymore

Gaspard:
Right right my bad

😌😌😌

Stop winking at me

Which means I'm not going either. My parents won't be cool with sending me off to New York City alone; even going with one other teenage boy was already a stretch. I won't get to see Cassie again this weekend.

Unless . . .

I open up my chat with Cassie and send her a message.

Gaspard is out for this weekend so shooting in Manhattan is a no-go ☹

I don't suppose I can get you to Flushing again, can I? I'm sorry it's so last minute. But maybe we can get some good shots of you playing against Dan Piao

Also I'll buy you bubble tea again

Cassie:

Arrrgggh

I'm so disappointed! I was super looking forward to it

I can ask my mom about Flushing, maybe she'll let me go

But forget bubble tea, I want something fancy for this. Peking duck. Or one of those overpriced fruit smoothies. EXTRA LARGE.

I'll even throw in one of those fake Rolexes they sell on the corner

Cassie:

We're talking THIS Sunday right? Like, in two days?

It'll probably be a game-time decision. I have an audition in the morning but I'll message you if I can make it

I won't get my hopes up, but at least there's a chance.

On Sunday morning, Cassie messages that we're on. My heart soars.

During the drive to Flushing, I tell my parents that I want to meet up with a friend after Ping-Pong practice. I mention that it's someone from middle school who's already working on college apps; we're going to critique each other's stats and essays.

"Did you bring your essay with you?" my mom asks suspiciously.

"It's on my phone," I say, without missing a beat. "I just have to share the link, and we'll look at it on *his* computer. Can I go? I think he knows a lot. His older brother got into MIT."

Eventually I manage to extract not only a yes, but also thirty dollars cash in case we go for snacks. That should cover the extra-large smoothie, if not the Peking Duck.

Now I just have to hope that my parents don't somehow find out that I was actually hanging out with Cassie, and we were very much *not* critiquing each other's college essays. I could just tell them the truth, but hanging out with a girl sounds suspiciously like dating, and I don't want to risk getting banned from New York City altogether.

In my Mandarin class, I can hardly sit still. We're learning a dialogue about finding a job: xīn shuǐ is "salary," pìn yòng is "hire," and miàn shì is "interview." All I can think about is how in an hour or so, Cassie and I will be hanging out again. When class is over, I practically sprint out of the classroom and to the front door of the community center. Through the glass, I see Cassie waiting for me outside. It's chilly, and she's wearing a beanie and fingerless gloves with pandas on the back.

"Cool gloves," I say after letting her in.

Cassie shows me how the pandas on the gloves unclip and fit over the fingers, turning the gloves into mittens. "My most prized possession!" she says.

It's only been one week since we filmed in Chinatown, but

being here now makes me realize that I've spent all week waiting for this moment.

"How was the audition?" I ask.

"Not bad. It was for all-state, so the odds aren't great. But as you know, that's when I perform my best." She winks. "Anyways, I already made all-city."

"How are things otherwise?"

"Busy," Cassie says, shrugging. "It's a good thing this weekend worked out, because I don't know when I'll be free again. College apps are picking up, and the bakery always gets so hectic around moon cake season."

The reference to moon cake season piques my curiosity; it makes sense that things at the bakery would get busier close to the Mid-Autumn Festival. So far, I've only seen the periphery of this part of her life: the pink box of pastries, the storefront, the way Cassie cried after fighting with her mom. It seems crucial to understanding her, and I want to ask her more about it. But before I can, Cassie changes the subject.

"By the way, I liked the clips you sent me. You actually know what you're doing, don't you? No offense, but I wasn't expecting this movie to be any good."

"Please. Gaspard and I aren't hobbyists. We're amateur professionals."

"By the way, can we go inside? I'm getting chilly." She points a panda-enclothed hand at the door.

We go downstairs and head to the basement, the scene of our

first meeting at the all-Chinatown Ping-Pong tournament. I take Cassie to see Coach Fang and ask him if she can participate.

"I remember you!" he declares when he sees her. "Your technique is terrible. But you play really well. Good mindset. Very aggressive. Almost beat Felix."

"Felix has told me a lot about you," Cassie replies. "He said that you played for China in the Olympics. It must have been a lot of pressure to represent your country."

Coach Fang puts his hand over his heart. "Opportunity, not pressure. Our team knows that China is going to win gold, silver, and maybe bronze too. The only question is, who? I was never the best, so no pressure on me. I was there to play on the B-team, and maybe steal a medal from Hu Bin. He was third best, but I always felt like I could beat him."

Cassie and I find a table and start to hit. As usual, Cassie is wielding her flimsy off-brand paddle. As we warm up, I feel a nervous energy gnawing at my brain. I can't help but think back to the last time I saw her, the walk around the block, the sense that we weren't having just any old conversation. There was a momentum to that day, like we were going somewhere, like if we kept talking we would uncover more and more connections between us. I want to do it again, but I don't know how to get back there.

"I can't believe that Coach Fang played in the Olympics," Cassie says from across the table. "*The* Olympics. I wonder what the food was like. Do you think that the athletes could go around trying food from other countries? They must have had it all. There's no way they only served one or two cuisines, that would be an unfair advantage."

"I don't know. He doesn't talk about it much. I guess we never ask him about stuff like that."

Once we're warmed up, I find someone to sub in for me so that I can film. I figure that having multiple opponents could come in handy for a montage, or another monologue. Dan Piao is busy doing footwork drills with one of the assistant coaches, but once he's free, I'll pull him in for the climactic showdown.

While Cassie plays, Coach Fang stops by our table.

"I played someone who holds the paddle like you once," he says to Cassie. "His name was Zheng Guoqiang, I think. Or maybe Zheng Jianguo. One of those patriotic names. He was very tall, too tall for Ping-Pong. Should have played basketball. Anyways, he always stands back from the table and plays long shots. He never makes mistakes. Was hard to beat him."

"Was this when you were training for the Olympics?" Cassie asks.

Coach Fang shakes his head. "No. Much earlier, when I was in middle school. Everyone has to pick a sport. I choose Ping-Pong, because I don't like running."

I've never seen him so talkative before. When he trains me, we usually get right down to business.

Cassie gets into a tight rally with her opponent, and she turns all her attention to the game. Eventually she wins the point, then smiles triumphantly at Coach Fang.

"Say, do you want to hit with me, Fang lǎoshī? For old times' sake?"

I'm not sure what old times she's referring to—the one time she and Coach Fang have met before was the all-Chinatown tournament. Unbelievably, though, Coach Fang breaks out into a smile. He never smiles.

"Sure. Will remind me of playing with Zheng Guoqiang. Or Jianguo. Whatever his name was."

As she and Coach Fang set up on opposite ends of a Ping-Pong table, Cassie winks at me. I get the feeling, familiar by now, that something unusual is about to happen.

Coach Fang and Cassie warm up, trading simple forehands across the table. As they get their rhythm going, Cassie backs off from the table to play longer shots, like Coach Fang's old opponent Zheng Guoqiang. I can see the pleasure dancing in and out of Coach Fang's features as they hit. He even gets some bounce in his step, rocking back and forth on his toes like he's dancing to some unheard music.

"Play on!" Coach Fang cries.

Now it's time for a real rally. Cassie and Coach Fang trade shots, opening the drill into a normal point. Gradually they turn up the intensity, placing the ball at the edges of the table, adding a little extra spin or power to each successive hit. The rally seems to have hypnotized them; they're both in the zone, flowing in rhythm like they're musicians, accelerating as the conductor waves the baton faster and faster.

Eventually the speed is too fast and the music runs off the rails. Coach Fang plays in a side-spinning shot that Cassie just barely gets to, sending a looping meatball back over the net. For a moment, as the ball floats gently down toward him, I see fire in his eyes. Then he unleashes a merciless smash, and the ball bounces off the table and shoots halfway across the room.

"Hyaaaa!" Coach Fang roars, pumping his fist and doing a short hop into the air. It's like he's right back in his glory days, playing with the furious hunger of an aspiring Olympian. He holds the pose for a second, knees bent, chest heaving. Then he wipes the sweat off his brow with the back of his hand, and he's back to being regular Coach Fang, teaching Ping-Pong at the Flushing Community Center.

Cassie shakes Coach Fang's hand, and the two of them start to chat. I film them surreptitiously from a couple of different angles, then wait for them to finish talking. But Cassie keeps asking questions about Coach Fang's life as an Olympic athlete, and he goes on telling stories about the training facilities, the other players, the international tournaments. I'm surprised how eager he sounds. Then again, it's not like I ever asked him about his past. I always just think of him as grumpy Coach Fang—a little scary, and not someone who is interested in chitchat.

Eventually I start to get anxious. Coach Fang is going on and on, and Cassie is listening with rapt attention. Time is ticking on by, and the two of us aren't even filming, much less hanging out.

A part of me wishes that I hadn't told Cassie that Coach Fang was a former Olympian.

It's nice to see Coach Fang opening up, I remind myself. And it's cool to see him through Cassie's eyes, as a legendary athlete with countless stories to tell. This might be their one chance to meet and have a conversation, so naturally they have to make the most of it.

But my time with Cassie is short too. We've hardly spoken since she arrived, and I don't know when we'll be able to meet again. I know I have no right to complain, but it still hurts me to sit and wait as the scarce minutes tick on by.

To distract myself, I take a lap around the room, shooting random B-roll of the rec center. I fill two paper cups with water from the cooler for Cassie and Coach Fang, so that I'm at least making myself useful. When I come back, the conversation is wrapping up. Cassie pulls out her paddle and offers it to Coach Fang. I set down the cups, open the camera on my phone, and film him examining the paddle, hefting it in his hand, and then offering it back. Then the two of them shake hands, and after I give Coach Fang his water, he goes off to circulate around the room again.

"Sorry, were you bored?" Cassie asks.

"No, it was okay! I shot some B-roll. Did you enjoy talking to Coach Fang?"

"His life was really interesting. He used to train in this hot, hot basement all summer, no air-conditioning or fans or anything. People fainted all the time. But the point was to make the players tough, so that they knew how to dig deep when they were in pain. They used to say, 'Training in ideal conditions sharpens your technique. But only by hardening the mind can you create an Olympic champion.'"

"That sounds like the kind of thing he says to us," I say.

Cassie and I rope in a few more people to shoot Ping-Pong scenes with us. Dan Piao himself agrees to play out almost a full game, although he balks when I tell him that he has to lose the final set. That finally puts a wrap on our afternoon of shooting.

"Want to go and get that smoothie?" I ask. "Or if you were being serious about the duck, I can take you to the place where we always go. It's in the mall, and there shouldn't be a line this time of day."

"Hmm, what time is it?" Cassie checks her phone. "Ah, I don't think I can. I have to head back to the bakery. I'm already running late; my mom is gonna be mad. It always takes longer than you think it will to get around on the weekends."

"You're leaving already?" I check my phone too; it's later than I thought. Somehow the time got away from us.

Cassie smiles. "Don't sound so sad! I was just joking about the smoothie, you don't have to buy me something every time I come up here. I'm just happy for my paycheck. You're paying me, right?"

I work hard to bite back my disappointment. "Totally. You can have twenty percent of the profits, plus one bubble tea for each day of filming."

"Twenty? I want one third and not a penny less. Otherwise your agent is gonna have to call my agent. You should know I normally don't get out of bed for less than five thousand dollars. Per. Hour."

Before we leave, Cassie says another goodbye with Coach Fang. I know I shouldn't be jealous, but I am. It feels like he got to hang out with Cassie more than I did.

I walk Cassie back to the door. Before she goes, she puts her panda gloves back on.

"I hope you got what you needed today!" she says cheerfully. "Let me know if you and Gaspard decide to come to Chinatown again."

This is the end. It's so sudden, so jarring. I put on a brave face, work out a smile.

"For sure. I think we definitely will be back. Catch you later, Cassie. Don't forget your music this time."

Cassie fishes around in her bag and pulls the music folder halfway out, to show me. Then she winks, gives a wave, and pushes through the door.

She's gone.

My mind sifts through the memories of the day, trying to find the happy moments, the moments of closeness. But I can't help but feel let down. The end of our shoot in Chinatown left me hopeful, optimistic; it made me confident that there was something special about our friendship. Today that feeling is missing.

I wait inside until my parents arrive. In the car, they put on their usual Chinese radio show. My Mandarin isn't good enough to keep up with it, so all I hear are snatches of phrases like "more than ten thousand," "exchange students," and "absolutely not."

It's not unusual for us to ride in the car in silence. But today the way we're all trapped in this metal box together, ignoring each other, makes me sad.

"So, what's up, guys?" I ask, raising my voice to be heard over the radio.

My dad shoots me a puzzled smile in the rearview mirror.

"Who are you calling guys? I'm not a guy."

"All right, what's up, bàba māma?"

"Nothing is up. We are the same," my mom says.

"Your mom and I are boring people, Felix."

"There's gotta be something new on your minds. Isn't anything interesting happening at work?"

"Why do you want to know about work?" my mom asks. "It's the weekend. Your baba and I don't want to think about work."

"Just trying to make conversation," I say.

"Oh. Why didn't you say so? We can talk about this news story. Nǐ tīng dé dǒng ma? There was a graduate student from China who came to—what's this university called? Lì something?"

"Lehigh," my dad chimes in.

"Right, Lehigh. Anyway, this boy didn't like his roommate. So he poisoned him! Can you believe it? The roommate even tried to warn him, 'I ate something that made me sick, so be careful.' He had to go to the hospital, and then the doctors got scared, because

115

the roommate was sick from something that people normally don't encounter. A special kind of metal. That's how the police got involved! And guess what the graduate student was studying. He was studying chemistry! So when you go to college, Felix, you have to be careful, especially if your roommate knows chemistry."

"Right. That's some great advice there, Mom. I know, I'll buy him a present, so he won't hate me," I say, barely disguising the irony in my voice.

"Yes. Good thinking," she replies, oblivious.

It still surprises me sometimes, the way we live on separate wavelengths. My parents conduct their entire lives in a language I hardly know; at their dental office in Flushing, their patients are mostly native Mandarin speakers. Their moody kid is the only English speaker they have to deal with on a regular basis.

"You should try to listen actively," my dad says. "I bet you can understand more than you think. You just need to focus, instead of thinking about girls all the time."

My heart skips a beat. What's that supposed to mean? Does he know about Cassie?

My mom shoots him a look. "Felix doesn't think about girls. He's too young."

"So what did you do in Flushing today? Buy any interesting groceries?" I say, a little too quickly.

My mom smacks her forehead. "Oh, I completely forgot. We bought lychees. Here, I took some into the car for you."

116

She reaches into a small plastic bag and pulls out a bulbous red fruit. She removes the peel, exposing the cloudy white flesh, and hands it to me. It's sweet and fragrant and has a nice bite to it.

"Oh, wait, where can I put the pit?" I ask after eating it.

My mom turns around. She casts a glance around the back seat, looking for a stray trash bag or napkin that we might've kept in the car.

"I can't just spit it back into the same bag. It's been in my mouth," I add.

"Here, give it to me," she says, holding out a hand. I look at her dubiously.

"Are you really going to hold it in your hand the whole way home?" I ask.

She looks back at me. "Yes. What do you mean? Nowhere else to put them."

"You don't have to hold my spit-covered pits, though."

She considers this for a moment. "I better hold it. I'll remember. You might forget and leave it in the car. Then it'll be here forever."

"Or grow into a tree," my dad says.

I feel guilty about it, but I still drop the pit into my mom's palm. Her fingers close around it, and then she turns and goes back to her radio program. I watch her in the side-view mirror—her fist pressed to her chest, her brow furrowed in concentration—until I feel a pang in my heart, and I have to turn away.

She does so much for me—comes up with grand plans to ensure my success, casually assumes any new burden or expense if only it will make my life easier. All because I'm the one that her hopes are riding on, the one who's supposed to absorb her attentiveness and care and use it to push the next generation even further. Her utter dedication makes me feel safe, like I'm wrapped inside a fortress of love, but it also makes me wish that I could be a different person altogether. Someone better, someone stronger, someone who is good enough to actually deserve it.

NINE

FOR OUR NEXT SCREENING, GASPARD AND I select *He Got Game*. Gaspard, international man of mystery that he is, prefers "le foot" over basketball, so I'm relying on Ray Allen and Denzel to bring him around. If I can't make him a fan of the game, at least I can give him an appreciation of one-on-one basketball as a uniquely cinematic canvas for depicting emotional drama.

The turnout for the screening is our best yet: Mr. Eggleston, one of the freshman history teachers, and two girls from the basketball team show up to watch. About ten minutes into the movie, I hear the door open for another guest. I turn to look.

It's Henry.

He slips into a seat in the back. I'm looking right at him, so that he must notice me, but he keeps his eyes fixed on the TV screen.

Now I can't focus. I don't want to keep looking back at him, but when I try to just watch the movie, I can feel his eyes on me.

What is he doing here?

The movie feels twice as long as it should, but finally we get to the climactic one-on-one between Jesus Shuttlesworth and his estranged father, Jake. Jesus hates Jake, and on the last play, he knocks him flat on his back before scoring the winning point. Then he says to him, point blank, "You ain't my father." Jake agrees to leave him alone, but offers him one last piece of advice: get the hatred out of your heart.

I don't hate Henry. I know Cassie thinks I should, and sure, maybe I wouldn't mind barbecuing him in a one-on-one game of basketball, but I don't hate him. We haven't spoken in years, but now he's right here, close enough for me to see the fraying edges of his shoelaces, the scabs on the backs of his knuckles.

After the credits roll, I turn the lights in the French classroom back on. Mr. Eggleston thanks us for playing the movie and shakes our hands. The two girls from the basketball team look fired up, like they want to go straight to the court to work on their post moves. Henry is already heading for the door.

"Hey, wait," I call. He stops in the doorway, and finally he looks at me.

"What's up, Henry?" I ask.

Henry shrugs in response.

"Did you like the movie?"

"Yeah, it was good. Been meaning to see that one," he says. His eyes shoot toward the door. I try to ignore this. It has to mean something that he came here.

"Are you still a Knicks fan?"

"Nah. Don't watch much basketball anymore."

Henry seems uncomfortable, but then again, he always had something of a shifty, nervous energy about him. His voice sounds the same. All in all, he hasn't changed that much. Being here with him feels the same as it did back then.

"We're thinking about watching *Lords of Dogtown* later this month, if you wanna check that out."

"Yeah, cool. I'll think about it."

"You know it, right? The skateboarding movie. If you want, you can—"

"Listen, I gotta go. I'll see you later, Felix."

Henry pushes the door open and disappears into the hallway. The finality of it knocks the wind out of me. He's still the same Henry, afraid to associate with me.

My chest feels numb. Two years later, and I'm still letting him do this to me. Why was I trying to be nice? As if coming to watch a movie was some act of kindness, enough to make up for everything he did to me. Why didn't I tell him to get the hell out of my screening the moment I saw him?

Gaspard raises an eyebrow at me. "What was that guy's problem?"

I shake my head. "Someone I used to hang out with. We used to be friends in freshman year. But he mostly hangs out with his skater friends now."

121

"Yeah, well, you dodged one there. That dude seems like a dick."

I shrug. "It's my fault. I don't know why I tried to chat with him. I know what he thinks of me."

"How was that your fault? You were being nice, he was the one with the attitude."

Gaspard looks pissed, which makes me feel a bit better. I tell him more about my brief friendship with Henry.

"I can't stand people that act like that. How hard is it to be a decent person?" He shakes his head. "It's his problem. Don't ever say it's your fault."

"Okay. You're right, I know."

"Do you?"

I pause for a moment. It is strange that I was instinctively nice to Henry, instead of running him out of the room the moment he walked in. On the surface, it kind of feels like a soft move, like I'm crawling back to him.

But the thing is, I wasn't. I don't need Henry, I know that. I was just being nice, and for all my flaws, that's not something I need to be ashamed of.

"Yeah, I do," I say. "Sometimes people just decide to leave, and that's on them. I'm not mad about it. It would have been asking a lot for him to stand up for me against his other friends. He didn't do it, and that's that."

Together we wheel the TV cart back into the media closet.

Then we head out the front door of the school and into the cold autumn night.

"Thanks for sticking up for me," I say. "About Henry."

He winks at me. "Us copresidents gotta have each other's backs."

"We've come a long way from our little marriage of convenience, haven't we?"

Gaspard chuckles. "Felix," he drawls, "I think this is the beginning of a beautiful friendship."

It's been almost a week since Flushing, and Cassie still hasn't messaged me. Not that I expected her to, but I was hoping for it. I'm anxious to find some proof that the distant mood we left off on wasn't definitive, that there are still more moments of deep significance ahead.

I open my chat with Cassie and try to think of something cool to say. For inspiration, I click through to her profile. I see that she and Gaspard are following each other now too, which makes me smile. Below that are her recent pictures, which I start to scroll through. There's a group photo of her at a friend's birthday party, some pictures posted by a summer program for kids where she was a counselor, and a picture that her mom posted of a nice dinner, with the caption "So Many Beautiful Memories!" Then I get to a run of mirror selfies that she and her friend appear to have taken while trying on outfits somewhere, and I click away, feeling like I've stumbled upon something too private.

Just say hi and stop being weird, I tell myself. Even so, it takes a good ten minutes of drafting and deep breaths to work up the courage I need.

> Is there anything that you've always wanted to do but never had the chance?

Immediately the typing bubble pops up over her name.

Cassie:

Make my mother proud of me

LOOOOL jk jk

I don't know, there's lots of stuff

I wanna feed a giraffe for sure

I would like to visit London and see if I can make one of those royal guard guys laugh

You know the ones who are supposed to stay completely still

Oh and I've always wanted to go camping

I heard you can see the stars way better when you're out somewhere with no lights

Also hi Felix

Lol hi Cassie

Cassie:

Was that a college essay prompt?

No, I just thought of it

I had a feeling you'd have a good answer

Cassie:

Because I've never done anything interesting before?

No! That's like the opposite of the truth

I just thought you'd have some cool ideas because
you're very original

Cassie:

I know I know just messin

Our messages feel the same as they did before: fun, easy. I
breathe a sigh of relief. At least this part hasn't changed.

What made you say "making my mother proud" as
your first answer?

Cassie:

I was mostly joking

I'm pretty sure I make her proud. Well, I really hope
so anyways. Sometimes I have my doubts

> What is your relationship with her like?

Cassie:

Oh wow getting deep

> Sorry

> You don't have to answer if you don't want to

But once again I find myself drawn to the topic of Cassie and her mom. I know there must be a deeper story there, because I've seen glimpses of it already.

So far our conversations have felt imbalanced, with her helping me as I talk through my move to Great Neck. Parental struggles, on the other hand, are universal. They're something we can work through together; they could add a new dynamic to our friendship. Already memories of my mom are surging up out of my subconscious. After holding on to them so long, it would feel so good to finally share them.

Cassie:

You know what's funny, I just wrote an essay that's sort of about her

Well it's kind of about my whole family but that's like 80 percent her

> Can I read it?

126

Cassie:

Idk it's very rough and I feel weird about sharing it

I guess that shows that I shouldn't use it to seek approval from an admissions officer

Aw you don't have to feel weird!

For an agonizingly long time, there's no response. As I wait, I start to regret asking to read the essay. It was an impulse, a startlingly powerful one—what did she write about, does she have a story that's similar to mine?—and I acted on it without thinking.

Finally the typing bubble reappears.

Cassie:

I had a feeling you were going to ask me something about this

Sorry, maybe I shouldn't have

Cassie:

It's okay

I can tell this topic means a lot to you, the way you talk about your parents

I guess I'd rather share with a friend first before deciding whether to use it

> Lemme just edit it a little bit and I'll send it you

> Thanks for being interested

As I wait, I try to sit back and understand what's happening. Something feels off about the conversation; there's an ominous undercurrent to it that I can't ignore. We're entering new and more personal emotional territory, and I want, badly, to keep going further—only I don't know if it's right to want that. I wonder if I'm pushing too hard.

Still, when the email from chow.u.doing@gmail.com comes into my inbox fifteen minutes later, I tear it open like it's a college decision letter.

> Here's my essay. Let me know if you find any typos. Also it's a little long so tell me what I can cut. Don't tell me what you think of it unless you like it.

A Conversation with My Ancestors

Grandmother on my mom's side (Po Po)

Do you ever feel like you got a raw deal? For hundreds of years, parents in your village could raise kids knowing they wouldn't move far away. They'd stay living in the house with you and take care of you when you got old. At worst, they'd move to the other side of the village, but you'd still bump into them at the market or the odd festival and say hello, I miss you, are you eating enough? But then you had a kid who moved all the way to the other side of the world. Were you happy for my mom, or did it hurt to see her go? I'm imagining having a kid of my own, in America, and hearing her say to me that she wants to move to the moon.

Great-ancestors in general

Geez, this is a tough one. I don't know what to say to y'all, because everything I've learned about Chinese history suggests that you guys had it rough. I hope that at least some of you got to be magistrates, or land-owners, or at least had an extra pig or two. Well, unless you lived in Communist times. Then I hope you were dirt poor, and you kept your head down and stayed out of trouble. Anyways, you would not believe the stuff we have in America. Did you know that you can buy an eight-foot-tall stuffed bear at Costco? Wild. I don't mean to make you jealous. I hope you're proud of me, or at least proud of my mom for making it all possible.

Mom

I'm going to say this, even if you don't believe me: Mom, I love you. Shocking, I know. Sometimes I ask myself why we fight so much. All we have is each other. We should be so close and in tune that every argument is instantly forgiven. But we're not. I think that's our destiny. It's like we're two opposite halves of the yin-yang symbol, always meant to be in opposition, but locked together with no way out. Even if that's how it is, I love you. I may be young and you may say I don't know what love is, but that isn't true. The feeling that I get when I look at you and you don't know I'm watching is warm, deep, unmistakable. It's one of the few things in this world that I'm absolutely sure of.

Dad

Do you remember what the last thing you said to me was? I do. We were at the airport, and you were in a hurry to go, so you said, "I need to go through customs." An excuse. Which, like, yeah, fine. You did. But is that all you meant by it? You didn't think I'd hear it as, "My only daughter, who I am leaving for who knows how long, even though you cried and begged me to stay, I'm so determined to leave that I can't risk five extra minutes for you, five stinking minutes of parental affection to tide you over for the rest of your life?" Are you kidding me? And yeah, maybe it's some consolation that I'm tougher, or wiser, or smarter or whatever because you weren't there. But I didn't ask for that. Because of you, I'll never know what it's like to grow up with a dad.

Cassandra Chow (that's me!)

Hey, Cass. I know you hate lectures, but I'm writing to you from the future, so you'll forgive me for offering some advice. Listen to your teachers more. They really do know better than you. Don't get so worked up about things. You'll never regret letting your anger go. And try to enjoy things more. I know you have a lot to complain about, but in other ways, you're so, so lucky.

I see right away what Cassie was saying. This essay is personal, painfully so. Before I messaged her, I was embarrassed to see the mirror selfies that her friend posted online, but this blows that out of the water.

I know what Mr. Qin would say about this essay—"Don't show them all this messy family drama, they're just going to think you're soft. Hating your dad isn't going to get you into Harvard." True, there's nothing about what Cassie has written that follows any kind of sensible essay advice. But screw Mr. Qin. How can anyone read what Cassie wrote and not want to root for her?

I read the essay over again, lingering on the section about Cassie's dad. So she too has a memory that is forever burned into her mind.

I need to go through customs.

So weak.

And about the way she was crying outside Golden Promises— she was upset with her mom, yes, but also frustrated that the two of them didn't know how to live together without hurting each other. That story feels instantly familiar.

> Cassie it's really good

> There isn't a single word I would change

Cassie:

You think?

Idk bro

Don't you worry that they'd say, 'oh, another Asian girl with inner turmoil. She wouldn't have all these problems if she wasn't so quiet and submissive.'

> You have to give them more credit than that

> Even admissions officers have humanity

Cassie:

Did your college coach tell you that?

> . . .

> Ok fine good point

> Idk though I feel like this is so much more than that

> And I don't think it's just because I know you

> Because I don't actually know what happened, but

> this still made me feel something

> Sorry this isn't very helpful

Cassie:

Haha it's fine

Maybe I'll use it, maybe not

My hands are practically trembling. It feels like we're picking up where we left off back in Manhattan Chinatown. That if we continue the conversation, it'll lead to some kind of revelation. Only this time, it won't just be about me, and my past. It'll be about both of us, finding answers together, finding some kind of healing.

> You're an amazing person and your dad is an asshole for leaving you

> Um, not to call your dad an asshole or anything

Cassie:

It's fine

I'm used to him being gone by now

It doesn't make me that sad to talk about it

> Would you feel comfortable telling me what happened?

Cassie:

There's not that much to say

My parents got divorced when I was little

They used to get into shouting matches like every other night

I was too young to fully get what was happening with the divorce

But my dad said he was moving back to Hong Kong

And that was it, he was gone

Now he's married again and has another kid

The part that hurt was that he didn't try to take me with him or fight for me or anything

He just said he was leaving and I was staying with my mom

I mean on the bright side at least I never blamed myself or thought I wasn't good enough or whatever

But it still hurt a lot

To have someone who was supposed to love me give up on me so easily

It's like dude, at least pretend

Anyway we hardly even talk anymore so it's whatever

I'm so, so sorry, Cassie

Cassie:

Thanks Felix

Wow I just told you so much about myself lol

Didn't mean to go off like that

Want to share some more about yourself to balance
it out?

Even though my own experiences feel totally banal compared
to Cassie's, I tell her the story of quitting Ping-Pong, and the way
my mom reacted. As I type it out, it reads like a stereotypical story
about a boy and his Tiger Mom. The only thing that makes it
interesting is that it happened to me.

I guess the biggest thing is, I feel like I don't have the
right to be upset

She kind of has a point, and obviously I owe
everything to her

You could argue that she's carrying me on her back
and I'm the one that's not holding up my end of the
deal

Cassie:

Hey don't qualify your feelings

You don't have to be right to be upset

Otherwise you won't be able to process it

> I just hate that I'm not able to tough it out when I have to do something hard

> I don't know how to get over that until I prove that I can stick with something all the way to the end

Cassie:

You shouldn't have to beat yourself up over not making the Olympics in a sport you don't even like that much

Plus you're like really good at Ping-Pong

Not everything you do has to end up on your college app for it to be meaningful

> If only I could convince my parents of that.

After Cassie logs off, I read over our messages again, trying to relive the humming, glowing thrill of talking to her. But even as I do so, my mind races to nitpick the words I chose, the things I didn't manage to say. I shouldn't have asked more questions about her dad; I should know by now that she doesn't like talking about him. I could have drawn a clearer connection between her mom and mine, to show her how similar we are. I could have shown her that together, we could figure out a better way to connect with our parents.

I can't sit still, so I get up and pace around the room. I've never felt such a strong pull toward another person before, and it frightens me how hard it is keep my emotions under control. I want Cassie to feel the same way, but I can't expect her to, not when what I'm feeling is so unreasonable, so big.

I just wish I knew where this was all heading. Will the feelings pass with time, so that we gradually drift apart from each other? Or will they grow stronger and stronger, expanding inside my body until I come apart?

TEN

GASPARD COMES TO OUR NEXT FILM CLUB MEET-
ing dripping with confidence. He sits me down, turns off the
lights in the French classroom, and play his latest edit for me.

"Once I realized that I had a special affinity for the game of
Ping-Pong, I needed to figure out what I was going to do," Cassie
monologues. "If you're an artist, it's rather simple—you just work
on your next painting, or your next story. If you play a sport, it's
different. Yes, there are some aims that you have in common with
an artist—namely, captivating your audience with the unbeliev-
able things you can do. But you also need competition. The only
way you can really make a statement is by beating someone.

"And thus begins the story of the Mandate of Heaven."

During Cassie's monologue, the camera lingers on her intro-
spective, brooding face. Gaspard uses a black-and-white filter to
crank up the moodiness, which I think is a bit much. When she
mentions the Mandate of Heaven, Gaspard adds another cut to
black. Then the music drops—fast, rippling piano that gives the

scene a dreamlike quality.

"Chopin," Gaspard whispers, wiggling his eyebrows.

At the moment the music begins, we cut to the footage of Coach Fang and Cassie, playing the fast, furious point from Sunday. As long as that rally was, Gaspard has spliced in additional close-ups of Cassie to make it even longer. The real audio from the game has been completely taken out, so all you can hear is the piano, and Cassie's voiceover:

"The old man at the rec center was unbeatable. Rumor was that he had once played in the Olympics for the Chinese national team. He had an old, beat-up paddle that everyone said must have been made using some secret Soviet technology. Called it the Mandate of Heaven. He kept a record of his victories using a blackboard that he hung up in the basement. He had one hundred and six consecutive victories before I got to him."

The music cuts out again for some slow-mo shots of Cassie lunging for a backhand, the ball skimming the top of the net and bouncing just out of Coach Fang's reach. Then there's a shot of a blackboard with one hundred and six tally marks being erased. Finally Coach Fang solemnly presents Cassie with the beat-up old paddle, passing the Mandate of Heaven on to her.

Once the sequence is over, Gaspard thumps his own chest and lets out a little roar.

"That was *money*, my dude. I'm un*conscious* right now. Please explain to me how I just edited those clips into a *masterpiece*."

I wipe Gaspard's forehead with an invisible towel, to help him cool off from his hot streak. It's true, he's done a great job. The lack of game sound and the deliberate pacing give the rally an almost unbearable tension. In real life, Coach Fang passed the paddle back to Cassie in a casual, disinterested way, but Gaspard has cut it and placed it at the exact right moment to seem like a miniature rite of passage.

"I mean, you asked, and I *delivered*," Gaspard continues. "You said this movie has no plot? Now we've got an origin story. We've got a *motivation*. Next up, the *call to adventure*. I'm talking the *hero's journey*. Ever heard of it?"

"You weren't kidding when you said you were incredibly humble," I say, rolling my eyes.

Still, I can't deny that I feel it too. Before, we just had interesting footage and a couple of cool filters. Now we have a character who's actually *doing* things. The beginnings of a story. My mind is buzzing with possibility, because it feels like we're finally on to something.

The Ping-Pong Queen is looking for challenges, seeking to put her imprint on the world, to prove she exists. She's not just talented, she's a *beast*, and that's what makes her intriguing. But to make her compelling, we need more than intrigue: we need conflict.

At home, I start brainstorming. *Sources of conflict: make money, defeat bullies, get into college.*

Parents.

I write down the last idea, and everything clicks into place.

It's the topic at the heart of my life in Great Neck. Cassie wrote her college essay about her parents, and I want to write my college essay about mine. This movie has to be about them. It's the best way, the only way, to make this movie meaningful, to uncover some new truths, to show the world who we really are.

I start by searching for a single statement to them. *Everything I do turns into something I have to do for you.* After that, the rest of the story comes easily.

After the Ping-Pong Queen starts building a reputation, her mom asks her to teach lessons, get a job at a Ping-Pong lounge. They need the money to help keep the family business alive. Ping-Pong is just a game, the mom says. If you're going to spend so much time on it, you'd better get your money's worth. People like us don't have time to play around.

But the more time she spends on these worldly concerns, the more the Ping-Pong Queen feels weighed down. It feels good to help her mom out, but in the meantime the pulsing, glowing ambition in her heart is starting to atrophy. She needs a better canvas for her abilities than teaching the basics to unruly kids, or hustling drunk college students at the neighborhood lounge. Her mom is using the extra money to buy new curtains, a toaster oven, a shoe rack. Life upgrades to be sure, but are they really worthy uses of the Mandate of Heaven?

So she tells her mom that she's quitting all her jobs to focus on her training. She needs time to hone her craft, to seek out new challenges. Money isn't everything, the Ping-Pong Queen declares.

That's where the trouble begins.

I pause and consider where the story will go next. Maybe the Ping-Pong Queen will run away from home, dashing through Penn Station with a backpack containing just her paddle and a change of clothes. She'll live on her own until she's made a name for herself. From time to time, she'll come back to the old neighborhood to watch her mother from afar. Eventually they'll reconcile, learn to see each other's perspectives, yadda yadda. Something like that.

Anyways, it's a start. The rest we can figure out together as we're filming. Right now, I'm just excited to share this idea with Gaspard and Cassie. This finally feels like enough material for a real movie, not just a funny class project. For all my doubts, for all the false starts and days spent messing around, this might actually work out after all.

First, there's the question of how to get a person to play the Ping-Pong Queen's mom. We need an actual adult in order for the movie not to feel completely bush league, preferably someone who isn't expecting to be paid. The easiest solution, of course, would be to get Cassie's actual mom to do it.

There are a lot of ways it could go wrong. If I had to ask my own mom to be in the movie, she'd probably do it, but there'd be the risk of her getting too involved, critiquing my decisions, starting a fight. We all know how that story ends.

Then again, Cassie's mom wouldn't do that. I'd still be the director, and even if she thought I was garbage at it, she wouldn't go after someone else's kid. Cassie might even enjoy being in that setting, acting out resolutions to conflicts, rehearsing the harmony that she talked about in her essay. It would feel good to help her do that.

At the very least, I can ask. If Cassie or her mom says no, I won't push any further, but if they both say yes, then we'll do it.

> I came up with some ideas for the rest of the movie

> Do you think your mom would be interested in being in it?

> No pressure

Cassie:

My mom?

Why do you want her to be in the movie?

> I came up with more plot ideas and thought she could be another character

> Basically someone important to the Ping-Pong Queen's life who doesn't want her to keep playing for fun

> So she has to choose between her family and her dream

Cassie:

Lol so dramatic

Hmm so you want my mom to actually play my mom?

What do you think?

Cassie:

I dunno if she'd have time

But I guess I can ask her

She usually likes meeting my friends

Okay! You'll let me know?

Cassie:

Oui oui

She doesn't sound very enthusiastic. Now that a few days have passed since I got this new idea, my own enthusiasm is waning too. It was naive to expect all the big threads in my life to come together so neatly.

Still, I can't just quit on this idea. I have to see it through, even if it gets difficult. Besides, maybe Cassie's mom will turn out to be perfect for the role. Cassie's essay did make it seem like they're close, at the end of the day.

In the end, Cassie says her mom is happy to help, if she has time. Adding a new cast member makes scheduling more difficult, but we manage to find a Saturday near the end of October for the next shoot. Gaspard and I make the journey into Manhattan once more. The trip goes faster this time, now that we're familiar with all the LIRR stops along the way. When we get to Chinatown, a light rain is falling. We come into Golden Promises damp and shivering, and Cassie's mom immediately jumps us, pulling off our coats and hurrying us to a table already set with steaming cups of milk tea and a tray of treats. It's like she's springing some kind of hospitality trap.

"Felix and Gaspard! So nice to meet you. You can call me Ms. Chow. Cassie tells me you used to live in Flushing. Now you moved, so you must not eat many good sweets anymore."

"M hou ji si, Ms. Chow," I mutter, trying to convey my polite upbringing with one of the few Cantonese phrases I know.

Cassie is standing a few feet behind her mom, looking embarrassed by all the fuss. "Eat up, boys," she says flatly.

"Come on, sit!" Ms. Chow pulls out another chair and pulls Cassie into it. "Keep our guests company."

A dark look crosses Cassie's face as her mom sits her down. She picks up a pineapple bun and bites into it, chewing hard as if to relieve some stress.

"Eat! Don't wait. And don't let Cassandra take something if you want it," Ms. Chow adds, looking dubious at the way her daughter is sharing in the treats meant for the guests.

"Thanks, *Mom*," Cassie shoots back. "We'll eat up and then let you know when we're ready."

Cassie's mom smiles one last time and then flounces back to the counter.

"So now you've met my mom. She said yes to this idea right away, by the way. I think she was flattered," Cassie says. "Sorry about all the pastries. Ideally you can finish most of them, or she'll ask why you didn't like them. At least try to eat half. But don't take a bite of something and leave it unfinished, or she'll *definitely* take it the wrong way."

"I shall do my solemn best," Gaspard says, double-fisting an egg tart and a coconut cream bun. "This is all delicious. You gonna eat that hot-dog one?"

I shake my head. I'm not very hungry all of a sudden. Cassie seems to be a little on edge with her mom around, and that's making me more aware of the possibility that today might go sideways.

Gaspard shrugs. "You're missing out," he mumbles through a mouthful of pastry.

While we're eating, a few customers filter in to order items out of the display case, and Ms. Chow fills their pink to-go boxes and ties them with string. There aren't any other customers sitting at tables, but it seems like the bakery part of Golden Promises is pretty popular.

After things quiet down, Cassie's mom puts up an On Break sign and disappears upstairs. When she comes back down, she looks different, and I realize that she's put on makeup.

"Mom, it's just a *movie*. You're playing my mom on a regular day. It's not like you're going to a fancy red carpet."

"Don't want to look old. Who says your mom can't wear makeup? Like you said, it's a *movie*," Cassie's mom says. She chuckles to herself.

Gaspard, meanwhile, seems utterly at ease. The pastry flight has him floating on his own cloud of Golden Promises.

"Why don't you two sit at the table in the back?" he says, gesturing easily toward the back wall like a game show host introducing the night's prize.

The back wall is wallpapered with a blown-up photo of a busy street scene in Hong Kong. The sidewalks are thronged with shoppers, and glowing neon signs advertise everything from watches and cosmetics to desserts and foot massages.

"That's perfect," I say, trying to match Gaspard's tone. "That's a lovely photo, Ms. Chow."

Cassie and her mom sit at the table. In front of the photo, they become two faces in the crowd, an island in the middle of a flowing river of humanity.

"Let's warm up with something simple," I say. "No lines or anything. Just try to have a natural conversation. Ms. Chow, you're telling Cassie that she's spending too much time on Ping-Pong. She needs to focus on more important things. Cassie, you're explaining that Ping-Pong *is* the most important thing."

Cassie and her mom exchange puzzled looks. After a moment, Cassie's mom suddenly brandishes an accusatory pointer finger at Cassie.

"You have to stop!" she cries. After a moment, she stands up and adds, in case it wasn't clear, "Playing Ping-Pong!"

Cassie bursts out laughing. Ms. Chow starts to laugh too. She mutters something in Cantonese, and Cassie laughs even harder.

"Mom," she sputters, gasping for breath. "What was *that*?"

"I'm acting!" Cassie's mom replies, mock indignant.

"It's good, it's good, we're all loosening up," Gaspard says. "Let's try it again, but a bit more subtle this time. Ms. Chow, maybe you can try folding your hands together, so you look sort of stern?"

The two of them try the scene again. This time, Cassie's mom begins with a much simpler, "We need to talk."

"I already know what you're going to say," Cassie replies. "You want me to quit."

"You don't have to quit. But you can't spend all your time playing Ping-Pong."

"If you want to be the best, that's what you have to do."

"It's just a game."

"Not to me."

For the next take, I suggest that they try to do the scene in Cantonese. Cassie's mom is quick on the uptake. She crosses her arms and starts speaking in an even, forceful voice. I can't understand what she's saying, but the rich caramel sound of the language is hypnotic—it reminds me of Maggie Cheung and Tony Leung in *In the Mood for Love*. It isn't just the words, either. Ms. Chow's facial expressions, rhythms, rises and falls in tone are different in her native tongue. Cassie's responses are slower and less confident than her English, and every so often she pauses to search for the right word. The conversation dynamics are shifted; Ms. Chow is in control.

"This is going great," Gaspard says.

I nod in agreement. "Now let's try something more scripted."

I tell each of them what to say: Cassie, that she has a dream in her heart that she doesn't want to ignore, and Ms. Chow, that there are realities to be faced, bills to be paid, that their lives will be much harder if Cassie can't contribute.

"Oh, that's easy. We have that conversation every day," Ms. Chow says cheerfully.

With that, we begin. Now that Cassie's mom has reined in her melodramatic impulses, she speaks with a quiet intensity that fits her role perfectly. Cassie, meanwhile, looks genuinely moody, like she's itching to get out of the shop and back to the rec center. They're good.

When we pause for a break, Cassie gets up and strides over to the table of snacks. She takes a big bite of her pineapple bun, chews furiously, and then drains her milk tea in two big gulps. Gaspard begins to chat up Ms. Chow.

"Your mom is a natural," I say, joining Cassie.

She looks at me with her nose wrinkled, like she's noticed something unpleasant for the first time.

"Where are you going with all of this?" she asks. "What is this movie about?"

I'm a bit taken aback by the question, but I hasten to explain my idea: the conflict between the Ping-Pong Queen's dreams of greatness and her mom, the voice of practicality, asking her to use her talents to help with the family finances.

"So it's about how we don't have enough money and I don't get to do what I want?"

"It's supposed to be about how your dream turns into something that you have to do for your mom. Like, even if you get to keep playing, you have to do it on her terms. Until it becomes another obligation."

"So that's a yes, then. That's what my life looks like to you, I guess?"

"I—I don't . . ."

"Felix, do you feel sorry for me?"

Only now do I realize, too late, that she's angry at me. Her eyes are flinty, like I've never seen before. Her anger isn't big and loud and engrossing, like the other parts of her personality. It's a quiet, hard thing, a stone barrier between her and me.

"Wait, wait, let me back things up. I didn't mean to . . . that's not what I—" The words die on my tongue. My brain is locking up, and my face is turning numb.

"So do you?"

I'm not sure how to answer her question. It doesn't feel right to say a simple yes or no. The question is wrong, the whole situation is wrong.

"I don't understand why this movie is about me," she continues. "Why not make it about *you*?"

"It *is* supposed to be about me. Both of us, I guess. It sounded like we both—I'm sorry. I see what you're saying, this is messed up. We don't have to do it this way. I wasn't thinking."

Before, when I was excited to finally have some direction for the plot, I didn't think too hard about where the inspiration was coming from. I thought I was making it up, being creative. Now I realize that the ideas came from my assumptions about Cassie, guesses about what it's like to work at a bakery, projections of stories that I've heard before. All adding up to a cartoonish, reductive view of her life.

Cassie sits down in a chair, looking exhausted. "I'm not saying we can't do it. I was just surprised, is all. It's a bit too real." After a long exhale, she adds, "I guess it's not *wrong* to tell the story like this. I mean, it's a good story, right? I see how it's, like, cinematic and stuff."

She gazes off into space. I sit down at the table across from her and stare at the crumb-covered plates, trying to think what to say. I want to show Cassie that I see so much more of her than this one mistake suggests. I want to undo the bad impression I've made before it hardens into a fact.

After a long while, Cassie finally speaks. "My mom is good at acting, huh?"

"Yeah. She's terrific."

"I'm not surprised. She always flashes hidden talents."

"Like what?"

"Sometimes a song comes on the radio, and she'll start singing along. She has a great voice. But if I try to tell her that, she'll just laugh it off and say no, she doesn't. Then she won't sing anymore. Although maybe she'll hum." She stands up. "Should we get back to it?"

"Are you sure you want to?"

Cassie shrugs noncommittally. "Let's at least finish out the day. My mom's having fun. She'll be disappointed if we stop now."

She seems eager to move on, but I can still feel the shadow of our confrontation hanging over me. When we start up again, I tell Cassie and her mom to act out a happy scene. Ms. Chow tells Cassie a story about when she was a baby.

"Whenever the TV was on, you only wanted to watch the commercials. Once the show came back on, you'd cry until I changed the channel!"

"You never told me that." Cassie laughs. "Why did I like commercials so much?"

"They're more eye-catching, so it makes sense. Brighter colors, louder voices, silly little songs. The person in the commercial would yell out 'Eat more yogurt!' and you'd repeat, 'More yogurt! More yogurt!'"

"That's so funny, I was like a little saleswoman."

"You were a funny baby. I laughed every day when I was taking care of you."

It's a cute story, and hearing it makes me feel better. If we keep focusing on happy times like these, the movie might still do some good for Cassie and her mom.

We get shots of two of them working together at the store, pouring custard into tarts, brushing egg wash onto pork buns, pulling fresh bread out of the oven. Then Ms. Chow flipping the sign on the door from Open to Closed, and her and Cassie sitting together at the back of the shop and sharing a cup of tea and a sponge cake at the end of the day.

As we're wrapping up, Ms. Chow dashes behind the counter and fills two pink boxes with more pastries. Gaspard happily accepts, with a dopey smile on his face like it's Christmas morning. The man loves Chinese pastries. When Ms. Chow offers me a box, I try to politely decline.

"Oh no, please, you already gave me that box of egg tarts."

"Don't be silly, Felix! That was for helping my Cassandra get her music folder back. She's always forgetting things. This is different, your family can try. Don't be so . . . how do you say it? Kè qi?"

I'm normally a pretty robust practitioner of the polite refusal, but in Ms. Chow, it's clear that I'm dealing with an expert. Her use of Mandarin is a devastating counter to my politeness, and I have no choice but to accept. The scents wafting out of the box are heavenly. My mouth waters, and I remember that I didn't get to eat any of the treats from earlier.

"Looking forward to the next time. I like you two. Glad to know my daughter knows how to make friends."

Cassie rolls her eyes. "I'm gonna walk them to the station. Be back in ten."

Gaspard and I say a polite goodbye. Then the three of us go out into the street.

"Felix, I'll happily take that box of pastries if you don't want it," Gaspard says.

"Oh, I didn't mean that I don't want it," I say quickly, stealing a glance at Cassie. I don't want her to be offended. "I was just being polite."

"Oh," Gaspard says sadly. He grips his own pink box a little more tightly.

"Okay, fine, you can have it. Clearly you'll get more mileage out of it than I will."

A twinkle jumps into Gaspard's eye, and he snatches the box out of my hands and balances it on top of his own. "Deal. No takebacks."

Cassie laughs, but it sounds forced.

"Listen. About this plot," I say. "We can change it. We *should* change it. I'm sorry, I didn't mean for it to come out like—"

"It's okay," Cassie says. "Like I said, I get why you wanted to tell the story this way. Anyways, it's your movie."

I open my mouth to say more, but Cassie silences me with a pat on the shoulder. "It's okay. I know you didn't mean it in a bad way."

Cassie leans in, and for a brief moment I feel her arms wrapped around me. A hug. It ends just as quickly as it began. Gaspard gets one too, but loaded down with boxes as he is, it's an awkward one-armed side hug.

She says her goodbye, and I say mine back in a daze. Did that just happen? I wish that I'd had some warning, so that I could have properly registered it in the moment. I don't know what it means. I can't forget how angry she looked, and I can't forget the horrible, sick feeling of having messed everything up.

And then she's gone, and Gaspard and I are heading home.

"What was that apology about?" Gaspard asks as we wait on the subway platform. I tell him what happened.

"Dang, we messed up with that one, huh? I should have said something. I had a little bit of a funny feeling when you told me your idea, but I couldn't put my finger on it."

"It's my fault. I can't believe I did that," I reply.

"Seems like she was okay about it. She did hug you at the end. Today still ended up being pretty fun, no?" He chuckles. "I liked meeting Ms. Chow. She and Cassie are sort of similar. Both full of surprises."

He looks down happily at his two pink boxes.

I sit in silence, trying to understand what happened. Above all, I feel like a child—like Cassie finally opened up to me about her life, and in response I made a crude crayon drawing of it, complete with a frowny-faced stick figure with the name "Cassie" written underneath. The worst part is how oblivious I was, how I actually thought that she would appreciate it.

For now, nothing seems to be broken between the two of us. But today is a reminder of the gulf between us, not just in how we saw the movie plot, but how we see each other. For all the

155

hopes that I've poured into our friendship, all the obvious signs I've shown about wanting to be closer, I still don't know what's going on in Cassie's head. The things that I want so badly—for us to be closer, to compare our emotional scars, to search for meaning—maybe she doesn't want them at all.

ELEVEN

IT'S A FACT OF LIVING TOGETHER WITH MY MOM that she and I are always dancing on the edge of some sort of conflict. There's a constant, low-level tension between us, and every so often it builds up too much and bursts. Once or twice a month, a parental lecture will go a little too far; a few times a year we'll have a bigger argument that might feature some shouting. Only one or two have been bad enough to leave a real emotional scar—I'm looking at you, Quitting Ping-Pong Incident—so in that sense, we're lucky.

In the middle of the week, I get my first AP Chem midterm back, and it's a B minus. My mom, who's honestly due for something like this, lets me hear about it.

"You told us that you only had enough capacity for one AP," my mom says at dinner. My dad goes on silently eating his rice. "We didn't force you to take AP US History. But the truth is, it's not about how many APs you take. You just don't want to work hard."

"Mom, that's not fair. I studied. This class is just really difficult."

"I know it's difficult. What's your point?" my mom snaps. "Are you saying it's impossible for you to get an A? That B minus is the highest grade the teacher will give you? Sure you studied. The point is, you didn't study *enough*."

"Mom! I—"

"Don't argue. You're wrong. Qiǎng cí duó lǐ." Strong words for a false argument. That shuts me up.

I sit in numb silence as my mom continues to lay into me. By this point in my life, I've learned that the best strategy is to just sit there and take it. My mom is incredibly skilled at arguing—her abilities were honed from being one of three siblings—so trying to fight back only makes it worse.

Besides, she's right. I still feel horrible, but I know she's right. After dinner I slink upstairs and stew in my room. My own harsh retorts are still trapped in my head, hot and sharp against the inside of my skull. I open my laptop to start doing homework, but I can't focus. Instead I spend a few minutes having imagined arguments with my mom; in one, I've gotten a B in AP Chem but nailed the movie and gotten into Yale. My mom apologizes profusely for ever doubting me, and she even thanks me for quitting Ping-Pong to open up room for my true, brilliant passion.

No, thank you, Mom. I needed haters to give me motivation. I ate all of that pain like carbohydrates and turned it into fuel. You made me this way. A straight-up savage!

There's a knock on my door, and I instinctively open a school-related tab in my browser—the dictionary where I was looking up vocab words for English.

"Come in," I say.

It's my dad. He's bringing me a cup of peppermint tea and an almond cookie. This is cleanup duty: in my parents' good cop/bad cop routine, my mom is the one who hits fast and hard. My dad's job is to follow behind, apply some ointment to the wound, and make sure that I've learned my lesson.

"You hungry, Felix? You didn't eat much at dinner."

"Yeah, well, I kind of lost my appetite."

My dad sets the tea and the plate with the cookie down on my desk. "You still need to eat."

"I'm sorry I'm always disappointing you," I say.

"We're not disappointed. We just want you to stay focused. You can't settle for bad grades, Felix. A B is a big warning sign for you. It means you have to change your habits, soon, to recover."

"I know," I say, staring at my cookie with absolutely zero appetite.

"Put more time into studying. Get an A on the next test. If it's an A minus, it's not the end of the world. Just don't accept this like it's normal."

"I will. I mean, I won't. Accept it. I will put more time into studying. I just wish Mom could lecture me without tearing me apart. Like getting one B means I'm human garbage or something."

"No one said you were human garbage. Your mom had a rough day. We're under a lot of stress at the practice. She's just pushing you because she believes in you."

I bite back more complaints about how much I'm being mistreated. My parents have told stories about their own high school experiences—getting locked into their bedrooms to study for their university exams, screaming matches with their parents, sudden collapses from exhaustion in the middle of the day—and so to them, a dose of yelling is par for the course. "I got you," I say feebly. "It's fine."

My dad nods. "Good. We know you can do it. A little more time with your textbooks, and a little less time talking to your girlfriend." He winks at me and then leaves the room, closing the door behind him. I'm still not sure if he knows about Cassie, or if he's just kidding around.

My head is still swimming with retorts: Why is it all on me? What about the way *you* took me away from my friends, dropped me into a new high school in a new town, and ruined the only thing I was ever good at? I could go downstairs right now, throw it all back in their faces, make them admit that they're responsible too.

But in the end, I do the only thing I can. I decide to actually listen to my mom, even though she just yelled at me. I take the heavy AP Chem review book off the shelf—the one that my parents bought for me at the beginning of the year with such high hopes—and, like a good boy, I study.

On Thursday, Gaspard and I screen *Terms of Endearment*. This time, we get a surprise guest—Ms. Haverchak.

"I just love this movie," she says. "I saw it in theaters, you know. The two of you have good taste. I'm glad the club is coming along."

"Coming along" is a generous characterization of two copresidents watching *Terms of Endearment* with their guidance counselor, but Gaspard and I will take it. I've gotten used to thinking of any screening with a guest as a successful week.

The movie is good, led by amazing performances from Debra Winger and Shirley MacLaine. Ms. Haverchak swoons over middle-aged Jack Nicholson, who I have to agree was surprisingly good-looking.

At the end of the movie, as Debra Winger is (spoiler alert) dying of cancer, she calls her two sons into the room. The younger one is in tears, but the older one is playing it cool, because he's eleven, around that age where you start to hate your mom for no reason.

"I know you like me," Debra Winger says to him. Even though he's spent the last year avoiding her, being moody whenever she talks to him, she tells him that she loves him. The kid sighs, looks away, does anything he can to avoid the embarrassing outburst of emotion from his mom.

Debra Winger goes on to remind him of the happy memories— the time she bought him a baseball glove even though the family was broke, the stories she read when she was putting him to bed. All the reasons he'll regret it if he can't get it together and be nice, one last time. Because one day, he's going to remember that he loves her, and he's going to look back on this moment.

"And maybe you're gonna feel badly because you never told me," she says. "Don't."

At this point, even though she's weak and sick, she sits up.

"I know that you love me," she says. "So don't ever do that to yourself, all right?"

Ms. Haverchak is dabbing her eyes with a handkerchief, and Gaspard is shaking his head like "Damn this is good."

When the movie ends, Ms. Haverchak thanks us and tells us to keep up the good work. Gaspard and I start cleaning the room like usual.

"Hey, Felix, do you wanna come to a party this weekend?" Gaspard asks.

"A party?"

"Yeah. At Lexie Han's house. Do you know her?"

"I know her from your Spanish video, but that's about it. Isn't she a senior?"

"Yeah, we have AP Spanish together. I asked, and she said she wants you to come."

I raise an eyebrow. "I'm pretty sure she couldn't pick me out of a lineup."

"Well, whatever, she's nice. Please come? I'm going and I don't wanna be the only junior."

"I would, but I know for a fact that I'd have a terrible time." I've never been to a high school party, but being around a big group of strangers from the year above me sounds more like an ordeal than an opportunity.

"Maybe you wouldn't, though! You gotta live a little."

"No thanks, I'm perfectly happy living at my current amount."

"I heard Cassie might come," Gaspard says, smirking.

"What is wrong with you?" I shake my head. "Anyways, it's not up to me. My parents would never allow it. I'm in the absolute doghouse right now because of AP Chem. I'm lucky my mom still lets me sleep indoors."

"How about you ask them? I'll make a bet with you. If they say yes, then you go. And if you don't, I'll buy you a milk shake."

He sticks out a hand for me to shake. I glance at it, shrug, then take it. "If you want to give away a free milk shake, I won't stop you. You don't know my parents, though. This is about to be the easiest W of my life."

We shake on it, and I tell him that there are no takebacks. So now at least I have a milk shake to look forward to.

After we split up, and I'm walking home, I'm still thinking about that hospital scene from *Terms of Endearment*. Part of it is the writing, part of it is the perfect acting from Debra Winger. But mostly I'm thinking about the kid.

I understand that kid. I even wonder if that kid is me. Not that my mother is dying of cancer, but I understand that feeling—of being confronted with a situation that you know is crucial, that you know you'll never get a second shot at, and yet still being unable to shake yourself out of your normal behavior and muster up what the moment demands. You *know* you're wrong. You *know* you'll regret it. You're practically yelling at yourself, "Wake up, you big dummy!" And yet still, what you need to summon out of yourself isn't there.

I felt something similar when I was in my final days of piano, when I told my mom that I was quitting Ping-Pong. Even now, I think I feel it.

When I look back at junior year of high school, maybe I'll feel the same regret, the same sense that I just couldn't quite get my act together, couldn't see the forest for the trees. My life feels so complicated, but in my memory it'll probably look simple. I'll wonder what I was so hung up about.

But right now, as the Felix Ma that exists in this moment, I feel lost. Whether it's college apps, my mom, Cassie, the movie, I'm just feeling around in the dark. I don't trust myself, and I'm acting and moving forward only because the march of time is pulling me along.

Wake up, I think to myself. *Wake up, wake up,* over and over again on the walk home, chanting it like a spell, as if maybe, just maybe, those two words will take on some higher power and set me free.

"Hey, there's something I wanted to ask. It's about this weekend. I was wondering—"

"Later," my mom says, waving her hand. I've just walked in the door, and I can tell something's off. My dad is wearing a nice sweater over a collared shirt, and my mom has her hair up in a bun and pearls around her neck. The kitchen smells like sweet-and-sour ribs, which my parents never make when it's just the three of us for dinner.

"Mr. Qin is stopping by tonight," my dad explains. "We invited him over for a group progress update."

"A *what*?"

Just when I thought things couldn't get any worse.

Things aren't going particularly well on the Mr. Qin front, either. It's still not clear how I'm supposed to win an award; I haven't even mentioned to him that we might need to scrap the story. He's probably coming over to rag on me. Just what I need, on top of everything else.

Mr. Qin arrives wearing a long black coat over a dark brown three-piece suit. He's holding a bottle of wine with a red ribbon tied around the neck. After looking only at his head and shoulders for so long, it's jarring to see the rest of his body. He's taller than I expected.

"Mr. Ma, Mrs. Ma, a pleasure to be here. This is a lovely home! Great neighborhood. And to top it off, you've got a great kid." He winks at me. "You should be proud of yourselves. This is the American Dream in a nutshell!"

Mr. Qin is a different type of slick when parents are around.

165

My dad hangs up his coat, and my mom offers him a drink: sparkling water, tea, Martinelli's? The fact that there's a full production to the evening only makes things worse. It's like an elaborate ceremony leading up to my decapitation.

We sit down to dinner, the steaming plate of ribs serving as the centerpiece of the table.

"As you know, my unique approach to college admissions is to help my students build a standout profile, centered around an unforgettable hook," Mr. Qin says gravely. "Now, everything starts with grades and test scores. That's your foundation. That determines what tier of school is even going to look at you."

"See?" my mom says, nudging my shoulder. Here we go.

"Felix is solid there. The B in chemistry, eh, of course we want that to be an A," Mr. Qin says. So he knows about that. I wonder if he and my parents have a secret group chat.

"But Felix has As in history and Honors English," Mr. Qin continues. "He's a humanities kid, we'll say. More of a sensitive, emotional type. It fits."

My parents both look at me like they're seeing me for the first time. Their son, the humanities kid. Who'd have thought?

"I have to say, Mr. and Mrs. Ma, you undersold your son. Felix is smart, passionate, and he's showing a lot of initiative. Once we settled on the film club idea, he and his friend decided to go and *make* a movie."

This sounds suspiciously like praise.

"We weren't so sure about that," my mom says. "Isn't the whole thing a little silly? A Ping-Pong movie?"

"As I always tell my clients, it's about the execution. But I wouldn't bet against Felix there. He has some deep ideas for this movie: some real *emotional* stuff, you know? Like I said, a sensitive kid. The important thing is, he's getting out there and making it happen. That's leadership right there. Colleges love that."

All of a sudden, the air in the room has turned from staleness and dread into pure oxygen. My dad's mouth is hanging open in disbelief, and my mom even strokes my head and smiles at me fondly.

This isn't a decapitation, it's a celebration.

What on earth? I look at Mr. Qin with wonder. The *power* this man has. He's just too, too good.

Mr. Qin says a few more pretty words about my potential, my bright future. Then, for the rest of the meal, he tells us funny stories about his other students. Last year he had a boy who couldn't do anything himself. He was applying to a prestigious summer camp, but after weeks of procrastination, Mr. Qin had to write the essay and fill out the application questions for him. The day that the admissions decisions came out, Mr. Qin texted the family anxiously to check if the boy had gotten in . . . only to find that the boy had forgotten to submit the application.

Mr. Qin, fully in his element, roars with laughter at his own story. "I never want to say anyone is a hopeless case, but at some point, you have to ask yourself: is this kid even ready for college? Is he going to be able to register for classes, show up on the first day, remember to feed himself?"

After the meal, my parents clear the table and go off to the kitchen to wash dishes. Mr. Qin and I stay at the dining table together.

"Thanks for saying all of that nice stuff about me," I say.

"Of course! Don't mention it, Felix. I meant every word. It's important to keep things in perspective. But."

And with that one little word, "but," he's back to the normal Mr. Qin again. "Remember, none of this works until you have that one signature achievement. Lucky for you, Felix, I've got a lead."

He produces his phone from his jacket pocket and unfolds it into tablet mode.

"You're shooting this film in Chinatown, right? It just so happens that there's going to be a short film festival at an independent theater very close by. A real classy kind of place that shows a lot of those old movies you like. Getting your film screened at a place like that is going to look really good, no awards needed. I checked, and they showed one student film made by an NYU sophomore last year, so you should have a shot. I think you need to enter your film into the festival, Felix. I'll email you the application form right after this."

Straight to business, as usual.

The thing is, though, I like this idea. It fits with my and

Gaspard's vibe. Mr. Qin gives me the name of the theater, the Ludlow, and shows me their website. At the top of the page is a blown-up still from *Pather Panchali*. Below it is a paragraph introducing their Satyajit Ray series, running every Thursday and Saturday this month. Beyond that, there's a Zhang Yimou series starting in a couple of weeks, and even, be still my heart, a screening of *2046*, directed by Wong Kar-wai, my favorite director. And there at the bottom of the page is the announcement: Seeking Submissions for the Third Annual Ludlow Theater Short Film Festival.

"This looks incredible," I finally say in response.

Mr. Qin nods knowingly. "Of course it does. I'm very good at what I do. Now, if you can get this in the bag, then your essay will follow. Didn't you say you wanted to write about your parents? You can talk about how proud you made them. 'From the stage, I looked for them in the audience. My mom was in tears. I knew I'd finally proved to her that I was tough or whatever, and I'd done it my way.' Now that's a great twist on the strict parents angle."

The trite summary of my emotional life aside, I'm with Mr. Qin all the way. I've never seen my parents act the way they did tonight—like I'd surprised them, and for once it was a good surprise. It *would* be amazing to see my mom, shattered by the piercing emotions of our film, breaking down in tears. *"I was always proud of you. I always believed in you, I just didn't know how to say it. But now I don't need to, because your movie said it all."* All the years of heartache, worth it.

My parents insist on packing up a giant box of leftovers for Mr. Qin to take home. He leaves laden with rice, cabbage, and sweet-and-sour pork ribs, enough for at least two more meals.

"Now, what was it that you wanted to ask us about?" my dad asks.

"Oh, that," I say, still feeling dazed. "Well, there's this party on Saturday . . ."

TWELVE

"I CAN'T BELIEVE HOW BADLY I BOTCHED THIS. IT would have been so easy to insinuate that there would be alcohol. Or drugs. Or even just a couple of very persuasive English majors."

Gaspard and I are coming up the walk to Lexie Han's house.

"Hate to say it, Felix, but you got cocky. You were riding the high of that surprise meeting, and you let it cloud your judgment."

And thus, here we are. Even though I'm complaining, I don't really mind being at this party. After that dinner with Mr. Qin, it feels like only good things are possible.

The house is one of those intimidating new ones that lords over the average neighborhood—two-door garage, attractively dappled bricks, giant windows ablaze with light from a crystal chandelier. When Gaspard rings the bell, even the chime sounds rich. It's a deep, languid *ding-dong* that takes its time to sound out.

The door opens and there's Lexie, Gaspard's padre-in-crime, wearing fuzzy pink slippers, her hair dyed with streaks of blond.

"Oh my gosh, hi!" she cries out, giving Gaspard a hug. Gaspard isn't particularly tall, but Lexie barely comes up to his neck, and he looks massive next to her. As they break apart, I wonder what I'm supposed to do in greeting—shake Lexie's hand, maybe.

"Hi, Felix! So good to finally meet you," she says, as if in answer to my question. She gives me a hug too, which is how I learn that she smells really good. I'm not quite sure how to process all of this.

"Shoes off! This is an Asian household!" she says casually as we follow her into the house. "You can choose your own pair of slippers."

Next to a messy jumble of shoes there's a tub of slippers. Gaspard fishes out two pairs that are equally as fuzzy as Lexie's. He gives me a baby-blue pair and keeps a lime-green one for himself.

"By the way, these are for you," I say to Lexie, holding out the gift that my parents made me bring—a twenty-four-pack of Ferrero Rocher hazelnut chocolates.

"Thanks!" Lexie Han smirks faintly as she accepts the gift. She knows.

The three of us shuffle down into the basement, where the party is happening. I'm not quite sure what to expect—I had a vague image of flashing strobe lights, red Solo cups, and heavy bass—but it certainly isn't what we find. Ten or so people are sprawled out on and around a vast couch, their feet clad in fuzzy slippers, all watching a K-pop music video on the TV.

"Ahhh, are you serious? You started watching without me?" Lexie shrieks, indignant.

"We're going to have to watch this video at least ten times

tonight, don't worry," another girl responds.

Lexie introduces me and Gaspard to rest of her friends, and the two of us stand off to the side and watch as a boy band twists, runs, and shakes through a series of colorful sets: a forest populated by cute, puzzled-looking woodland creatures; a city in the clouds; and a world where everything is made of dessert. When the beat changes and the rap verse starts, a couple of girls rap along.

"I'm *obsessed* with Jimin," one of the girls says. "He's criminally underutilized in this video."

This sparks a debate about who the most appealing member of the group is. Even the only two other guys in the room—two hulking offensive-lineman-looking dudes sitting by the window—weigh in with their opinions. The arguments grow heated, reaching an impasse, until Lexie points out magnanimously that, "It's really about their group chemistry, and their genuine love and support for one another."

This is not the party I was expecting to walk into. There is no alcohol, there are no drugs, and the lights are very bright. Most of the attendees are wearing sweatpants. Thankfully, my parents didn't make me dress up.

We watch another music video, then another, which makes it easy for me to remain silent without feeling awkward. I'm not exactly comfortable, but I'm not intimidated anymore either. Something about watching people geek out over a boy band is very disarming.

"All right, people! Hope all of that boy candy got your hormones going. Now it's time for the main event!" Lexie announces.

The main event, it turns out, is a game called The Renegades. Each of us is given a secret card indicating whether we're Revolutionaries or Fifth Columnists. The Revolutionaries are trying to overturn the old world order, while the Fifth Columnists try to stop them through sabotage. Because everyone's identity is secret, it's a game of wild accusations, backstabbing, and general mayhem.

There's no time for tentativeness, because almost immediately Damini (the girl who's obsessed with Jimin) falsely accuses me of being a Fifth Columnist.

"Oh, hell yes." Gaspard jumps in, delighted. "Felix absolutely cannot be trusted. He is a man of sweet words and false deeds."

"Why me?" I protest. "If you're accusing me, that means *you're* the traitor."

"I don't know, Felix, you seem very *suspicious*," Lexie adds, smirking. "Is that why you brought Ferrero Rochers? To throw us off the scent?"

"Oh snap, there's Rochers?" one of the two boys asks. His name, I learn, is Reggie, and his friend is Nasr. They seem chill, but they look like cartoon versions of high school seniors: huge, muscular, capable of squishing my head like a melon with their bare hands.

We pause briefly so that Lexie can open up the twenty-four-pack of chocolates. "It's cool if we eat them now, right?" she asks.

"Unless you think they're poisoned," I say, half joking and half bitter that our revolution is being threatened by Damini's maybe-suspicion-maybe-subversion.

After four rounds, the revolution has failed two out of four missions, which means it all comes down to the final round. We've determined that Lexie, Reggie, and another girl named Yael are definitely Revolutionaries, and that Nasr is definitely a spy. I'm still under heavy suspicion.

"Guys, if we want to win this mission, then you *have* to pick me," I plead. "I know there's been a lot of unfair accusations, but that's water under the bridge. All I care about is the victory of our glorious revolution. I've given my life for this cause. I've been undercover deep within the state. I haven't seen my family in *four years*. We're so close. Please don't let this be the end."

"I am shocked, *shocked*, by this man's audacity!" Gaspard roars, indignant. "We have nothing more to say to him. The only thing he cares about is preserving the wretched order that has broken the backs of our people for far too long. Out with the old! In with the new!"

I'm outraged. It's so obvious that he's a spy. Now I know intimately how painful it feels to be falsely accused.

Lexie shakes her head. "To be honest, I don't know which of them to trust. Gaspard is advocating hard for himself. A little *too* hard. As for Felix, his record is spotty, but he *did* bring us these chocolates, which as we know are a classic calling card of the revolutionary. The safe choice is to vote for me. We've succeeded on both of the missions I've been on. Revolutionaries—I *got* you."

The votes come in. Gaspard: rejected. Felix: rejected. Lexie: approved.

With heavy hearts, we send the operatives on their mission. I should have been among them, but at least Gaspard isn't with them either. The operatives each play their card. We flip them over. Three successes, one fail. There was a spy on the mission.

"No!" Gaspard and I both groan.

Gaspard frowns at me. "Don't groan like you're sad about this. It's over, Felix. Go ahead and celebrate with your old world order friends."

It's time to reveal our identities. I flip over my Revolutionary card with a wounded sense of self-righteousness. Gaspard flips his over. Also Revolutionary. Damini is too. Lexie, though? A damn Fifth Columnist.

I meet eyes with Gaspard and see my own disbelief mirrored in his face. We've been played.

"How could you?" I ask her.

She winks. "Nothing personal, boys. I'm a mercenary at heart. Turns out Fifth Columning pays a lot better than revolutioning."

It's a cold, cold world.

"By the way, you guys are fun to play with," Damini adds. "I liked your speech. Where did you come up with that? Have you played this game before?"

I shake my head. "We just watch a lot of old movies. Gaspard and I co-founded the film club."

"Oh, no way! That's so cool. My mom and I like to watch Audrey Hepburn movies together."

"Funny, Gaspard and I were just talking about showing *Charade*. We do screenings on Thursdays if you want to check us out."

We're all too tired of yelling at ourselves and each other to play another game of The Renegades, so instead a split-screen game of Starfall starts up. Gaspard and I team up against Reggie and Nasr, but they're way too good for us to handle. After a particularly ugly double assassination, they start guffawing and calling us scrubs. It doesn't help that I'm shy about killing them in a video game, like they'll come back for me in real life. Meanwhile, Lexie and Damini bring down an electric kettle and packs of Shin Ramyun for us to eat. This, apparently, is a Han house party tradition.

"This is a much more wholesome party than I expected," I whisper to Gaspard.

"You watch too many movies, Felix," he says, his lip twitching. "You're glad you came, right? Sorry I was going after you so hard in that spy game. You have to admit, you were acting *mad* suspicious."

"Yeah, but haven't you ever read, like, an Agatha Christie book? It's never the one you suspect. And yes, I am glad I came."

Over noodles, Reggie and Nasr tell the party about their senior prank idea—to rearrange the letters of the Great Neck Edmund J. Cooper High School sign to spell out "Green doo doo iN tHe Emu Shack."

"They'll talk about it forever. It's been ten years since we had a decent prank at this school. The superintendent probably brags to the parents about how law and order have returned to our district," Reggie admonishes us.

Nasr shakes his head sadly. "We've gotta remind him about that age-old truth—that between kids and teachers there's an endless war, and kids always win."

"It's about respect," Reggie says, finishing what I can only assume is their rehearsed, two-man pitch. The crowd applauds.

After the Shin Ramyun, the party enters its final act—karaoke. Reggie kicks things off with a sweet rendition of "Stay" by Rihanna, and then Lexie and Damini keep the energy going with an impressive rendition of a K-pop song, capped off by Damini's flawless delivery on a rap verse all in Korean. Then it's to me and Gaspard. We huddle up and plot our strategy.

"Do we try to turn it up or take it down?" I whisper.

"Let's go for a classic. Something slow. To show them how refined we are."

We go for "I Will Always Love You" by Whitney Houston. As we softly sing our way through the intro, the room goes dead silent. When the drums come in, Reggie and Nasr pull out their phone flashlights and wave them in the air; soon everyone else is swaying along.

Once we hit the first chorus, though, Gaspard and I realize we're in trouble. The notes are pretty high, and Gaspard and I don't exactly have Whitney-level vocal range. Gaspard's voice cracks right in the middle of "lo-ove," and he ends up doubling over and sneezing. Meanwhile, I shift into a falsetto and just barely manage to hold on and hit the final "you." Lexie and Damini whistle their approval.

For the rest of the song, Gaspard and I limp along. Before the final chorus, there's a break in the music, and we exchange worried looks. No way we're hitting those high notes again. The drum kicks back in, and both of us jump in for the final "and I-I-I-I-I-I-I—" a full octave lower. It's not exactly a triumphant, soaring finale, but at least we're in tune.

At the end of the party, Nasr comes up from behind and claps me on the back. For a second my knees go wobbly, and I have an unwanted flashback to getting backstabbed in Starfall. Out of the corner of my eye, I see Reggie, dapping up Gaspard.

"You two are so pure. The last of the innocents," Reggie says, wiping an imaginary tear from his cheek.

"Reminds me of a younger me," Nasr agrees. "I was losing hope, but maybe the next generation will be all right."

They approve of us, it would seem.

"No sweat," I say. "The war never ends. Green doo-doo in the emu shack."

Reggie and Nasr exchange a knowing look. They both shout, "Amen!" Then they give each of us one last fist bump before bounding up the stairs with all the confidence of the masters of the world. As for me, it feels like I've passed some kind of test.

In the foyer, Gaspard and I wait for our rides. Lexie is seeing Damini off, and Damini, already bundled up in winter clothes, stops to give Gaspard and me a hug each.

"I'm glad you came! It was a genuine pleasure to meet both of you."

After we say goodbye to Lexie and head out of the house, I feel a happy buzz in my chest. I was assuming that I wouldn't have fun tonight—at worst, that I'd get bullied somehow. I definitely didn't expect to be right in the middle of things, tossing around denunciations and performing a pop super ballad for an audience. But it's like Mr. Qin said—I shouldn't undersell myself.

The story that I've told myself for so long is that I'm not supposed to be living in Great Neck. I never found the right people, the right activities; the things that worked back in Flushing don't work here. But maybe this year, I've finally found a way in, a new path forward where I don't have to rely on rooting through the past for clues. Or maybe it was always there, and only now am I realizing that I've been on it all along.

THIRTEEN

"THE GAME OF PING-PONG IS, AT ITS HEART, A conversation," Cassie narrates, over a shot of her walking down the street, jacket zipped up against the cold. "I say 'top spin,' and you say 'slice.' We go on like that, exchanging ideas, switching our words to keep each other guessing."

The camera follows Cassie into the community center and downstairs into the basement, where she sheds her sweats, blows on her hands, and unzips the Mandate of Heaven from its carrying case.

"The conversation has rules. If I say 'loop,' and you say 'push,' then unless you've got something clever planned, you're in trouble. The trick is who can string together words into sentences, force the opponent into a dead end, then end the conversation with a period or an exclamation point. That's where the artistry of the game lies."

The music comes in, and there's a series of fast-paced clips to illustrate Cassie's point—rallies shot from an overhead angle where it's clear that Cassie is pinning her opponent (me) to one side of the table before rocketing a kill shot to the other side; or applying a sequence of devastating spin until the opponent (me, in a different shirt) helplessly hits the ball into the net.

Cut to black.

"The game of Ping-Pong is, at its heart, a conversation."

An exterior shot of Golden Promises. Then an interior shot of Cassie's mom, looking wistfully at the front door, as if wondering when Cassie will come home. Then Cassie and her mom, sitting across from each other at the table.

"The conversation has rules. If I say how I feel, and you say the wrong thing back, then we're in trouble."

Cassie and her mom begin speaking to each other in Cantonese. Gaspard and I have added subtitles, using a translator app and a healthy dose of creative license.

"I need you to do more around the shop. We're struggling. Can't you see that?"

"It's your fault. We were doing fine before. We never should have moved into this bigger space."

"That's over now. If you keep spending time playing games, then we could lose our livelihood. Don't you understand?"

"You should have taken better care of us. It's not fair."

"What do you know about fairness?"

As the emotions rise, the sounds of a Ping-Pong rally slowly build. Squeaking rubber soles, the thwack of the paddle against the ball, the smaller echo of the ball hitting the table. The overlaid sound builds and builds until it overwhelms the voices. Near the end, the original audio is buried altogether, and it's just lips moving wordlessly, close-ups of eyes and clenched hands and teeth.

Finally, at the end, we kill the Ping-Pong effects and cut the real conversation audio back in. Ten seconds of loud, glorious Cantonese. Then, the clip ends.

At our last film club meeting, Gaspard and I debated what to do about the movie. After we realized the problems with the plot, it was tempting to call the whole thing off. In the end, we decided to at least edit the footage together and take stock of where we were.

Then came the email from Mr. Qin.

Listen, Felix,

I took a look at some of the past entries into Ludlow. Bottom line is, the judges care a lot about your process. They did an interview with one of the student directors, a college kid. He told this very interesting story. Said he was shooting a sad scene, and the main actress wasn't giving enough emotion. So he yells cut, pulls her aside, and starts screaming in her face. Cursing her out, spit flying everywhere. Says she can't act, she should just go home. Mind you, the director is a big guy, very intimidating. So by the end, the girl is in tears, ready to quit. But instead, the director puts her back in there. She's all shaken up, and they get the rest of the scene in one take. Now, I'm not saying you have to go screaming at people, but a little bit of color like that might help your case. Think it over.

It's the type of anecdote that you often hear about these creative types who are geniuses, but also assholes. Like Steve Jobs, screaming at his engineers about broken iMac demos, or Michael Jordan, chucking the ball at his teammates' heads. I wonder if the opposite anecdote will work: i.e., I made this movie because my mom was screaming at *me*. Somehow, it seems more impressive to be the one doing the screaming.

And then the final paragraph:

Now, I know this project is somewhat whimsical, but I can't overstate how important an opportunity this film festival is. You only have a limited amount of time remaining to build up your admissions profile, and a selection at a legitimate event like this could be the linchpin of your candidacy. It's no exaggeration to say that what you do now will have an outsized impact on the rest of your life. Good luck.

Michael Qin
B.A., Harvard College
J.D., NYU School of Law

I've been at this point before: found some early success with an activity, got my parents' hopes up. That's the easy part, when everything is still fun and the excitement is carrying me forward. Once there's real momentum and importance behind the project, that's when the pressure comes in.

When Ping-Pong became something serious, and I understood the climb that I needed to make to get up in the U18 rankings, the difficulty of the task closed in on me like a vise. I knew how good the kids at the top were, how much improvement I'd have to squeeze out of my body to catch up to them. At practice, if I didn't play well, the pressure and frustration were so heavy that I couldn't breathe. And then the urge to quit seeped into my mind. It was so embarrassing to think about, and yet it was such a relief. The idea took hold, grew bigger and bigger, until I knew that I needed to do it.

Things can't go that way this time. This is probably my last chance. I have to make it count. I have to keep pushing forward, no matter what.

Now that some time has passed, the footage from our last shoot doesn't seem so bad anymore. Yes, the setting is based on Cassie's life, but the conflict comes off as stylized, like a fairy tale, too abstract to be distasteful. Really, the movie is about a person who is searching for something, who won't give up until she finds it.

With that in mind, I write a new ending.

The Ping-Pong Queen finally manages to talk her mom into letting her play in a big local tournament.

She goes, and it's exhilarating: real scorekeepers, real competition, real prize money. Just one taste, and she's hooked.

She asks if she can go to another one, an even bigger one, but her mom says no, absolutely not. "You've had your fun, now it's back to reality." The P.P.Q. faces a choice. Does she obey her mother's commands, or go against her, try to prove her wrong?

The day before the tournament, she packs her bags. In the middle of the night, she creeps downstairs. The light in the living room is on, but her mom is asleep. She's passed out on the couch, with a pile of bills in front of her. The P.P.Q. tiptoes over, pulls the blanket up to her mom's chin. On the table she leaves a note. "I have to do this, for me. When I win, then you'll understand."

(Montage)

The P.P.Q. steps out into the world. She boards the evening bus, sleeps fitfully on top of her backpack, wakes up to the first rays of sunlight. She feels guilty about disobeying her mom, but on the walk to the tournament, she finds only affirmations of her choice. A woman selling paintings by the train station. The faint sound of piano music coming from an apartment window. Kids playing basketball in the park, their small bodies slick with sweat. Reminders that she is not alone, that she too is among the ranks of the dreamers, the people who are following the inner voice that calls them to greatness.

Then, the tournament. The P.P.Q. is playing on an empty stomach and no sleep, and her first games go badly. She wonders if she's made a mistake, if she's not who she thinks she is. But then she remembers that there's no turning back. It's either win here, or come home empty-handed. So she locks in, finds a new level of focus.

After that, it's simple. The Ping-Pong Queen sticks to her guns, until she wins! She brings home her prize money, her mom looks at her daughter with tears of pride, and life is grand. Perhaps it feels a bit too clean, but doesn't the hero have to win in the end? And isn't this basically what's happening in real life, right now, with me and my parents?

This will work, I tell myself. Cassie will like this; her character will get to follow her dreams instead of having to give them up. We just need one more day, one more shoot, to bring the story to an end.

———

Gaspard and I are on the LIRR, watching rows and rows of sub-urban houses go by, when my phone rings. It's Cassie. She's never called me before, and that's a thrill all by itself.

"Hello?"

"Hey. Did you guys head out already?" she asks. Her voice sounds different: thinner than normal, like she might be sick.

"Yeah, we're on the train."

"Oh. Okay."

"Is something wrong?"

"We had a late night, is all. I just woke up, actually." Over the line, she coughs once before covering the speaker.

"Does today still work?" I ask.

There's a pause, like she's thinking it over. "Well anyways, I'm up now, so it should be fine. My mom is still a bit pissed at me, but I think she'll act normal once you get here."

"Oh. I'm sorry."

"No worries. It's my own fault, I guess. Sorry, I should have sent you a message or something. I don't want you to come all the way out here for nothing."

"We can still cancel," I say. Even as the words come out, though, I can hear my own insincerity. I don't really want to cancel, to risk letting the energy behind this movie fizzle out.

"No, it's fine. I better start getting ready. I'll see you soon, Felix."

I wish she sounded more enthusiastic. But I shouldn't get too in my head about it—she said it was okay. Instead of worrying, I remind myself that today could turn out great. We might get everything we need to nail the final cut of the movie. Cassie and her mom might love it. I need to be more optimistic. There's power in optimism, in saying yes.

"Something up?" Gaspard asks, looking up from his book. The man is reading *The Lightning Thief*—or, to be more precise, *El ladrón del rayo*, because of course his Spanish is that good.

"No," I reply. "We're still on."

It's cold, even for late fall, and our breath turns into fog as we emerge from the subway station. In Chinatown, people are bundled up, hands shoved in their pockets, walking around with the extra bit of speed that comes from not wanting to be outside. Even the people hawking fake designer handbags and watches on Canal Street look unenthused, half-heartedly waving their print-out catalogs at us like "You know the drill."

At Golden Promises, there are three more steaming mugs of milk tea waiting for us at our usual table. This time, there's even another customer, a lǎo tài tai reading a newspaper.

"Every summer, I forget how much I hate winter," Cassie says as we try to warm up over our milk tea.

"Does business pick up around the holidays?" Gaspard asks.

"Yeah. We get orders for parties and things like that. The busiest times are probably Chinese New Year and the Mid-Autumn Festival. Golden Promises makes a mean mooncake. If you had started this shoot a few weeks earlier, my mom probably would have force-fed you four or five each."

Gaspard nods ruefully. "If only."

Despite the warm welcome, I'm feeling so nervous that it's hard for me to speak. Being back here reawakens the memories of last time, the glint of Cassie's anger, the feeling that the ground was opening up under my feet, and the question that she asked: "Is this what my life looks like to you?" In the moment, my thoughts were too confused to compose into a simple answer. I knew how I *felt*, but I couldn't find the right words. The question was phrased so that I wasn't supposed to say yes. But I wanted to object to that—*I'm not just some outsider, judging at a distance. I grew up in a place like this one. I'm just like you.* I wanted her to see that, but I was afraid she'd tell me that I was wrong.

Cassie's mom comes out. She's wearing a mischievous grin, like she's been looking forward to the shoot, and for a moment, I see the family resemblance to Cassie. They have the same smile, a smile that makes it look like they're up to something.

"Hello, Felix and Gaspard. Nice to see you again. This must mean I didn't scare you off last time. Cassie was afraid you wouldn't come back."

"Not what I said!" Cassie pouts.

"Oh, I'll come back for these pastries as long as you let me, Ms. Chow," Gaspard says sweetly. I think he's laying it on outrageously thick, but Ms. Chow beams.

"Cassandra and I are ready. We learned a lot from acting together the first time."

"Yup, that's true. A couple of pros is what we are." Cassie nods.

We warm up with some filler scenes: a series of mood-setting shots that we can use for montages or to set up a voiceover. Cassie and her mom setting out buns in the display case. Cassie's mom rolling dough in the back kitchen, finishing with a theatrical wipe of her brow. Cassie and her mom sitting on the kitchen floor, smiling over cups of milk tea after a hard day's work. I can see traces of fatigue in their movements, in the lines of their faces, but on the whole they seem game enough.

Then we move on to some simple story beats, which we'll slot in during editing to round out the overall narrative. At the counter, Cassie hands her mom an envelope full of cash, labeled Tutoring Money. Cassie's mom nods her approval and counts the cash into the register. Cassie smiles back, pleased, but as she walks away, her face darkens. Cut.

"If my daughter does this in real life, I'll be happy," Cassie's mom says. Cassie sticks out her tongue in response.

Cassie puts up an Out to Lunch sign on the front door, and the four of us head upstairs into the apartment to shoot footage at home. It's my first-ever glimpse of the Chow family domestic life. Their apartment is small, and made more cramped by the stacks of baking supplies, books, and papers in their living room. We pick out a path to the couch, where I shoot Cassie and her mom, faces illuminated by the glow of the television. In the corner of the room is Cassie's saxophone case, set down next to a music stand holding a familiar sheet music folder.

"Okay, now can I get the two of you to hug?"

Cassie raises a dubious eyebrow. She and her mom lock eyes and swap skeptical glances. But then her mom spreads out her arms, pastes on an exaggerated smile, and wrinkles her nose as if to say, "Oh, come here." A grin breaks out across Cassie's face, and the two embrace.

"Aww," Gaspard says.

"I *love* you, Mommy," Cassie says in a sticky-sweet voice. She plants a loud kiss on her mom's cheek, and her mom laughs.

"Don't be fooled, boys. My daughter never, ever does this. I'm lucky if I can get just a card on Mother's Day."

"Mother's Day cards aren't a right, they're awarded based on annual performance," Cassie quips back.

There's an edge in her voice that takes me aback. Yes, Ms. Chow is making small jokes here and there, but they feel like ordinary banter, perhaps played up for Gaspard's and my benefit. Yet Cassie seems reluctant to play into this dynamic. It's like she's trying to convey a silent message—"Not now, not here."

Next, we move on to the meat of the day, the new ending arc.

"Did you get a chance to read the script that I sent you?" I ask. "I thought you'd like it more than the last one."

"Oh, yeah. Well, I kind of skimmed it. We didn't have time to memorize it or anything. I don't remember much. Sorry," Cassie replies.

"That's fine," I say. But her answer makes me nervous. I was hoping that she'd say, "Yes, I read it, I liked it." That she'd give her approval, and take some tension out of the air.

"Speak for yourself. I read it," Ms. Chow says.

"You did? When?"

"This morning, while you were sleeping."

"Oh. You didn't say anything." Cassie frowns.

"That's fine," Gaspard cuts in. "We can give you instructions."

I give an overview of what the first scene should be, and we start filming.

"I want to enter the Branchburg Open," the Ping-Pong Queen says. "It's a tournament in New Jersey. I need forty dollars for the entry fee, plus the money for the bus ride there and back."

"I can't take you all the way out there!"

"I know. I'll go by myself."

"I'm not letting you go by yourself to New Jersey."

"I'm not a little kid. I know how to ride the bus. If I win, I'll get points in the youth rankings. That's how you get your name on the map. Plus there's a cash prize."

They argue back and forth for a bit, but finally her mom relents.

In the next scene, the Ping-Pong Queen comes back happy from the tournament. "It was amazing! The best players I've ever played against, by far."

"And how much did you win?"

"Ah, I got fifth. Prizes start at third place. I was so close! But there's another tournament in a month. If I train really hard, and go back, I can—"

"Ai-yah, you're already thinking about the next tournament? What makes you think you can take all this time off? Your work is already so sloppy."

Ms. Chow pauses, as if considering how to drive home this point. Then she breaks character for a moment, her face brightening as if she's just thought of an idea.

"This morning, before you left, you forgot to put a filter into the coffee machine! Do you know what happened when Ms. Lam came in for her morning coffee? Coffee grounds all over her nice Chanel jacket! And no coffee, that goes without saying. I've never apologized so hard in my life!"

This wasn't in the script. The Ping-Pong Queen pauses for a moment, startled. She looks unsure how to respond, casts a glance around the room as if searching for someone to defend her.

"Ms. Lam's jacket isn't real Chanel," she grumbles at last.

"That's not the point! There was one thing you had to do!"

After we call cut, Ms. Chow continues. "Hope you don't mind me improvising. That story came back to me all of a sudden. It's true, you know. Cassandra really did that once. The grounds burned and got stuck in the percolator. It took forever to clean the thing out."

"You always bring that up," Cassie says, looking unhappy.

"The problem is, she's too lazy about some types of work. She just tries to get it done as fast as possible. In a bakery, you have to be precise with everything, and Cassie doesn't like that. Plus, she's clumsy. That comes from her father."

194

"It was only once, out of how many thousand times?" Cassie snaps. "And it wasn't because I was lazy, it was because I was tired. How long are you going to keep telling that story?"

Ms. Chow waves her hand dismissively. "Sorry, I didn't mean to. It just came out."

Cassie shoots me a glance, like she's checking to see whether I was paying attention, how much I heard. I wince in sympathy, hoping to convey that I get it, I go through it too.

That story fit the scene perfectly, I think to myself. Even that final, off-camera exchange about the percolator hints at how much history there is behind the tension and frayed nerves on-screen. It would have been a perfect illustration of something my mom does too—making the implication that a mistake isn't merely a mistake, but rather a reflection of your character, proof of the flaws imprinted inside you that you can't shake off.

"What's next?" Cassie asks.

I describe the climactic confrontation, where the Ping-Pong Queen asks to enter the Baltimore Open, but her mom says no.

"Another fight?"

"But it's leading up to an ending where you go off and win a big tournament, and your mom sees that you had what it takes all along," I say quickly. "That's the new ending."

"Oh." She considers this for a moment. "Well, let's keep going. Home stretch."

The next scene opens after the Ping-Pong Queen's mom discovers the entrance forms for the Baltimore Open. She waves them in front of her daughter's face and starts on another lecture.

"You always want life to be easy. But nobody's life gets to be easy. Everyone has to struggle and make sacrifices. When you run off to play your game, you think that the bakery just goes away? I'm left here, working twice as hard, so you can go and have fun. Is that what you want?"

"It's not like that. Ping-Pong isn't just a game for me. It's my calling. Maybe it won't win us money just yet, but if I keep playing, I know I can make it as a pro."

"Ai-yah, your calling? What is a calling? When your stomach is empty, is that a calling too? You can't put all your hopes into such a small basket. What if you decide you don't want to play anymore? Then what will you have to show for it?"

"That won't happen. I can feel it."

"You're a child. You don't know any better."

The Ping-Pong Queen looks dazed. She doesn't respond for a while, and she seems to be retreating inside herself. Eventually she looks at the camera.

"Cut!" Gaspard calls.

Cassie shakes her head. "Sorry. I kind of zoned out for a second there. I'm still tired."

"You want some tea? Maybe you need to eat something," Ms. Chow asks.

"I'm not hungry."

"Let's take a quick break," Gaspard says.

The two of us go off to the side to confer.

"This is getting kind of heavy," Gaspard says. "It might be hard to keep going. Do you think maybe we have enough?"

I feel uneasy with how today is going too. Cassie is clearly tired, and acting out conflict with her mom is making her upset. On the other hand, the shoot is going well. Cassie's mom has incredible delivery; all of her words have the right weight, the right timing. Mr. Qin had a point—when the actors bring real emotion into the scene, the performances become much more compelling.

"We still have to get to the part where her mom says no about the Open. After that we'll be done with the heavy stuff. The part where she sneaks out will lighten the mood."

Gaspard nods. "That's true. Okay, let's make it quick."

One last push, and the rest will be easy.

"We're almost there," I say to Cassie and her mom. Ms. Chow gives a thumbs-up. Hopefully that positive energy will be enough to carry us.

I remind them where the scene is going, how it needs to end. "But make sure to work your way into it," I say.

I yell action, and the scene picks up where it left off.

"Mom, you don't get it. It's like you don't see me at all. This is the one thing that makes me feel like . . . like I matter. How can you ask me to give it up?"

"You're being selfish. You're the one who doesn't see. Do you know how much work goes into keeping the lights on, putting food on the table? You want people to take care of you your whole life? Everything I do is for you. And you say that you don't matter? How can you not see it?"

"I *do* see it," Cassie hisses, narrowing her eyes.

Cassie turns and looks at me, like she did at the end of the last scene. This time, her eyes are making an entreaty, like she's hoping I'll call cut.

There's a thread of tension in the room that's been pulled tight. Any more, and it could snap. We could cut now, skip straight to the important lines about the Baltimore Open, and then move on.

I hesitate. It feels like we're on the verge of capturing something big, something important. Something like the memory of what my mom said to me after I told her I wanted to quit Ping-Pong: zhème ruǎnruò. So weak. A searing moment that could become the heart of this story. It's inches away. We can push for a little more, hope the thread holds for just a bit longer.

I shake my head, mouthing, "Don't look at the camera." Cassie turns back. *If she needs to stop, she'll stop,* I tell myself. Ms. Chow has a defiant look in her eyes, like she knows she has the upper hand. In the face of this challenge, Cassie seems to muster one more wave of resolve.

"Of course I know how much you do for me. I wish you didn't have to. I *want* to take care of you some day," Cassie continues. "But what about how I feel? I'm the only person at school who has to wake up at five a.m. to make the dough, start the coffee, and set up all the chairs. Everyone else at school gets to have their *thing* that makes them special. Playing an instrument, or singing in the choir, or speech and debate. Something they can put their heart into. I want to have that too."

"You get to go to school. You're in a very good high school, you'll go to college, and then you won't have to do this anymore. You got to play Ping-Pong for so long already. When will it be enough?"

"It's the only thing I have!"

"Only thing you have?" Ms. Chow is matching Cassie's intensity now. They're clashing, and suddenly I can imagine how truly terrible it must be when they fight, when they turn the full force of their personalities onto each other.

"You must not need me, then," Ms. Chow continues, her voice low and flinty. "If you walk out the door with your Ping-Pong paddle right now, you won't be losing a thing. Go on, go. Do it. Let's see."

They're just pretending, I tell myself. They're still talking about Ping-Pong, a conflict that isn't real. In the back of my head, though, is a growing feeling of dread. There's too much emotion now; they're going beyond what's needed for acting.

"Stop! Just stop!" Cassie yells, so loudly that I wince. "Why do you have to talk like this, Mom? You know I'm not going to just walk out of the door, so what's your point? You think I don't get it, but I do. It's just that it sucks, and I'm tired, and sometimes I want to find an easy way out. But you never let me have that, it's not enough if I do my work, I even have to say the right things, *think* the right things. And I'm your *kid*, you're supposed to encourage me, and inspire me. I'm the one person in the world who should get to have that from you. But no, you're so nice to everyone else, but for me, the one person who lives with you, who . . . who loves you, you have no problem making me miserable."

"Cut!" Gaspard cries.

For a moment, the room is completely silent. The air feels heavy, oppressively so, as Cassie and her mother sit across each other from the table, breathing hard, glaring. From across the room, the lǎo tài tai spares us a brief blank glance before returning to her newspaper.

Finally Ms. Chow turns to us. "Did we get it, Mr. Director?" she asks, smiling cheerfully.

Only then do I unfreeze, shake myself out of my stupor, and come back to the real world. What just happened?

Cassie goes upstairs without excusing herself. We still haven't gotten to the Baltimore Open, not to mention the remaining scenes that I had planned, but it's obvious that we're done for the day. That scene was too draining. All of the air has been sucked out of the room.

With no other option, Gaspard and I call a wrap, check the LIRR train schedule, and politely refuse another set of to-go boxes from Ms. Chow. Only when our coats are zipped and our bags are packed up does Ms. Chow say, "I'll tell Cassie you're leaving," and go upstairs herself.

"We messed up," Gaspard says.

"It's my fault," I reply. My heart is pounding, but mostly I feel numb. This wasn't supposed to happen again. I changed the ending of the movie. I planned for this. I care about Cassie, and I've been trying all along to show her that.

But I also pushed us to this point. All day I saw the warning signs, and I ignored them, hoping it'd be okay. Part of me is still praying for an easy way out: Cassie will reappear, tell us that she was just in the bathroom, there's no reason to worry, I'm tough, this kind of thing rolls right off me.

When she does finally come back down, she looks normal. No puffy eyes, no burning anger. She only sounds a little distant as she says, "Sorry, I won't walk you to the station today. It looks nasty out there. Plus, I need to eat."

"Cassie—" I begin.

"I thought you changed it," she says, cutting me off.

"I did. I made the ending about how you get to follow your dreams and prove your mom wrong."

"But it's still about me and my mom. It's, like, just our life. The only thing you made up is the Ping-Pong part."

As reality sinks in, I search back through the events leading to today in disbelief. When I was here just a few weeks ago, the only thought in my mind was *I messed up, this can't ever happen again.* Was one nice dinner with Mr. Qin and one high school party really all it took to fill me up with delusions of grandeur, to make me lose the thread so badly?

"We should have stopped the scene earlier," Gaspard says. "I'm sorry. It's my job to do that, when Felix is the one filming."

"No, it's my job too. I should be saying sorry. Especially since—"

"Really it's me and my mom who need to get ahold of ourselves. We shouldn't be talking to each other like that in front of other people. It was probably awkward for you." She looks at me as she utters this last phrase, and I feel her eyes boring into me, as if to add on an accusation—"But this was what you wanted, wasn't it?"

Because I was the one holding the camera, hiding behind that cold metal eye, watching the violence and trauma of this event as a bystander, never intervening, just taking it all in. Cassie looked to me for help while we were filming, but I wasn't looking at the real her, I was looking at the version of her on my screen.

Now she's reaching for the door, and this is all coming to an abrupt, painful end. It's happening quickly, too quickly for me to gather myself, find the words that can change the situation. Cassie turns and waves one last time, and the door shuts. And I realize, with dread, that I don't know what happens next.

The sky is already dark. Gaspard and I are mostly silent as we schlep back to Penn Station. It's like we just committed a crime together, and we're each waiting for the other to say what we've done out loud.

"That was really bad, wasn't it?" I say as the LIRR hurtles out of the tunnel into Queens.

He nods. "We shouldn't have let them have a real fight like that. It was too intimate. We weren't meant to see that. And it makes it worse that we were filming."

This isn't news to me, but hearing it put in such stark terms by another person makes the truth hit me. Suddenly it's hard to breathe. I shift in my seat, try to straighten out my body, look down and see my chest rising and falling as I suck in oxygen.

"Maybe it's not all bad, though," Gaspard adds quickly. "I get the feeling that Ms. Chow is pretty unflappable. I doubt she'd let something like this bother her. It *was* for the story, after all. There must have been a part of each of them that was just pretending."

But only a part. The feelings, the words, they were all real. They were real because I asked Cassie to star in a movie based on her own life. They were real because I didn't stop filming, even when I saw that she wanted to stop.

Out the window, I stare at the dark shapes of trees passing by. There's something that I'm finally beginning to understand.

When Cassie asked me, "Is this what my life looks like to you?" there was a small voice of protest in my head. *Yes, I suppose it is, but why is that a bad thing? I think you're amazing and your mom is amazing and you're close in a way that I've never been with my parents. You talk and joke and understand each other. That essay you wrote about her, those words would never come to me because I don't feel things the way you do, I don't have the same energy, the same spark; no one does. This life at the bakery, just the two of you with your larger-than-life personalities, it's special, it looks like a movie, like* Lady Bird *or* Turning Red *or even, yes,* Terms of Endearment. *It's like my story, only ten times bigger and better.*

That's what I wanted to tell her. But there was something she was trying to tell me. That it was still her story, and it wasn't mine to tell. That was the problem, more than the corny plot. Admiring her, thinking she was cool, feeling like I understood her—none of that gave me the right to make this movie the way I did.

The day feels like a bad dream, and I'm still clinging to a faint hope that it wasn't so bad, that Cassie may have been shaken up for a moment, but she'll be fine and the wrongness of that final argument was all in my head. But I know, deep down, that it wasn't.

FOURTEEN

AT HOME, I TRY TO KEEP BUSY. I OFFER TO HELP my parents cook dinner, even if their blatant disregard for my kitchen skills means that they only give me the most menial tasks: washing rice, breaking the stem tips off long beans, setting the table with a spoon and set of chopsticks for each person. I throw myself into studying for chemistry, which leads me to the infuriating realization that studying a lot makes all the homework and tests easier. In short, I do whatever it takes so that I don't have to think about the movie.

I'm in the cafeteria, spending my free period doing my reading for *The Crucible* when I hear someone sliding into the booth across from me.

"Can we do movie stuff later? I still want another day or two before we work on it again," I say, assuming it's Gaspard. We have the same free period, although lately he's been using it to work with Lexie on Spanish Club activities. The man is already copresident of one club, but I'm pretty sure he's gunning for treasurer or at least secretary in another.

"What?" an unfamiliar voice replies.

I look up from my book. It's Henry.

"Oh." I pause, and there's an uncomfortable silence. After a moment, I ask, "What's up?"

"Not much," he says. His eyes dart around the cafeteria. "Saw you here. Thought I'd say hi. What's up with you?"

"I'm good."

"Nice." Henry nods. He eyes me briefly, then looks down and starts fiddling with his backpack straps. "Watching anything good at your movie club?"

"We might do *Rashomon* soon. It's about four characters at a trial that each have to tell their version of the same story."

Henry glances at me again, and nods. Then he starts tapping on the table. "Sounds legit."

"We might also do *Hoop Dreams*. It's a documentary about these two high school kids that play basketball at a prep school. They both want to make it into the league. You still follow basketball?"

Henry shrugs. "Nah, not really."

"Yeah, well, you're not missing out. The Knicks are garbage, as usual."

Henry laughs, flashing his teeth, showing dimples on his cheeks. Now it's all coming back to me. Yes, Henry had this annoying habit of always looking around, like he was afraid of being seen with me. But he was also an easy laugh, and he had the kind of laugh that made you *want* to make him laugh.

"What's up with you?" I ask.

"Nothing much."

"Nothing?"

"I got my driver's license. And I'm thinking about applying to culinary school."

"Culinary? You cook?"

He shrugs. "My parents have a restaurant. You might know it, Victory Café?"

"That's your place?" I sound too excited, and I wonder if I'm coming off as fake. But it's just that shocking to hear that Henry has an interest in cooking.

"My granddaddy opened it when he first moved out here. Now it's my mom's. Someday it'll be mine, I guess. Anyways, for now it's a job that I can't get fired from."

"True." I let this new piece of information about Henry sink in. I remember meeting his parents a couple of times, eating the snacks they made, smelling the dinner they were prepping and wishing I could stay to try it. "How about your skateboarding? You still hang out with Gus and Matt Wyatt and all of them?"

Henry gives me a longer look, like he's trying to detect any hard feelings I still might have. I did my best to keep any hostility out of my voice, but it's still there, an itch at the edge of my brain.

"Yeah. The crew. We're all good. I did a fakie heelflip the other day."

"Fakie heelflip?"

"Yeah, it's a heelflip but you ride fakie. Like, backward. And a heelflip is a kickflip. But backward."

"So you're riding backward and doing a kickflip backward. Doesn't that just turn it back into a kickflip?"

"No." He frowns. "Wait . . ."

His face twitches, and I understand right away that he's doing the trick in his head, visualizing himself on the board. Back in the day, when I tried, awkwardly, to talk to him about skateboarding, he used to do the same thing.

"Nah. Nah," he says, laughing. "It's two different kinds of backward. It's like if you were a righty, and you wrote something backward, with your left hand. Two different kinds of backward. See?"

"Hey, you good?"

I look up. Gaspard is walking toward us from across the cafeteria, his eyebrow raised. I remember how he immediately didn't like Henry when they met at film club. Now that Gaspard knows the full story, he must like him even less.

"Yeah, we're good. We were just catching up. No sweat," I say quickly. Henry, meanwhile, is fiddling with his backpack straps again.

Gaspard nods, although he still looks hesitant. "You sure?"

"Yup."

"All right, well, I gotta go meet up with Lexie. But I'll catch you after school?"

"Yeah, after school."

Gaspard shoots one more dirty look at Henry, then passes through the cafeteria to the foreign languages wing.

"I better bounce," Henry says. His nervous energy seems to have turned into actual nerves now.

"All right. I'll talk to you later, Henry."

"Yeah," he says. He gets up from the table and heads out to the quad. As he goes, he fishes his lighter out of his pocket and starts messing with it. I watch through the window as he flicks it on and off in his hand.

I remember why I liked Henry: he always seemed so cool to me. Back when I was a freshman, wondering who I was going to become in Great Neck, the idea of being friends with this skater dude was so surprising, so much more than I expected. It's a bad habit of mine, it seems—to meet someone new and fall head over heels for them, to lose all sense of proportion.

And then our friendship ended, and the questions came: Why was it so easy for you to get rid of me? Why don't we even talk anymore?

And why are we talking again now?

Now the ugly feelings bubble up—all the time that I spent fantasizing about screaming at Henry in the hallway, shoving him into a locker, tackling him off his skateboard.

I take a deep breath. I don't want to get back into that right now. *Push it down, push it away. We just talked in the cafeteria, and that's it.*

I have plenty of other stuff to deal with.

More than a week after the shoot in Chinatown, Gaspard and I finally watch the new footage.

At first it's okay. Cassie and her mom have little skirmishes, arguments narrowly avoided. They each have dark looks in private moments, but they keep their composure when talking to each other.

But then there's the argument. The lines of dialogue feel both familiar and painfully fresh. The resentment, the real venom that washed over me in the moment is there, on the screen, coming back full force. This is footage of two people who know each other inside and out, who are genuinely trying to hurt each other.

"Turn it off, dude," I say, shaking my head.

Gaspard closes his phone. "It's very intense. Maybe we can weave it in with other moments that tone the emotions down. Like, the two of them working together in the shop, making up and hugging, doing things for each other around the house even though they're mad. You know, just make it one part of the tapestry."

"We can't use this," I reply. The problem isn't just the intensity. It's that it isn't cinematic intensity—it's just ordinary, raw pain. It's like watching a snuff film, too gory and intimate for the eyes of an audience. "It's not right."

"We need something to get to an ending, though," Gaspard says gently.

"It doesn't matter. It can't be this."

He sighs. "Yeah, I think you're right."

With this clip gone, we don't have much to show from the last trip to Chinatown. But even if we had nothing, I wouldn't want to include it. I wish it had never happened, that the footage didn't exist. If only it had been shot on real 35mm film, I'd burn it.

I know I should message Cassie, but every time I start to type out an apology, the harsh reality of the words—*I went too far, I didn't think enough about your feelings, I used your story when it wasn't mine to use*—scares me. I can't bring myself to send them, to admit that they're true. With each passing day, my sense of dread grows. I feel like we're drifting apart, that I'm letting my only opportunity to make this right slip further and further away.

After a week, Cassie messages me first.

Cassie:

I don't think I can handle doing any more shoots for the movie

I've been feeling pretty terrible since the last one

I wish I had just canceled, I knew it wasn't going to be a good day

Sorry about this but hopefully you already got most of what you needed anyways

Now the wound has been ripped open, and there's no time for me to weigh my words or overthink how Cassie will respond to them.

> Cassie I'm so so sorry

> I shouldn't have let that last scene with your mom get to that point

> I've been feeling terrible too, I should have messaged you right away to say something

Cassie:

It's not your fault, I could have stopped the scene myself

I thought I'd be fine, but it just bothered me more than I thought it would

Like I thought going through all of this might even help me and my mom work through our stuff

But instead it's like we open up the box and the bad feelings come spilling out, and when we finally manage to put them away nothing is solved and I just feel worn out

I feel like that's the big difference between you and me and I'm finally realizing that

> What do you mean?

Cassie:

Idk. I guess it seems like for you, it's therapeutic to talk about the shitty stuff that happened to you and to be able to share it with someone

Which is totally normal! And I get it. I'm glad that I was able to be someone you could tell things to

But I'm not like that

Like even with that essay I wrote about my family

To be honest, after I sent it to you I regretted it. It's so private and I shouldn't have shared it with anyone. I would never want an admissions counselor to read that, it's like sending them my diary or something

I thought Cassie might be angry with me, that she'd send me some strongly worded message like "Yeah, you DID go too far," or just "Eff uuuuu." But this calmness, this refusal to blame me, is worse. It makes it seem like the problem between us isn't just one movie shoot gone awry. It's something deeper, something that's been there since the beginning. That all along, my compulsion to be closer to her, to find more pieces of my story in hers and hers in mine, was wrong. Reading Cassie's essay was strangely thrilling, it made me happy in a way that I still can't quite put into words—but for her, it was a mistake.

Now my mind goes frantic. I look desperately for a way out, an opportunity to repair the damage.

> Can we hang out again soon?

> Not to shoot, just for fun. No deep conversations or anything, just something relaxed

Cassie:

I think I have to pass for now

I have a lot of stuff I need to do that I've been putting off. And tbh I just need a break

I really will be okay but for now I just want to not think about the movie for a while

Sorry, Felix

Say sorry to Gaspard for me too

Also tell him my mom thinks he's lovely, lol

Cassie's status blinks from green to gray. She's offline.

I sit, stiff with shock, as the next wave of realization hits.

All along, I thought that there was something bright and beautiful ahead of us, some euphoric meeting of the minds that we had to keep pushing toward so that our friendship could reach its true potential. But in reality, I was forging ahead myself, on a path that

Cassie didn't want to follow. And now it's over. Not just the movie, but everything. I'm not delusional—I've seen enough movies to know what "I just need a break" means.

The one person I would have given anything to spend time with, the person who I wanted to be closer to than anyone else—now she's out of my life altogether.

PART THREE

FIFTEEN

OVER THANKSGIVING, MY PARENTS TELL ME
that we'll be going back to China to visit my grandparents for
winter break. It will be our first trip back in almost seven years.

I have some faint memories of the last trip: it was summer, and
unbearably hot, and my parents were fighting because the dental
business wasn't doing well. I can't picture my grandparents' apartment, but I remember camping out by the electric fan, trying to
stay cool, as my parents and aunts and uncles cracked sunflower
seeds at the dining table. I remember waking up in the middle of
the night with my legs covered in bug bites, rubbing ice cubes over
the angry red bumps to relieve the itching.

The weeks pass by quickly. As much as I try not to, I think
about Cassie every day. Exactly one time, just to torture myself, I
look through our old chat history.

Now, in the cold light of what's happened since, the messages
read completely differently. My own voice sounds distinctly like a
past version of myself, filled with an unchecked exuberance that I

now find embarrassing. It's always me reaching out, me who wants more. Cassie's messages, meanwhile, are transformed.

Cassie:

> You know what's funny, I just wrote an essay that's sort of about her

> Well, it's kind of about my whole family but that's like eighty percent her

> > Can I read it?

> Idk it's very rough and I feel weird about sharing it

> I guess that shows that I shouldn't use it to seek approval from an admissions officer

> > Aw, you don't have to feel weird!

Cassie:

> I had a feeling you were going to ask me something about this

I thought there was some depth to her sadness, that if I could get to the heart of it, we would reach some feeling of poignance together. But I shouldn't have given in to that urge, I should have thought more about her. Her reluctance was obvious, but I couldn't see it—no, I could have, but I didn't want to. I wish I could go back and shake myself by the shoulders: *Wake up, damn it, make yourself listen to what she's saying.*

When Gaspard learns that we won't be doing any more shoots, he gets creative. Using the footage we've already gathered, he stitches together a *La La Land* "what if" ending, showing two potential futures for the Ping-Pong Queen. In one, she gets a job tutoring math (Gaspard stretches literally a *single second* clip of Cassie solving quadratic equations with Kevin Ding from Chinese school as far as it will go) and gives her mom her earnings. Her mom is proud of her. Cassie smiles back, but it's a strained smile.

In the other, she runs away from home. We splice together some shots of her walking hurriedly down a subway staircase with an exterior shot of Penn Station, hands purchasing a LIRR ticket from a ticket machine, ending with a shot of a train pulling out of the station (which, incidentally, is a shot of our train coming *into* the station that he's sped up and reversed). For both futures, he's used the 8mm filter and added some discoloration, light leaks, and black specks to give the footage a feeling of unreality.

Finally the film cuts back to the present. It ends on a shot of Cassie, standing outside Golden Promises. In her hand is the Mandate of Heaven. Is she going to go inside or turn away? The camera lingers on her face, then her eyes. Before we learn what she does, the movie fades to black.

When it's time for us to fill out our application for Ludlow, the questions "What inspired you to make this movie?" and "Why is your film a good fit for the Ludlow Film Festival?" and "What is your movie about?" all seem impossible to answer. After I put in

221

the honest answers—"college applications," "it's pretentious," and "my own mediocrity"—Gaspard tells me to drop it.

"You're wallowing right now. Wallowers make bad applicants. Go to China, eat some of that good good food, and leave the promotional stuff to your uncle G."

There is one bright spot, though. To my surprise, the film is fun to watch. Cassie and I haven't spoken since she told me that she needed a break, but I still get a happy feeling seeing her play the Ping-Pong Queen. Her monologues don't get old, and on each watch-through a different clip triggers memories of our days of shooting.

My biggest fear now is that our friendship was a figment of my imagination, that Cassie was merely an unwilling participant in the whole movie enterprise. Some of that is true, that much is obvious. But there were good days too. There in the movie are clips of us undeniably having fun, feeling carefree, being creative together. So it wasn't all bad. That, at least, is something I can hold on to.

Before I know it, my parents and I are stuffing our suitcases into a taxi, riding to the airport, getting on a plane to Beijing packed with what feels like every other Chinese family in Nassau County. The safety announcements in two languages, the duty-free carts, the meal choice between penne alfredo and soy-sauce chicken; it all brings memories from my childhood rushing back.

After three straight movies, my eyes are burning and my head aches, and I still can't fall asleep. A flight attendant wheels a snack cart stealthily through the dark cabin, dropping pretzels and ham sandwiches into sleeping passengers' laps like an economy-class Santa Claus. Toward the end of the flight, I manage to pass out for an hour or so, but then before I know it the lights are back on and the flight attendants are asking, "Eggs or dim sum?" "Jīdàn hái shì yǐnchá?"

When we land, I'm bleary-eyed from the trip, but our journey still isn't over. After clearing customs, we go from the airport straight to the train station, where we get on the bullet train to Shenyang. It's broad daylight, and my mom keeps telling me not to fall asleep, but I do anyway. We get to Shenyang in the evening, and all of a sudden I'm wide awake. The first night, as my mom reminds me, is always the hardest.

By the time we arrive at my grandparents' apartment, a full twenty-four hours have passed since we left home. My grandparents have prepared a comically extravagant feast to greet us. Among other things, there's a steamed crab for each of us, plus a mountain of sweet-and-sour ribs and a whole catfish swimming in sauce.

"Yǒng yong, nǐ pàng le," my grandma tells me. I'm startled; it's been a long time since anyone has called me by my Chinese name.

"Lǎo lao hǎo," I mutter in return.

During the meal, I keep dozing off, dreaming I'm back in America. Then I jolt awake, and find myself sitting in an unfamiliar apartment, my stomach bulging uncomfortably with food, my ears full of Mandarin. My grandfather rubs my cheek and says how good it is to see me, and my grandmother piles more and more food onto my plate, even as she comments over and over on how much weight I've gained since my last visit.

It's all blazingly surreal, especially with the mixture of dissociation and nausea that the jet lag is giving me. I can't quite wrap my head around the fact that my parents and I have just launched ourselves into the sky and landed on the other side of the planet in such a short amount of time. And yet here we are, among family, who've been waiting for weeks—or really, years—to see us.

I wake up around eleven a.m., having spent hours tossing and turning in the dark before falling asleep. My parents are already awake, rearranging their suitcases now that all the gifts we brought have been taken out for distribution. On the dining room table is a steaming cauldron of lukewarm rice porridge and a couple of cold yóu tiáo. I help myself; my grandparents are out on their morning constitutional with the other retirees in their apartment block.

I'm just a couple of bites in when my parents come sweeping out of their room, already bundled up, and tell me to hurry and get ready.

"We're late," my mom says. My dad rips off a hunk of yóu tiáo and stuffs it into his mouth, chewing vigorously as if to demonstrate the urgency of the situation.

"Late for what?" I mumble.

"Your uncle is already outside. We're going to see your cousin. Are you still hungry? You ate a lot last night."

I remember all of the nǐ pàng le comments I got last night and put down my spoon. My parents stuff a hat onto my head and pull my arms into my winter coat, and we're off.

My uncle is waiting outside in the car. It's freezing; the ground is icy, and the pale winter light filtering through the polluted air gives the snowbanks a rosy hue.

"Yǒng yong pàng le," my uncle says. Great. Hi to you too, uncle. Yǒng yong is the pet version of my Chinese name, Yǒnglín, which means "eternal forest." Pàng le is their way of telling me that I look prosperous, aka that I'm gaining weight. Not that I was hoping for a hěn shuài (so handsome!) or anything, but still.

We drive to my aunt and uncle's apartment. It's coming back to me now: sān yí, who was pregnant during our last trip, and sān yí fu, my uncle, who used to have much more hair. When we get to the door, a kid half my height barrels into me and almost knocks me over.

"My name is Charles! I am seven!" he cries, in English, when he sees me. My uncle laughs and explains that he's starting English lessons at school.

After my sān yí greets me and tells me nǐ pàng le, she, my uncle, and my parents stake out the kitchen table for some steaming hot gossip.

Meanwhile, us kids get to play with each other. Charles shows me his favorite toy, which is a kind of inflatable punching bag that's weighted so it always gets back up when you knock it down. My cousin shows me how to give the punching bag a threatening speech ("Yāoguài! Nǐ bù xǔ chī tángsēng ròu!") and then charge after it, showering it with punches and kicks, caving in its cartoon face over and over again. As he pursues his target around the living room, I shoot a video.

"All right, let me at him!" I cry, leaping up off of the couch. Charles roars in delight as I give the punching bag the old one-two, yelling, "Say hello to my little friend!" "You feeling lucky, punk?" "I'm taking you to the bank . . . the BLOOD BANK!" From the adult table, my mom frowns at me, but my aunt is laughing, so it's okay.

While the two of us play, I try to eavesdrop on the adults' conversation. I can't appreciate the finer details, but I catch my mom and aunt saying bà and mā enough to understand that they're talking about my grandparents. The two sisters speak with animated hand gestures; every once in a while my aunt will say something, and my mom will slap the table and point at her like, "That's it! You've hit the nail on the head!" Meanwhile, their husbands nod along politely.

Later, my second aunt and my other younger cousin show up. Her name is Meijia, and the last time I saw her, she was a seven-year-old girl. Now she's fourteen and going through some type of cool preteen phase. She's cut her hair short, and she's wearing a sparkly shirt that says Don't Talk To Me, in English. I wonder if she knows what it means.

"Yǒng yong hǎo shuài!" my second aunt says. Nice. I remember now why she's my favorite aunt. She pinches my cheek, which feels a little age-inappropriate, then asks my mom, "Tā yǒu méi yǒu nǚ péngyou?" "Does he have a girlfriend?" My mom eyes me suspiciously and shakes her head, but my dad winks at me. I'm still not a fan of the random teasing that he suddenly started doing this year, but at least I know there's nothing behind it.

My second aunt puts the TV on for us kids and then joins the adult table. The TV is playing a dubbed version of *The Lion King 1½*, much to the delight of Charles. When Pumbaa passes gas and says, "Bù hǎo yì si," Charles breaks out in a fit of giggles. "Nà zhī dà gōngzhū fàng pì le!"

Meanwhile, Meijia pats me urgently on the arm. "Do you like Taylor?" she asks. She says each syllable of the name distinctly, Tay-lor.

"Taylor?"

She frowns. "Taylor. You must know Taylor."

She pulls out her phone and searches on Baidu. When she shows me the result, I can't read the Chinese characters, but I recognize the face.

"Oh, Taylor Swift! Yeah, everyone knows her."

"Do you like her?"

"She's okay."

My cousin frowns, like she's personally offended. "No, I mean, she's great," I add, to mollify her. "Everyone likes her."

"Which songs do you like?"

"'Shake It Off,'" I answer. Meijia raises a suspicious eyebrow, like my answer is exactly what someone who's only *pretending* to like Taylor would say.

"We call her méi mei," she explains.

"Like, pretty? Měi lì?"

"No!" Meijia shakes her head. "Like dǎo méi." She types the characters into her phone and holds up the translation. The nickname means "unlucky."

"Unlucky? She seems pretty lucky to me."

My cousin shakes her head vehemently. "Bù duì! She never finds love. *And* people are mean to her, even though she's so pretty. But not me. I always like Taylor."

I have to fight not to laugh.

"Oh!" Meijia's face lights up all of a sudden. "Do you have Instagram? Can I use it?"

"I do have it. But it's blocked right now. You can't use it in China."

Now she frowns. "When you go back to Měi guó, can you comment on Taylor's Instagram for me?"

"What do you want me to say?"

"Say . . . 'Taylor, I support you. I like you. You are my favorite. Love, Meijia. From China.'" There's a fervor in her eyes, like everything rests on my completion of this task.

"Okay, I'll do it if I remember."

She looks thrilled. When Charles gets bored of the movie, he invites her to hit the punching bag, and she rolls up her sleeves and gives it a good smack.

At the adult table, the presence of my second aunt seems to have had a calming effect. She's telling the table about her ex-husband's demanding parents, how they're giving her a harder time than ever now that she's no longer their daughter-in-law. It's a sad topic, but she's smiling and making jokes that have the other adults in a good mood. I even understand one of them: "I used to think they'd hound me until they died. But now I know that when it comes to my father-in-law, even death won't stop him. He'll come back as a ghost just to keep telling me I'm a terrible cook."

I steal a glance at Meijia, but she's got her headphones in and is watching a grainy video from a Taylor Swift concert. I wonder if she's old enough to pick up on our parents' conversations. On my last visit, I was too young to care about what the adults were saying—I was too busy playing Pokémon on my 3DS. This is the first time I've registered all of the family drama that they're absorbed in.

One good thing about Shenyang—life feels easier here. Nothing I do here can be used against me in court, to prove or disprove that I'm a loser. Nothing I do here counts toward college. I'm completely helpless, and my only job is to be a passenger, hang out with the other kids, and ride this whole China thing out.

Throughout the day, my brain keeps on conversing with an imaginary Cassie. I laugh with her about poorly translated street signs

(No Littering, Violators Will Be Fine), muse about what life would have been like if we'd grown up here rather than in the US. It's an embarrassing habit, and I wonder if I should be trying harder not to think about her. But I can't bring myself to stop, and truthfully there's a part of me that enjoys it. In the evening, when I'm lying in bed, unable to sleep, the thoughts get so intrusive that I decide to write her an email.

Dear Cassie,
Greetings from northern China! It's cold here. People still burn coal to stay warm, so the pollution is horrible. I'm eating like a king, though. I haven't been back to Shenyang since I was in fourth grade, so it's like I got these two snapshots of all my relatives to compare. One of my cousins transformed from a girl who never talked into an edgy teenager who loves Taylor Swift. I'm not sure, but I get the sense that it's very hipster or even slightly emo to like her here. My other cousin wasn't born yet last time, and now he's a little ball of terror that likes to beat up an inflatable punching bag. My aunts and uncles look pretty different, you can tell they got older. My grandparents, on the other hand, look exactly the same.

I wonder what you'd think of all of this. I see a lot of hilarious stuff here, and it's cool to see my relatives, but mostly I just feel lonely and out of place. There's nothing to do here that really feels like it belongs to me. The most satisfaction I get comes from talking to my cousins, because it feels like I'm doing my job as the oldest kid in our generation. I need to work on my Chinese though.

Sincerely,
Felix

I won't send it, but just finishing the email feels therapeutic, like I've brushed off a seed burr that was clinging to my mind. At the same time, though, I know I'm just being self-indulgent. The reason it feels good to write this way is because it's an escape, a way to pretend that I live in a world from before everything went wrong. But it isn't real, it's just a daydream—one that I can't linger in for too long.

The next morning, I wake up around ten, almost a reasonable hour. My grandparents are still around, and we all sit down to a breakfast of dòu huā and sesame shāo bǐng. As we eat, my grandfather makes an innocent comment about how much time we're spending over at my aunt's house. Maybe a little *too* much time.

"Well, us sisters don't get to see each other often. When we get together, it's like old times," my mom responds.

"You don't get to see us often either!" my grandmother snaps back. "But every time you're here, you sleep late and then dash out the door. Like this is a hotel!"

The table goes silent. I freeze, staring at my grandma. She still has a placid expression on her face, totally incongruous with the biting tone of her voice.

"I told you we could stay at an actual hotel. You're the one who insisted we sleep here," my mom replies.

My grandmother clicks her tongue. "Why would you say that? Think about it, Liping, what would it look like for a daughter to stay at a hotel in the city where she grew up? Don't use the word 'insisted,' like it's my fault."

"There was no other option," my grandfather adds. "You can't bring up staying at a hotel like it's a real possibility."

My mom stares down at her food. I can practically hear the retorts forming in her mind, but she holds them back. Maybe she doesn't want to upset the people that are, after all, hosting us. Or maybe she's absorbed the same lesson that I have: in this family, you can never win an argument with your mom.

After the meal, my mom calls my aunt to let them know that we're staying at our grandparents' place for the morning. Her voice is flinty as she delivers the news, but by the end of the call she's smiling, probably at some sucks-to-be-you sibling sympathy.

As a gesture of apology, my mom offers to do the dishes. My grandparents only refuse once before accepting, and peace is restored. While my dad sits with my grandparents, eating sunflower seeds, I follow my mom into the kitchen so that I can help. I offer to scrub out the pot of dòu huā, but my mom brushes me away. I try to rinse out the bowls in the sink, but it's too small, and after we bump elbows once, my mom shoos me back. Eventually I find my role: receiving wet dishes from my mom and placing them in the drying rack.

"Are you okay?" I ask.

My mom shrugs. "It's fine. We need to spend some more time here. We shouldn't have stayed all day at your sān yí's house yesterday. I should have known your grandmother wouldn't like that."

"Do you and grandma always fight like this?"

My mom peeks out of the kitchen to make sure her parents aren't listening. In a low voice, she continues. "This is what she's like. She's always finding something wrong. Nothing is ever good enough for her. And my dad always takes her side. He'll let her get away with anything."

After a moment she adds, "But like I said, they were right about this. You need to spend some time with your grandparents too. Try to tell them about your school, what you think of America. It'll mean a lot to them."

I wonder if she's thinking about *our* fights too. To me, the connection is obvious: she's talking about my grandma, but she could just as easily be describing herself, fighting with me, right down to the part where I, the child, grudgingly admit that she's right.

We go back out and lounge in the frosty apartment. My mom and my grandmother converse on and off, digging in and probing each other like trench warfare. They talk about how I'm doing in school, how the dental practice is holding up, how my grandparents are enjoying their retirement. Meanwhile, the two husbands stand by to provide backup.

In the afternoon, my grandparents take their daily nap, and I pull out my computer. I try writing again, only this time, I don't shy away from what happened.

I messed up. I knew after the very first shoot with your mom that the idea for the movie was wrong, but I went on anyways because I thought the movie had to be good, and I hoped you'd be okay with it. That was selfish. I hate that I have it in me to act like that. I feel like I never got to tell you how special I think you are, and how much it meant to me to meet someone like you. I always wanted to be close to you, and to feel like you saw me the same way—as someone who understands your story. But maybe that wasn't what you wanted. I wasn't a good enough friend to you, and I think maybe I wasn't a good enough person

Suddenly it's too hard to keep on writing. I snap my laptop shut.

I was hoping to find some lesson in the words, some hidden combination that would comfort me and show me the way. But instead they're a deep well, and digging deeper only brings up more regret, more pain.

When my grandparents come back out from their nap, my mom pulls me by the arm to sit and drink tea with them. The room in front of me feels distant, unreal, like my true being has shrunken down and is buried deep inside my body. It's only by a great effort that I keep myself present, and explain to my grandparents in broken, stilted Chinese how great American high schools are.

In the evening, we pile into the car and drive out to meet the rest of the family for dinner at a fancy hotel. Things are still tense between my mom and my grandma, and the ride across the city feels interminable. We arrive at the hotel at almost the same time as the rest of the family. I spot Charles, running circles in the revolving door at breakneck speed, and Meijia, chattering away on the phone with one of her friends, and I feel a rush of relief. Time to be a kid again.

In the restaurant, the run of extravagant food continues. My grandmother offers me a soup dumpling, and when I make the mistake of saying it's good, she adds another two orders of them, on top of the various lamb, beef, and chicken dishes that we've already got. Barely ten minutes into the meal, my stomach is so full that I can't even stand up straight.

"The food is delicious, Grandma," I tell her, careful not to single out any more items.

"This is nothing. There's a much better restaurant at the Shangri-La Hotel. Our friends took us once. I wish I could take you, Yǒng yong! But my kids can't afford it." She raises her voice for this last declaration, clearly meaning for the whole table to hear.

My mom and her sisters go quiet. The only sound comes from Charles and Meijia, who are watching a Taylor Swift video on Meijia's phone. Meanwhile, my grandma pops a shrimp into her mouth like nothing's amiss.

"Yes, we're all big disappointments," my sān yí says. "We know how you feel, Mom. You worked so hard your whole life, and look at what your kids did with it."

I can feel the disaster developing in slow motion. My sān yí is joking, but she wasn't there for the argument this morning; she doesn't know that my grandma is already close to her tipping point. My mom is trying to shoot her a look, like "drop it," but it's too late.

"You say that like you're proud of yourself! If you really know how I feel, the least you can do is pretend to feel guilty about it," my grandma shoots back. Somehow, her face *still* looks placid. In a way, it only makes the bombs she's dropping hit even harder.

"Anyways, thanks for the dumplings, Grandma—" I say, trying to head off the argument.

"Are you kidding me?" my sān yí cuts in. "You want us to hang our heads in shame, because we didn't buy you a mansion and a BMW? We're doing fine, Mom. Honestly." Unlike my mom, she doesn't seem to possess an instinct for self-preservation. Maybe, as the youngest, she never quelled her rebellious side.

"Mom doesn't mean it," my second aunt adds. "She knows how

hard we work. She's probably just feeling tired."

I'm pretty sure she's trying to be a peacemaker too, but my grandma smacks her chopsticks down onto the table, like this is finally the declaration of war she's been waiting for. My stomach sinks. All of this because I had to compliment the damn food.

My grandma raises an eyebrow at my grandpa, like, "Are you really going to let our kid talk to me like that?" In response, my grandpa takes a swig of tea and clears his throat.

"Your mother had high hopes for you. When you kids were growing up, you had opportunities that she and I could only dream of. We knew what kinds of changes were coming in this country. Your generation was going to have a real shot at living a good life!"

"You always say that," my second aunt says. "We know, there were such high hopes. We didn't live up to those hopes. But we all did fine! We had some good times, and we're all still here, living it down. At some point, that has to be enough!"

"You don't listen!" my grandma snaps. Clearly my grandpa wasn't bringing enough heat for her. "What about your kids? Little Meijia? Do you think 'fine' is good enough for her? You don't think of anyone but yourself. That's why your husband left you!"

That comment sucks all the life out of my second aunt. She goes mute, and her brow twitches as she presses her lips together. This is ten times worse than anything my parents have ever said to me. I sit in stunned silence, cursing myself for being so careless. I should have just talked to Charles and Meijia about *The Lion King*.

My mom and third aunt jump in to defend their sister, and soon the table is going at a full boil. My dad tries to get involved, but my grandma kneecaps him right away with a comment about how he's living off my mom's superior dentistry skills. My uncle gives him a knowing look, like "We have to just keep our mouths shut."

When I was little, I didn't care what happened at the adults' table. I was too busy EV training my Garchomp into the perfect killing machine to try to eavesdrop on their conversations. But in the mornings, I'd see the tired looks on my parents' faces, the little piles of sunflower shells that my aunts and uncles had left behind from a late-night conversation. Things must have been just as dramatic then as they are now.

Charles is playing a game on Meijia's phone, oblivious to what's going on. At least there's one kid whose happy innocence is in no danger at all.

But Meijia is sitting stone still, staring at the adults. There's a look of dread in her eyes, and I remember that she must have seen some version of this before, her parents fighting, her dad asking for a divorce, her world coming apart. This isn't just chipping away at her innocence. It's full-on demolishing it.

I have to do something. Maybe I can't make the adults stop fighting, but at least I can take care of us kids.

"Let's go check out the hotel," I say loudly. I get up and start walking, pulling Charles and Meijia along with me, and we exit the restaurant before anyone can stop us.

The lobby of the hotel is eerily quiet. In one corner of the room is a businesswoman talking on the phone, and by the door is an adult couple waiting with their suitcases, but otherwise it's deserted.

"You ate a lot!" Charles says, switching back to English again. "I wanted to eat the xiǎo lóng bāo, but you took all of them!"

"My bad, Charles. Grandma kept making me eat them. It was a tight situation. I'm not too proud of it either, so let us never speak of it again."

"It's okay!" Charles cries, even though I'm pretty sure he couldn't understand most of what I said.

Meijia is blinking in the light. Her expression is glum, but perhaps not more so than usual.

"Let's go take a picture with the tree," I say, pointing to the back of the lobby. There, in a dimly lit corner, is a Christmas tree. It's big, but only sparsely decorated with lights and plastic bulbs.

"The tree!" Charles says. He lets out a battle cry and goes dashing across the lobby, drawing alarmed looks from the hotel staff. I take Meijia's hand, let out a much smaller, indoor cry of my own, and we chase after him.

"Come on, give me your phone," I say to my cousin, when we're in front of the tree. Meijia hands it to me, giving me the chance to admire her sparkly phone case up close.

Charles puts his hands behind his back and straightens his spine. For an instant, he looks like a miniature version of my grandpa. Meijia poses behind him, putting a hand on his shoulder.

"Come on, say qié zi!" I say. Charles flashes his teeth, and after a moment Meijia throws up a half-hearted peace sign.

"Make sure you use the filters," she says.

I fumble around with the buttons until I turn on beautiful mode, which softens the light, clears up the skin, and generally gives Meijia and Charles the plastic-y look of a Chinese pop idol.

"Now, say Merry Christmas!"

"Merry Christmas!" Charles and Meijia both cry. It's only December twenty-third, but good enough.

Since Google is blocked in China, I use Bing to find the Taylor Swift Christmas single and play it for the two of them. Meijia yelps in delight when she hears her heroine's voice, then closes her eyes to lose herself in the music. I take each of them by the hand and the three of us dance in a circle.

Maybe, if we're lucky, Meijia won't even remember the bad parts of the night. When she looks at the pictures, all she'll think of are the tree, her baby cousin, and her strange older cousin from America. If I can give her that, then at least I'll have done one thing right on this trip.

When the song is over, I hand Meijia her phone, and take mine out to snap my own picture of my cousins. That's how I see that I have a new email. I feel a momentary panic, thinking that perhaps I ended up accidentally sending my message to Cassie earlier. But the new email isn't from her, it's from Gaspard. I open it; it's a forwarded message; the only text he's written is "Holy crap!!!"

There's an image attached. I open it, and wait for it to slowly download to completion on the hotels' faint Wi-Fi. It's a screen-shot of the Ludlow Theater website, with the header *Third Annual Ludlow Theater Short Film Festival*. Under the fifteen-to-thir-ty-minute category, I see *The Ping-Pong Queen of Chinatown, Felix Ma and Gaspard Pierre-Duluc.*

Holy crap indeed. We made it. We're in.

SIXTEEN

"THE IMPORTANT THING NOW IS TO MILK THIS for all it's worth. Don't get lazy! Ideally, you'll win the top prize. But you can't control that now. I'd say you should focus on networking. When you get to the festival, you have to talk to as many people as you can. Matter of fact, you should look through the list of participants and dig up as much as you can on them. Send emails. Don't be shy! I mean, the worst that can happen is they ignore you, right?"

Mr. Qin is smiling so wide that his teeth take up half of the screen. It's a smile that says, "I told you so," or maybe even, "Thank goodness you listened to me instead of moping around like a loser."

It's January first, the start of a new year, and I'm back on Long Island. When I told Mr. Qin the good news about the film festival, he scheduled an impromptu call for the same day.

"Anyways, the most important thing is to enjoy it and have fun. What's the point of life if you can't have a little fun? This takes a lot of the pressure off of you. The eagle has landed, baby!

I hope you and your friend are going to go out and celebrate. If it was me, I'd be eating a cheeseburger and drinking a nice Oreo shake. But hey, do what makes you happy."

I imagine Mr. Qin updating my spreadsheet row with the final stage: Felix Ma, EAGLE HAS LANDED. After this meeting, he'll have dinner with his family at his big house in Syosset. He'll take big slugs of red wine as he tells his wife about another college application optimized. "I'm the king of this business! The Ivies aren't ready! These kids keep me young!"

Maybe I should be celebrating too. All of the foolish ambition that Mr. Qin tried to stir up for me has paid off. Somehow, we did it. But I don't feel happy.

After we hang up, I call Gaspard. We haven't talked on the phone before, but I want to hear from someone else, someone who isn't expecting me to pretend to celebrate.

"Mr. Ma. What an unexpected delight," he says after he picks up. "To what do I owe this pleasure?"

He asks about my trip, and I tell him stories about my cousins. He tells me about his older sister, who's visiting home from college in California, and his own cousins, who run a plant-based café in Flatbush.

"They're way cooler than I am. Every year they're into some interesting new hobby. This time, they came over for Christmas and brought us homemade vegan chocolate."

"Hey, don't sell yourself short, you're pretty cool yourself," I say. "You're a filmmaker."

"I could say the same about you," he replies.

"Thanks again for filling out the Ludlow application. I'm sorry I made you do that alone."

"Don't apologize. It was fun."

"Seriously though, you must have done a good job answering those questions. I still can't quite believe you got us into this thing."

"First of all, the movie is good. That's what got us into the film festival. For the application, I just kept it simple. Came straight from the heart, you know?"

I chuckle. "And what did your heart say?"

"I said that the director grew up in Flushing and the lead actress grew up in Chinatown, and they both played competitive Ping-Pong in real life. It meant a lot to them to tell their stories and show the places they came from on the screen. And it was especially meaningful to the director to talk about his parents—to be honest about how painful some moments in his life with them were, but also to show the happy moments, and understand that beautiful, valuable things about himself, like his ambition and his work ethic, also come from them."

"Wow."

It's not that Gaspard has said anything shocking; what he wrote is more or less exactly what I would have tried to write. And there's a bitter tang to this moment because, good intentions aside, the movie hurt Cassie too. But it's still surprisingly nice to hear Gaspard speak from my perspective with such clarity, to feel so thoroughly seen by him.

"Thank you, dude," I continue. "That's so—that's beyond what I deserve, to have you say that on my behalf. You know, I feel like a narcissist, because we made this whole movie about me, and I never really even asked if you wanted to put yourself into it in any way."

"Nah, don't worry about that. The emotional part of the movie is your thing. The editing and the music are the most interesting part for me. Besides, we can do the Gaspard bio-pic later. But with professional actors, not amateurs, no offense to Cassie. I'll be played by Daniel Kaluuya. Speaking of Cassie, are you gonna invite her?" Gaspard asks.

"I don't know. I don't think she wants anything to do with the movie anymore."

"She is the star, though. She's a big reason that we got into the film festival, maybe even bigger than the two of us. We should at least let her know about it."

"We'll see."

I've been thinking about what to do next too—not just because of the film festival, but because today, New Year's Day, is her birthday.

Happy birthday, Cassie, hope you had a nice Christmas!

The message has been sitting there all day, typed out but unsent. I've come close to sending it several times already, telling myself that it shouldn't be a big deal, because no one would ever get mad over receiving a birthday message. But right there above the typing bubble looms the last exchange in our conversation history, her telling me that she wants space. Each time, that stops me.

I go back and read our messages again, this time from the beginning. The music folder, the bubble tea, the very first time she mentioned the movie. These messages still feel unspoiled by what's happened since. They make me smile. It's coming back to me, the inexplicable, giddy excitement that I felt about getting to see her again, one extra time, then another.

I read all the way up until that night I asked to read her essay—the very first time when I asked her something that was a little too personal. I don't want to go past that moment, see the cracks starting to form. Maybe another time, but not tonight. The last message I read before snapping my computer shut is:

> I've always wanted to go camping. I heard you can see the stars way better when you're out somewhere with no lights.

But right before bed, I open up my messages with her one last time. It's occurred to me that if I don't say anything, Cassie might think that I've forgotten about her birthday. I don't want that, especially when it's such an easy day to remember. Now that the day is almost over, I don't have to agonize over whether or not she'll respond, whether or not it's a mistake—I'll send the message, go to bed, and by morning she'll have either written back, or not.

> Happy birthday, Cassie

And then, because I agree with what Gaspard said, that Cassie deserves to at least know, I add,

> We got into the film festival

Not ten seconds after I turn out the light, my phone lights up with her response. I jolt up in bed to read it.

Cassie:

> Damn bro you're cutting it REAL CLOSE with that eleventh hour hbd

> But yes, thank you, Felix

> And that's great, congrats! Happy for you

I'm glad that she responded so quickly, but I wish she'd said something more like "We did it!" That "Happy for *you*" is like her way of keeping herself at arm's length, of saying, "This is your movie, not mine."

> If you want to come, I can send you the details

Cassie:

> When is it?

At the Ludlow, in Chinatown

Cassie:

Oh I've heard of it

Okay I'll think about it! Thanks!

In the dark, a smile creeps across my face. For this brief moment, it feels like we're friends again.

I know that the wound between us is still there, that it could never be this easy. If we're going to stay friends, we're eventually going to have to talk, really talk, about what happened. But at the very least, this feels like a good sign. The thread holding us together isn't completely broken. Maybe, with time, we can build it back up to what it was before.

In the morning, I have one new message from Cassie. I open it, and it's a doozy—a wall of text. It takes me three thumb swipes to reach the top. My heart pounds as I begin to read.

Hey, Felix, first of all, congrats on getting into the film festival. I'm genuinely happy that you got this far with it—remember when we were first joking about Felix Ma: The Movie? I still remember how amusing it was when you told me you were actually going to do it.

It felt a little random that you wanted me to be the star, but it was nice too. I think I told you, I just had a feeling something like this would happen. When you meet someone by chance just once, it's whatever, but once you get up to two or three times, it starts to feel inevitable.

I pause for a moment to let the words sink in, enjoy the happy buzz of reading something written by her, for me.

Getting to know you has been really, really fun. You gotta remember, my impression of you started as this polished, put-together piano god, so I was curious to know what you were actually like. For one thing, you're much more of a softie than I expected. But also, I feel like something clicked right away about us. I think we complement each other. I'm always trying to entertain people by having wacky ideas and acting confident, and I feel like you respond to that energy, and it brings out this creative, confident side of you too. I'm a little worried that that sounds like an arrogant thing for me to say—like I'm so wonderful that I unlocked all of this potential in you—but I'm trying to put it as truthfully as I can, from my point of view.

The words still read nice, but a seed of doubt is growing in my mind. There's something ominous about where this is heading, like these kind words are just the spoonful of sugar that comes before the medicine.

After a while I started to notice something inside of me that I didn't like. We first met as piano rivals, then as Ping-Pong rivals, right? And I realized that there's a part of me that still compares myself with you, and competes with you. It's not a very nice thing to admit, so I'm sorry. When you showed me the edited clips of the movie for the first time, I felt jealous. Like, yeah, I can come up with silly ideas and do useless stuff like eat spicy chicken wings, but you guys are built different, you can make something that looks *this* legit and it's just effortless. Seriously, you both know a lot about movies.

I never thought of the movie as something Cassie would be jealous of. It always felt like something that never would have been possible without her, that all stemmed from her force of personality. But maybe that was the problem.

When I realized how much of the movie was based on my life, I got upset. I was like, this movie is already your thing, but now you're taking something from me for it? It felt like you were breaking the rules somehow. But the weird thing was, I was also flattered. It was like you were admitting that you couldn't do this without me. You were making it my thing too. So I went along with it. And that was a mistake. You asked me and my mom to have a fight on camera. I should have said no. I realize now, that's a part of my life that's only for me and her to see. No one else gets to ask questions about it, or give advice, or make me talk about it if I don't want to. I know I started it by sending you my essay, so I'll take some of the blame. Anyways, the point is my own boundaries are clear to me now, and I have to spell them out.

Even in this terrible moment, as my heart is sinking like an anchor, getting a glimpse of Cassie's thoughts still has a powerful allure. A part of me wants this message to go on forever, no matter how painful it is. Only now, that urge is familiar to me. It's already led us to a dark, terrible place. I have to outgrow it.

I'm not saying that the movie was all bad. But I did have a lot of negative thoughts because of it, and I don't like being in that headspace. Being around you feels so good in some ways, but it also makes me feel guilty, and inadequate, and lately it makes

251

me angry. I'm not saying it's your fault, and maybe it's unfair for me to even tell you all of this. The point is, things have gotten complicated with you, and I just want things to be simple for a while. Sorry I just wrote you this super long essay. I realized that I can't make it to the film festival anyways, because that's the first rehearsal for all-state concert band. I hope it's fun though. Seriously, congrats again, it's a big deal.

There's a thudding finality to the end of the message. After I'm done, I go back and reread the latter half again, because this can't be the end, it can't be over just like that.

And then I feel sadness welling up inside. I manage to stand, lock the door, and dive headfirst into my pillow before the tears start to come. After that, it's horrible—my whole face goes numb, there's tears and snot and sweat pouring from my face, and I get these deep, throat-rattling hiccups that make me cough and gasp for air after each one. The last time this happened, my parents saw me; at least this time I get to be alone. But this is much, much worse than the end of things with Henry. Then, at least, the problem was other people bullying me. This time, I'm losing someone I care about, and it's all my fault, the problem is me.

SEVENTEEN

ON THE DAY OF THE LUDLOW FILM FESTIVAL, MY parents and I drive into Manhattan. My mom insists that I wear a button-down shirt and slacks, and she keeps telling me how handsome I look. We spend a long time looking for parking but still manage to arrive at the theater a half-hour early. Gaspard and his parents show up shortly afterward. He's wearing an actual suit, which I'm pretty sure has been tailored based on how well it fits.

Mr. Qin shows up too. Gaspard quickly steers his parents away to the concession stand, before they can figure out what Mr. Qin does and try to hire him. Mr. Qin claps me on the back and congratulates me for making the big day happen, but it's hard for me to match his enthusiasm. Not that I can blame him for what happened with Cassie, but I wish I hadn't taken his advice so much to heart. If I hadn't let his praise go to my head, if I hadn't built up the movie as this massive turning point in my life, then maybe things would have gone differently.

Once our parents are settled, Gaspard and I head to the

entrants' reception to do some "networking." Luckily, Gaspard is much more comfortable with this than I am. That, plus the fact that we stand out because of our age, makes it easy to mingle with the other filmmakers. Nothing super promising happens—no one offers to let us read their script or collaborate on their next project or anything—but we do talk to some interesting film students and artist types. The most popular person there is Aung Khin, a documentary filmmaker whose entry follows two girls from the Burmese countryside as they prepare for tryouts for the national football team.

When the screenings start, we take the reserved seats on the balcony. The day starts with the animated shorts. I've never seen low-budget or indie animated movies before, and it's interesting to see how the filmmakers have to work within constraints. One of the shorts, for example, has a beautiful illustration style that looks like a Renaissance oil painting. As the characters move from room to room, the style changes to mimic a stained-glass window, then a Byzantine mosaic. The movements are jerky, with a copy-pasted feel to them, but it fits the style well enough. Another short has somewhat simplistic backgrounds, but incredibly detailed animations of water—rain glistening in the sunlight, droplets sliding down a glass window, puddles reflecting the clouds.

When the live-action shorts begin, Gaspard and I are called down in front of the screen to give a speech.

"Um, it's great to be here today with so many amazing filmmakers," I begin, blinking under the lights. In the audience, I spot my parents—my dad filming with his iPad, and my mom smiling with unadulterated pride. For her, this is my big moment, my long-awaited triumph.

"I just want to say a big thank you to our friend Cassie. I wish she was here today, but she couldn't come because she had rehearsal for the all-state band. She was the heart of this movie, and she had to suffer a lot when we were making it. If we were to start all over again, we'd probably do things differently. But what you're about to see is the movie we did make, for better or worse."

There's a lump in my throat, so I pass the mic over to Gaspard.

"And thanks to Cassie's mom, Ms. Chow, for being in the movie and letting us film in her bakery. You guys gotta check it out if you're hungry after the film festival. Golden Promises, on Elizabeth Street. And of course, thanks to our parents for supporting us. Also shout-out to FiltroPro! It's this rad app that lets you edit movies on your phone. Wait, maybe I shouldn't have admitted that. Anyways yeah, thanks to the theater people for picking us!"

We get some polite applause as we hurry off stage and go back up to the balcony.

When the movie plays, it's jarring to see the footage we've shot projected onto the big screen. In front of such a big, serious audience, the artsy shots and serious monologues we put together feel hokey—too much like a random jumble of ideas. I wonder if it's obvious that we didn't go into the movie with a plan, that we whipped it up as we went along. The Ping-Pong Queen and her mom seem to whiplash between extremes, coexisting happily in one scene, then yelling at each other in the next. It doesn't really make sense, if you don't know Cassie and her mom personally. I crane my neck over the edge of the balcony, looking at the people below, taking in their reactions to something *we* made. It's weird. When it's over, we get about the same amount of applause as the other short films. A couple of the filmmakers around us lean in to whisper, "Nice job."

As for me, I feel like our movie isn't all that good. To hurt someone I cared about in the name of creating some small piece of art that only a few people will ever watch, that no one will remember, all because someone else told me that it had to exist—it wasn't worth it.

When the screening is over, we go out for celebratory dim sum with Gaspard's parents, my parents, and Mr. Qin. As the carts roll past our table, my mom goes off on ordering, piling our table high with bamboo steamers of dumplings, ribs, and buns.

Mr. Qin asks casually what Gaspard's parents do. His mom, it turns out, is a dermatologist, and his dad is a marriage lawyer. At the mention of these two lucrative professions, Mr. Qin's eyes grow wide like saucers, but he's classy enough to refrain from making his sales pitch to them on this occasion.

My mom passes around a dish of egg tarts, which makes me think of Golden Promises. Their egg tarts are better. If Cassie and her mom were here, they'd probably say so too.

"Did you hear me, Felix?"

I snap my head up. The whole table is looking at me.

"I said that the editing was impressive," Mr. Qin repeats. "The way you spliced scenes together, so you could see how Ping-Pong was a metaphor for interpersonal relationships."

"Oh. Well, Gaspard did most of the editing. He gets all the credit for that."

"No way, Felix was the idea guy," Gaspard says, with a wave of his hand. "I just clicked and dragged when he told me to."

"That's the most amazing part. They made the whole movie on their phones. These days, you don't even need a computer."

"There was just one thing that could have been better," my mom says, smiling mischievously. "The speeches. Next time you talk in front of so many people, you better prepare something."

The adults at the table chuckle, and I'm pretty sure I'm supposed to laugh too. The joke is that even now, at the supposed height of my success, she's nitpicking. But I don't feel like laughing, and I don't have the energy to pretend.

"Oh, yeah. Sorry. Next time."

She raises an eyebrow, and confusion creeps into her smile. "I'm kidding, Felix! What's wrong with you? You don't seem happy."

This exact scenario, this moment, is what I've wanted for years. Being celebrated, getting taken out to dim sum, finally proving that that comment my mom made isn't true. And now that it's here, it feels completely wrong.

"This movie was fake. It was all just a game. Why are we out to dim sum for this? There's nothing to celebrate."

My mom looks stunned. Quickly, my dad hops in. "What do you mean, fake? You put a lot of work into it. It turned out so well. You can't say something like that, your friend is right here."

Gaspard shrugs. His parents look mildly confused, and they cast questioning glances at their son, like, 'What's the deal with this Felix kid again?"

I ignore them and turn to Mr. Qin. "Was this really the only way to do things? Do you make all of your students go and dig up a fake achievement somewhere?"

"Felix!" my mom says sharply.

"It's all right, it's all right," Mr. Qin says, smiling calmly. "I understand having hang-ups about this process. The truth is, Felix, college admissions *is* a game. Sure, we'd like to think that admissions officers are thoughtful, humane people who don't need some flashy award to recognize each applicant's unique brilliance. But with the volume of profiles they have to sift through, it's just not realistic. I know that my approach may feel artificial, but for something as big as your choice of college, it's worth it to play ball just a little bit."

"How do you know the Mas, exactly, Mr. Qin?" Ms. Pierre-Duluc asks.

Gaspard stands up. "Felix, why don't we step outside for minute? We should get some air. Don't worry, Mr. and Mrs. Ma, he'll be fine. It was tough working on this project, you know. A lot of false starts, some times when we thought about giving up. We pushed through it anyways, because we wanted to finish. But I think we'll need to decompress for a bit before we can fully appreciate it."

I stand up too, before my parents can protest. The idea of getting some air sounds welcome. I hear my mom mutter something like, "Why didn't they say *that* in their speech?" but I ignore her.

"We'll be back in a bit!" Gaspard says cheerfully as we head for the exit.

Outside the restaurant, I let out a small, mangled groan. "Why did I say all of that stuff?"

"It's okay, it wasn't that bad," Gaspard says, patting me on the back. "Still cut up that Cassie didn't make it, huh?"

"Among other things."

"Why don't we stop by Golden Promises?"

"She's not there; she has band practice."

"Well, we can go and see Ms. Chow. Honestly, we probably should have invited her to the film festival, since she was our second star. It's the least we can do."

We go to the bakery, and for once, there's a line. There's a customer at the cash register with two big pink boxes of pastries, and he and Ms. Chow seem to be having an argument. The customer keeps waving his hands over the boxes and gesturing into the back of the shop, and Ms. Chow shrugs, like, "I hear you, man, but what do you want me to do about it?"

Eventually, the man takes his boxes and leaves in a huff. Since it's almost the lunar new year, she sends a cheerful "Gong huy fat choy!" after him. But once the door swings shut, she rolls her eyes and exchanges a tired smile with the woman who's next in line. When she spots the two of us, her eyes light up.

"My two favorite customers! I'll be with you in a minute."

I feel the smallest bit relieved. There was a part of me that worried that since Cassie is mad at me, Ms. Chow would be too.

When she's finished with the last customer, she comes around to the other side of the counter to greet us.

"Cassandra didn't tell me you were coming today! She's not here. I assume you know that."

"We know." Gaspard nods. "We're here for the film festival, so we thought we'd come visit."

"Yes, yes, she mentioned it. Congratulations! Thanks for coming to see me," Ms. Chow says. "Ah, wait just one second. I have something for you."

She runs into the back of the shop, and a couple of minutes later, she comes out holding a small cake. It says CONGRATU-LATIONS, FELIX AND GASPARD! in frosting. It must have already been ready, because there's no way she could have whipped it up on such short notice.

"I had a feeling you'd stop by sooner or later," she explains.

"But what if we didn't?" I ask.

"Easy enough to scrape the words off. Or just eat it. In your honor, of course!"

Ms. Chow sets the cake down at the table in front of the pic-ture of Hong Kong street, the same table where we filmed the movie. She cuts three generously sized slices and lays each one on a paper plate. The three of us sit around the table to eat with plastic forks and knives. While we eat, Ms. Chow tells us about Cassie's plans for college.

"I want my Cassie to study economics. She's smart, and she's good with numbers, and after she graduates she can work on Wall Street. Ms. Leung from the bookstore, her daughter studied economics, and now she works at Goldman Sachs. She just bought Ms. Leung a Lexus! That made me really jealous. If Cassie can buy a Lexus for us, then I'll park it in front of the bookstore every day, even if they give me a ticket." She winks at us. "I'm not a jerk. It's just because Ms. Leung is a show-off."

"I'm thinking of Spanish and linguistics," Gaspard says. "I don't think I'll be buying my parents a Lexus, but maybe I can get them a used Toyota?"

"How is Cassie?" I ask.

Ms. Chow blinks. My question is a bit out of the blue; based on the flow of the conversation, I should have started talking about my intended major. But I can't go through the motions of talking about that like it matters to me right now, when it doesn't.

"It's funny—she seems tired lately," Ms. Chow says. "Quiet. She's been very well-behaved. Doesn't complain as much when I ask her to do things, which is always a bad sign."

My face falls. "It's because of me," I say.

"What makes you say that? There's a lot going on in her life right now. It could be any number of things."

I shake my head. "It was the movie. I pushed her too hard. It was wrong to base it so much on your lives. I owe you an apology too, Ms. Chow."

"Oh, no need to apologize to me. I had fun. I don't mind having a movie made about my life. It's about time someone did that, in fact," she says, smiling.

"What Felix is saying is, we should have asked for permission first. And we should have given you a better idea of what you were getting into. Cassie suffered a lot more than she needed to because we didn't do that."

"It's possible." Ms. Chow taps her spoon against her chin thoughtfully. "I guess it did start this time after finishing the movie. I thought she was sad that it was over. But maybe it was because of you."

She smirks, like it's all a joke, but after she sees the look on my face, her expression grows more serious.

"Did she say anything? Does she hate me now?" I ask.

"No, she didn't. She hasn't mentioned you in a while." She sighs. "It happens, Felix. I'm sure you didn't mean any harm. It's just that Cassandra . . . most of the time, she has so much energy. She's always surprising me with what she can do. I learned never to say, 'You can't do that,' around her, because she always takes it as a challenge. But when she's down, she's really down. Her energy disappears, and she hides in her room a lot and doesn't talk to me. That's when I worry about her.

"But that doesn't erase the good times, either. I know it was good for Cassandra to spend some time with you boys. Whenever she talked about you, I could tell she was happy. She'll be all right again, once some time passes."

I must not look convinced, because after a moment, she adds, "I'll tell her you came by, she'll appreciate it. And I'll talk to her. I can't promise she'll forgive you right away, but I think she'll come around eventually. I know she cares about you."

When we finish eating, Ms. Chow refuses to let us pay for the cake, but I outfox her by slipping a twenty into the tip jar while she isn't looking.

Outside, Gaspard and I pick a direction and start walking aimlessly down the street.

"Feeling any better?" he asks.

"No."

"Look at me, son."

I frown. "What?"

"It's not your fault," Gaspard says gravely.

"What's not my fault?"

"No, no. It's not your fault."

"I don't get it."

"It's not your fa—"

"Are you trying to do that scene from *Good Will Hunting* on me?"

Gaspard smiles guiltily, eyes shining as he channels his inner Robin Williams. "Is it working?"

"No, it doesn't fit the situation at all. Matt Damon was abused as a child in that movie. He needed someone else to help him confront it. This is totally different; everything *is* my fault. You need to pick a different movie."

"Damn." Gaspard shakes his head. "That was the closest I could think of."

"Thanks for trying."

We walk in silence, but I can practically hear the gears in Gaspard's head turning as he searches for a different emotionally climactic movie scene to mine for ideas.

"It probably has to be, like, a romantic comedy or something. The pep talk before the guy gets the girl back, or vice versa," I suggest.

"That doesn't fit either. This isn't romantic; you said it yourself," Gaspard replies.

"Thank you for finally acknowledging that."

"You're welcome." He winks. "Okay, how about this: Felix, you messed things up, big time. But try not to think about that right now."

"Are you sure? I think I should be thinking about them a lot. I have to at least learn something, right?"

Gaspard raises a hand to shush me. "Don't interrupt. Think about . . . think about the things she taught you. They're a part of you now. That's what you have to take away from this. You have to carry them forward."

"But what did she teach me?"

Gaspard shrugs. "Don't ask me. You'd know best."

"I don't know . . . believe in myself? If I wanna do something, I should just do it? Also, don't make a movie about someone else's life without permission?"

"Just focus on those first two for now," Gaspard says. "Listen, I'm serious. Cassie might forgive you, and she might not. You heard what Ms. Chow said; it's gonna take some time. Meanwhile, how are you going to find some positives out of this? What's something you can do to balance out the mistake, to make the world a little bit better?"

Even though we're on Canal Street, and the sidewalk is packed, I stop in my tracks to look at him. "What movie is that from?"

Gaspard grins. "It's not from a movie. I made it up. Do you like it?"

"It's not bad, I guess."

"So do you know what to do?"

I look at the people streaming around like we're an inanimate obstacle, the lights twinkling on in the windows of buildings, the cars rushing noisily by. I feel small, but solid. Present.

"Maybe."

EIGHTEEN

IN FRESHMAN YEAR, WHEN HENRY WAS GET-
ting more and more into skateboarding, I developed this
little routine with him. Basically, he'd start talking in his special lingo—"I just got these new trucks, the turning is hella deep
but they still have awesome pop"—and I'd intentionally, exag-
geratedly misunderstand. I'd pretend he was talking about actual
trucks, or ask what his pop had to do with it. I don't know if
Henry knew I was doing it on purpose, and I don't even know if *I*
knew I was doing it on purpose. It was just a habit I developed as
an awkward freshman.

Henry didn't mind it, but his friends did. When they talked
about skateboarding at lunch, I'd make my usual ignorant comments. No one laughed, and occasionally this kid Alex Economos,
who had a fuzzy mustache and a mop of skater hair, would say,
"Who is this kid?"

There was one guy in the group who seemed quieter and mood-
ier than the others. He put up with me for a while, but then one

day, it was like he finally got fed up. I made a corny joke about ollies and nollies, and he called me an idiot to my face. It felt like getting punched. I was completely stunned, even when everyone else started laughing at me. The worst part was that Henry didn't stand up for me. He laughed too.

If I focus on those memories, they still make me angry. But I also remember the time that Henry let me ride that new skateboard with the new trucks, how patient he was when he was teaching me. How after I fell and scraped up my palms and knees, he congratulated me and said that now that I'd wiped out, I could call myself a skater.

At school, I want to talk to Henry again, but it's hard to catch him alone. He's always with his skater friends, and I'm not interested in getting anywhere near them. Henry doesn't come to any more film club screenings, and he's nowhere to be found during free periods. I wonder if maybe he regretted talking to me during the last one.

Normally I'd just give up. The only thing that keeps me going is what Gaspard said. Look for some positives, do something to balance out the mistake. Take all that desperation to undo what happened with Cassie, and channel it into something else, something healthy.

I find Henry's social media profile, but it looks like he doesn't post much. His profile picture is dated to four years ago, and the last sign of any kind of activity is a video he was tagged in back in sophomore year, of Alex Economos eating it at the skate park.

I add him as a friend anyways. After he accepts, I message him.

> Want to hang out?

> We could go to the mall or something

After a day, Henry responds.

Henry:

Nah I don't want to go to the mall

Womp womp. No counter-offer, not even a sorry. I try to think of someplace he might like to go to, other than the skate park. The trouble is, I don't know much about him. Our friendship always hinged on proximity and the fact that we're both Asian. Which is why things fell apart in the first place.

> What about shakes at Atlas Diner?

Last-ditch effort. If this doesn't happen, then at least I can say I went out giving it all I could.

Henry:

How bout you come to Victory Café

I'll cook you lunch

> I'm in!

Looks like Henry and I aren't done with each other yet after all.

"So what do you taste?"

"Um . . . everything?"

"Anything specific?"

"I think coconut milk? And chicken? Also . . . the ocean. It tastes like being on the beach on a hot day. Also it's really spicy. I'm sweating." I wipe the sweat beads off my upper lip.

"All of that stuff is in there." Henry nods. Over his usual hoodie and ripped jeans, he's wearing a gray apron. "Well, I don't know about the beach part. But there's dried shrimp and chili paste. Also lemongrass."

"Okay, I think I'm getting that."

"Did you taste the secret ingredient, though?" he asks eagerly.

"I think I've already exhausted my abilities there. This is delicious. That's all I can say."

I showed up to Victory Café around two p.m., when the stragglers from the lunch crowd were finishing up their food and asking for their checks. Henry peeked out from the kitchen, spotted me, and told me to have a seat. Ten minutes later, he brought out a steaming bowl of Indonesian laksa.

"There's saffron," Henry says. "I thought it might add an extra kick."

"Ohhh. Well, I'm sure I'd have gotten that, if I knew what saffron tasted like. There's plenty of kick, that's for sure. Arguably too much. I'm dying here. Do you have any water?"

There's a delayed onset to the heat, and I'm starting to suffer. As flattered as I am that Henry wanted to cook for me, he's badly overestimated my spice tolerance. There's a reason I didn't participate in that wings challenge in Chinatown.

"Yeah, just a sec." Henry dashes off to the kitchen, then comes back with a glass of fizzy pink soda. It's sweet and thick and provides instant relief.

Henry dips his own spoon into the laksa and has a taste. "It's not bad, but it's basic. Maybe too basic. I want to figure out a way to make it more surprising." He scratches his head. "I want it to stand out."

After this last admission, he looks down at his feet like he's just given up some big secret. He goes back into the kitchen, and when he comes out, he's taken off his apron.

"So how do you apply to cooking school? Is there like an audition, where you have to make the perfect scrambled eggs? Or some kind of competition?"

"Nah, it's not like that. Most people who apply can get in. I don't think it's that competitive," Henry says.

"Could you do one of those cooking competition shows though? You could go on TV and stuff."

"I don't think so. I'm just learning how to make the stuff we serve here. I'm not trying to cook in a fancy restaurant or anything."

"Oh. Well, it's still cool that you knew to put saffron in the laksa."

There's an awkward silence. I realize that I sound like Mr. Qin, trying to turn Henry's activity into a source of accolades. Now there's a terrifying thought.

"How'd you meet that guy you do the movie club with?" Henry asks.

"His name's Gaspard. He just showed up to the first meeting when I was trying to start the club. That was the first time I ever talked to him. But he's into old movies like I am, so it worked out."

"He seems kind of uptight," Henry says. "But maybe I just don't know him enough."

I remember the two times they've interacted; both times, Gaspard was coming on aggressive, trying to have my back. "He's not uptight. Maybe the nice clothes give off a certain impression. But he's chill when you get to know him."

"Yeah. Makes sense." Henry fidgets with the soup spoon, scooping out his laksa, examining it, then pouring the soup back into the bowl.

The comment about Gaspard puts me on edge, and counter-accusations start popping into my head. A pulse of anger runs across my mind, and I blurt out a question just as Henry speaks again too.

"You haven't changed much," he says.

"Why did you have to stop talking to me altogether?"

Henry looks at me, surprised, then quickly looks back down at the soup. A part of me wishes I could take it back, and a part of me wants to hear the answer.

"I don't know," Henry says quietly. "It just happened. It's not because I . . . it wasn't about y—"

He cuts himself off, chewing on his lip.

He was about to say, "It wasn't about you." But he didn't. Because it *was* about me. Henry wasn't just trying to protect me from getting bullied. I was an inconvenience, an obligation, and he didn't want me in his life anymore. Nothing will ever change that, it's a scar that will never go away. Thinking about it brings back all the anger, all the times I'd see Henry in the hallways and fantasize about attacking him, then going one-on-six against all of his skater friends. I used to imagine getting beat up by them, going down like a tragic hero. At least then Henry would have to feel bad for what he did.

"I guess I didn't have to just stop talking to you," Henry continues. "But I did. Sometimes I thought I should just say what's up, but I didn't. Then it got harder and harder, and eventually it just felt like it was too late."

He's scowling down at his hands, like he's mad that he can't come up with a better answer. I wanted to get everything out in the open, but this conversation isn't getting us anywhere. We can't dig this up and expect the sunlight to heal it. It's too painful.

"But you still did it in the end," I say. "You came to the film club. And you talked to me in the cafeteria. Thanks. Thanks for trying."

Henry shrugs. "Yeah. No problem."

We're both silent for a moment, looking in different directions, wavering on the line between fighting and being friends. I can feel the temptation to let my anger loose, to finally have it out with Henry after all these years. But I want to find another way.

"By the way, do you have a video of that trick you were talking about? The fakie heelflip?"

For the first time all afternoon, Henry grins. The dimples show up in his cheeks, and he looks like a different person. "Yeah! Here, I'll show you."

He whips out his phone and finds the video.

"Oh wait, no, I wiped out on this one," he narrates, as his video self stumbles on the landing.

"It's this one," he says, swiping to another video. "Oh wait, no, I *ate it* on this one." The Henry in the video tumbles to the ground heavily. It looks painful. I say a silent thank you that I didn't really try to get into skateboarding just so we'd stay friends.

"Damn, I gotta delete some of these," Henry says as the skateboard slides out from under his feet on landing and he tap-dances backward before taking a seat on the ground. "But I can't."

"Why not?"

"I just can't. See, I'm looking at the delete button right now. Can't do it. Just have to keep it, I guess."

I raise an eyebrow at him, and we both laugh.

"Oh wait, no, it's for sure this one," he says, swiping to a fourth video.

"I've heard that one before."

But this time, video Henry nails the landing. His arms shoot out a little for balance, but it still looks clean. He tries to play it off in the video, but at the end, just before it cuts out, he raises up his arms and yells, "Ah—"

"Yessir," he says. "I remember how it felt."

"How did it feel?"

"You know. Good."

"Hey, I have a question. Do you get frustrated while you're doing tricks? Like, if you keep messing up and wiping out, do you get annoyed?" I'm thinking of Ping-Pong, and piano, when you're alone out there and you feel like a prisoner in your own head.

Henry smiles. "Nah. You don't wanna be that one dude at the park who takes it way too seriously. Who yells and has a stick up his butt."

"Even if you almost get it, but don't?"

"Almost getting tricks feels good. It feels the same as getting the trick. Almost." He drums his fingers on the table, thinking. "I have an analogy. Getting a trick is like eating the whole cupcake. Almost getting a trick is like eating just the frosting."

"Wow. That sounds awesome."

"Everyone is different, I guess. Some people get frustrated. But not me. I only get mad when I eat it. That hurts. Come to think of it, maybe I am gonna delete the one video where I fell."

He opens up the video, and we watch Henry fall again. Henry winces, and his finger hovers over the delete button. He looks at the button, then back at me, then back at the button.

"Can't do it?" I ask.

He grins. "Nah. Just have to keep it, I guess."

In mid-March, on the eve of college acceptance season, Cassie posts a photo of herself and a friend from school. They're wearing bandannas and face paint for some kind of spirit week, and they look happy together. Cassie is tossing her head back and laughing, while her friend pats her shoulder and smacks her own forehead. The caption, written by Cassie, is:

Four years of making fools of ourselves XD love you so much, gonna miss you next year

Her friend, whose name is Melody Tiew, has commented a row of heart and sparkle emojis, and the rest of the comments are variations on "awww so cute."

Seeing the photo makes me feel a pang of jealousy. Melody Tiew never had to contrive a movie project to be friends with Cassie; she had the good fortune of going to Van Der Donck, of hanging out with Cassie every day.

It's been almost two months since the film festival. I haven't messaged Cassie, and even though I miss her, I've gotten used to life without her, and without the movie.

But then, out of the blue, she messages me.

Cassie:

Hey I've been meaning to say thanks for stopping by to see my mom after the film festival

It meant a lot to her, I think. She really likes you two

Or maybe she was just happy that you proved her right for making the congratulations cake. She loves being right

I was so sure I was gonna have to eat the whole thing myself. I did have a couple slices lolol

I type my response so fast that my thumbs start to cramp up. Feeling her presence again, even just digitally, is like water for a person who's dying of thirst.

That was the highlight of the day! It was so nice of your mom to make us a cake when she didn't even know if we'd stop by to eat it

We missed you that day, would have been fun if you'd made it

And then, a miracle:

Cassie:

Things are pretty hectic right now but when they calm down a bit we should hang out again

> It'd be nice not to just leave things off where we did

For a while now, I've had this idea about how I can make things up to her. It feels a little corny and fantastical, but it's also a grand gesture, something meaningful. I was planning to save the idea for later, give Cassie a bit more space. But after her message, I can't wait any longer. I gather up all of the information I found online and send her a message detailing my proposal.

Cassie:

> Omggg is that for real?

> Wow I didn't even know you could do that haha . . . I feel like we have to

> I'll think about it. But honestly, it's almost definitely a yes

NINETEEN

"AND THIS IS THE *ONLY* WAY TO MAKE THINGS right? We can't just go to Chinatown to see her, or even Flushing?" Gaspard shakes his head.

"It's not the only way. But it's a good idea. It'll mean a lot to her. We're basically helping her realize one of her dreams."

"But do *I* have to come?"

"Yes. Please. The group energy is better when you're around. She'll be expecting you."

"It's *March*. The whole point of living in the modern era is that we don't have to experience these deprivations anymore. How is it even legal to go *camping* in the winter?"

Because of course that's my idea. *I've always wanted to go camping. I heard you can see the stars way better when you're out somewhere with no lights.* It turns out you are allowed to go camping in the winter in Long Island—with caveats. The biggest one being that you have to go with the Boy Scouts. So sayeth the law of Suffolk County Parks and Recreation.

As it turns out, Mr. Qin has an old student who was an Eagle Scout. After I apologize profusely to both him and to my parents for my unusual behavior at the dim sum restaurant, Mr. Qin is nice enough to help hook us up with a troop from Smithtown.

After that, the trip comes together surprisingly quickly. I reserve a tent site at the scout camp in Nissequogue, and pay a twenty-four dollar fee on the Boy Scouts website. We'll be joining Scout Patrol 312, affectionately known as the Drippopotami. The reservation even comes with a free rental of a heavy-duty, weather-proof tent.

I keep waiting for Cassie to back out, but she doesn't do it. Every so often, she messages me a question like "Will there be poison ivy even though it's winter?" or "How many pairs of socks do I need to bring?" The sticking point, it turns out, is Gaspard.

"Is it really gonna take *this much* to make things up to her? I get it, we messed up, but why does that mean we have to stay outside *all night*, in the cold?"

"It won't be that bad. We'll be safe, with the Boy Scouts around. And it won't be that cold, we'll be by the fire and then in an insulated tent. There's a ton of reviews for this campsite that talk about how nice it is in the winter."

Even though we're on the phone, I can practically hear Gaspard shaking his head on the other end of the line. "I mean, just listen to yourself. This is madness. There has to be another way."

"Hey, I came with you to Lexie Han's party. I didn't think I'd have a good time there, but look how that turned out."

"How dare you, that's *completely* different—"

In the end, though, he relents.

And then suddenly it's the third weekend of March, and Gaspard and I are at the Great Neck LIRR station, waiting for Cassie to arrive. At 4:01 p.m., her train pulls in, and there she is, bundled up in comically thick layers of jackets and scarves, her backpack stuffed to the brim with whatever survival gear, nonperishable food, and extra socks she decided to pack.

"Wow, a welcoming committee," she says as she piles into the back seat of Gaspard's car. "I'm wearing literally every single jacket and scarf that I own right now."

She unwinds one, two, three scarves from around her neck, and underneath I see no fewer than four different collars, fanned out like playing cards. She wasn't kidding.

My house is a ten-minute drive from the station. When we pull onto my street, Cassie whistles.

"Dang, this is where you live?"

"Yeah. We're that brick one at the end of the street," I say, pointing.

"Are you for real?"

I chuckle. "Is something wrong?"

"This street looks like the set of a movie or something. The bushes are absurdly well trimmed. How are the houses so pristine? Were they all just built?"

"Most people use landscapers, I guess. Not us, my dad makes

me mow the lawn in the summers. Anyways, this is nothing. You should go and see Linden Street, where Gaspard's friend Lexie lives. Now *those* are some nice houses."

"I'm not sure if I want to," Cassie says.

Inside the house, my parents are waiting in the living room. They've already set out three cups of tea, some slices of Asian pear, and a plate of almond cookies.

"Ah yee hou, shu shu hou," Cassie says. "This is a beautiful home!"

"Thank you," my mom replies, beaming. "It's nice to meet another one of Felix's friends."

"Felix doesn't have many friends who are girls," my dad says. I find this comment very unnecessary, and I'm glad Gaspard is around. Otherwise, my dad would probably make more jokes about me having a girlfriend.

Thankfully, my parents don't stick around long before heading upstairs.

"So this is your life," Cassie says softly. She looks around the living room, tracing her eyes over the skylight on the ceiling, letting them linger on the brush scrolls, the framed dentistry awards, the oil painting of a sailboat on a rough sea.

"Yeah."

She sighs, then sinks back onto the couch. For a while, we're all silent. Normally Cassie has a lot to say, so it's easy to sit back and let her drive the conversation. Today, though, her eyes are distant, like her mind is somewhere else.

"We should probably leave around six or so," Gaspard says. "Are you all packed, Felix?"

"Yeah, I'm packed. My parents bought me a sixty-four-ounce thermos for this, can you believe it? Supposedly it'll keep water hot all night. But it's going to be heavy."

I look at Cassie, waiting for her reaction. *Wow, sixty-four ounces? You're going to have to pee so much!* Nothing.

"I learned how to tie a knot for this. The fisherman's knot. You use it to tie two ropes together. That's my contribution to the group," I say. "The guy in the video was dead serious about knots. 'You have to understand, there will be situations where this knot is what's separating life and death.'"

It's not like I think this is some irresistibly interesting quote, but it's still deflating that Cassie doesn't so much as nod in response. Normally, just her presence is enough to make everything feel more exciting—she'll put her own take on whatever you say, make you feel like you're funny and original. Now, though, it seems like she doesn't even want to be here. I wonder if I was overeager about this idea, if I should have let more time pass instead of pushing for it as soon as she reached out.

"I guess I knew your house would be like this," she murmurs. "But it's still different to see it."

I don't know whether I should accept this compliment or politely decline ("Oh no, it's nothing, it's not that nice," like my parents would say). Both options seem faintly annoying, so I just reply, "Thanks for coming."

She sits up. "I got into Stony Brook. I found out today."

"No way, that's, like, right next to where we're going camping!" I blurt out.

Cassie looks at me sourly. "Thanks, I'm aware of that. Aren't you going to say congratulations?"

"Oh. Sorry," I say, frustrated with myself.

"Congratulations, Cassie," Gaspard says.

"Yeah, congratulations," I add hastily. "That's awesome, it really is. Was it your first acceptance?"

"No, the second. I got into Cornell too."

"Wait, that's amazing!" I smile. "Way to bury the lead, Cassie."

She shrugs. "Well, I'm not going there anyways," she replies flatly.

"Why not? That's an awesome school!"

"They didn't give me enough money. I got some grants, but none of the scholarships I applied for came through. And I absolutely refuse to take out loans that big."

"But there has to be a way, right?"

"Well, it's not like I'm going to find thirty thousand dollars a year under my mattress."

I open my mouth, then close it again. It's unfathomable to me that she could get an opportunity that good and not be able to take it.

Gaspard sucks his teeth. "Sorry, Cassie. That sucks."

"Yeah, sorry." I pat her on the shoulder—gingerly, and just once.

Cassie shakes her head and waves me away. "No, it's fine. I didn't mean to make you feel sorry for me. I didn't want to go that bad, and it's kind of far away anyways. I just applied because my guidance counselor asked me to."

She sighs. "Sorry, sorry, I'm being a downer right now. It wasn't like this in the morning, I swear. The point is, I'm happy about Stony Brook. They basically gave me a full ride, when you add it all up. Let's talk about something else. Tell me about your Christmas breaks—I never even asked about them."

Gaspard tells us about the big family gathering at his aunt's house in Westchester County, and I talk about my cousins and my aunts and my grandparents. Cassie laughs about the punching bag and the Taylor Swift story. She seems to relax a little, once she doesn't have to be the center of attention.

At six o'clock, we load our bags into the car and begin the drive down the Northern State Parkway. The scout camp is about an hour away, and it feels strange to be setting out on a long drive so late in the day.

"Holy crap, it's twenty-nine degrees out," Gaspard says, pointing to the thermostat reading on his dashboard.

"It's only going to get colder," Cassie says from the backseat. "Hold on to your butts."

As the houses get more sparse, and the trees start to close in around us, the air in the car begins to feel too quiet, almost lifeless. I try to think of something positive to say, something that will brighten the mood.

"Hey, I talked to Henry," I say, turning to face Cassie.

"Who?"

"My friend from freshman year. The one I told you about."

"Henry . . . oh, him? The one I wanted to punch? Did you punch him?"

"No. We just talked. It was nice."

Cassie frowns, like she wonders why I'm telling her this.

"He came to one of our screenings awhile back. I kind of took it as a sign that he was still thinking about what happened, even after all this time. And I was right. It was nice to be able to get some closure there."

I'm trying to convey this idea that something good happened in the world, something that can be traced back to her, but I don't think it's coming through. I glance anxiously at Gaspard, on the faint hope that he might be able to help me explain, but he looks to be at a loss for words too. A part of me worries that the story is coming off as insincere—like, "Hey, I forgave that guy Henry, so you should forgive me too."

Finally Cassie shrugs. "That's nice, I guess. I probably still would have punched him."

I force a smile and turn my eyes back to the road. For the rest of the drive, we're mostly silent.

The scout camp isn't exactly the frontier of the wilderness, as it turns out. When we arrive, there are a few vans parked in the lot already, and lights blaze out from a lodge building. Behind the lodge there's a system of ropes and platforms built into the trees, an outdoor climbing wall, and an archery range with a row of red targets.

"Oh, so it's the *bougie* scouts," Cassie quips. "No wonder they're so chill about camping in the winter."

We park the car, grab our bags, and hurry over to the lodge. The inside is warm and inviting; when we open the door, we're greeted by the buzz of excited adolescent voices and the smell of cinnamon and chocolate.

"And you must be our guest campers," says a stout man with a salt-and-pepper beard who's waiting by the door with a clipboard. He's one of only two adults in the room. "Felix Ma, Cassie Chow, and Gaspard Pierre . . . De-luck? Am I saying that right?"

"Duluc," Gaspard replies primly.

"Excellent. Name's Greg, and that over there is Scout Leader Amos. Plus we've got Ethan over there, he's an Eagle Scout. Point is, you're in good hands. Is this your first time camping in the winter?"

"It's our first time camping, period," I say.

"Well, you're in luck. As you can see, we've got just about the whole troop here tonight. No one wants to miss out on a warm night like this one."

Gaspard turns to me and mouths, *"Warm?"* There are about ten other scouts in the lodge, including some that look like they're in middle school and one or two that look like they might still be in elementary school. All of them are in uniform: red neckerchiefs, brown button-down shirts with patches sewn onto the sleeves.

Greg invites us to help ourselves to some hot chocolate and apple cider donuts while the scouts have their meeting.

"This is so bizarre," Cassie whispers as the meeting begins. The scouts begin by saying the Pledge of Allegiance, then raising three fingers and doing the scout oath.

"What, the culty rituals, or the fact that we're about to go camping when the temperature is below freezing?" Gaspard asks.

"Both."

"I don't know, it's kind of cute," I suggest. Both Cassie and Gaspard shoot me funny looks. "They seem genuinely into it, right? Being part of a group like this seems fun."

Scout Leader Amos, who with his mustache and flat-brimmed hat looks like the Platonic ideal of a Boy Scout leader, goes over a list of rules and safety tips for the evening.

"Remember, we have three guests with us this evening," he says, extending a hand toward the three of us in the back of the room. "Let's take good care of them and show them the Patrol 312 way."

The boys shout out, "Drippopotami!" And with that, the meeting is adjourned.

When we go back outside, the air feels colder than it did before. Every gust of wind is agony, cutting straight through my layers of pants and long underwear, stinging my cheeks and making my eyes water.

"Is it too late to call it and go home?" Gaspard asks. "If we leave now, we can still make it back by nine or so."

"Absolutely not, Gaspard," Cassie says. "It's too late to turn back. The only way out is to make it through to the other side."

Gaspard and I look at each other. At the exact same time, we both say, *"Daaaaamn,"* because we know that we can't give up after a statement like that. The troop starts off on the trail. The three of us stay in the back, with Greg taking up the rear. The sight of the elementary-school Boy Scouts marching ahead of us is strangely encouraging. If they can make it, then what's our excuse?

The hike to the campground is only a half mile on the map, but that's more than enough time for us all to get very, very cold. Twenty-nine degrees isn't exactly unusual for Long Island in the wintertime, especially out here in the woods. But it's not a temperature that you normally stay out in for more than five or so minutes at a time—the walk from the bus to the front door of the school, or the very beginning of the car ride before the heat kicks in. On this half-mile hike, I discover the way even a moderately cold night can infiltrate your layers of clothing, freeze the snot in your nostrils, and make your face turn numb.

"You know the great thing about camping in the winter?" Greg asks cheerfully, from behind us. "No mosquitoes!"

When we get to the campsite, the boys spring into action. They get to work pitching the tents, which are enormous—ten foot by fifteen, with four thick canvas walls and a high pointed roof.

"These are the same tents the infantry used in the Ardennes, you know," Greg says cheerfully. "So, did you bring winter-grade sleeping bags?"

The three of us look at each other.

"I just brought a regular one," Gaspard says.

"Me too," Cassie adds.

I remember, with a sinking heart, the drawstring bag that I was supposed to carry into the car. I know for sure that I didn't bring it. It's still at home. "I forgot mine."

Greg roars with laughter. "A bunch of city slickers! No worries, we always bring extra. Hopefully there's enough. Otherwise, you boys might have to share."

Two of the scouts help us set up our sleeping bags. They're long and narrow and thick, with only a small round opening at the top for your head.

"You look like a mummy once you get inside," one of the scouts says. "But they keep you mad warm. If anything, you might over-heat."

"We're gonna start building the fire now," says the other. "You can stay inside here if you're cold. It'll be ready in about ten minutes. There'll be s'mores, and soup."

"You cook the soup over the fire?" I ask.

The scouts both snicker. "No, we have the stove for that."

When they're gone, Cassie gives me a funny look. "You didn't even bring a sleeping bag?"

"I had it ready, I just forgot to bring it into the car."

"What were you going to do if they didn't have extra?"

"I don't know. Freeze."

"Oh my god," she says, shaking her head.

In my head, a retort forms in my mind, that none of us was really prepared, and the Boy Scouts bailed us out. But I don't want to fight with Cassie.

While we wait for the fire, we unpack our bags for a bit. I take out a big bag of potato chips, a flashlight, and my sixty-four-ounce thermos. When I open it, steam gushes out. The thing works, at least.

When we hear the crackle of burning wood, we go back outside. Cassie stops and tilts her head up toward the sky. It's dark, much darker than it gets in Great Neck, but I don't see any stars.

"Oh shoot, it was cloudy today. I forgot," she says. "Wow, that sucks. That was like the number one thing I was looking forward to."

I take this comment more personally than I should. This whole trip was my idea, and I want it to go perfectly.

"Maybe it'll clear up later," I say.

We go over to the fire, where the Boy Scouts are passing around long metal skewers and bags of jumbo marshmallows. When we get close enough, the flames bathe our fronts with sweet, delicious warmth.

"I've never figured out how to get this right," Gaspard says as he's holding his marshmallow out over the fire. As if on cue, it bursts into flames, and he quickly pulls it back to blow it out.

"You have to hold it far away and keep on turning it," Cassie says. "It's all about patience."

"Have you done this before?"

"Not specifically with marshmallows. But I've, you know, used heat to cook food before."

Gaspard tries it again, but again the marshmallow ignites.

"Give me that," Cassie says, snatching the skewer out of his hands. "You're wasting all of these perfectly good marshmallows."

Gaspard takes it like a champ, smiling and shaking his head sheepishly. But I wince. Cassie isn't usually moody like this, and I know that the sleeping bag and the wasted marshmallows aren't the real reason why. I can't keep waiting and hoping that things will go back to normal; it's time to confront the situation.

When the marshmallows are done, we assemble our s'mores. My marshmallow is a bit overdone on one side, but Cassie's are an even golden brown all around. By this time, our fronts are hot, and our backs are cold, so we turn our backs to the fire and look off into the darkness of the woods. I wait until we're done eating, in the hope that the sugar will be a mood lifter. Then I take a deep breath, gather up my courage, and say the words.

"Can we talk about what happened?"

It's too dark to make out Cassie's facial expression, but I can sense the way her shoulders sag.

"What do you want to talk about?"

"I think we should . . . you know, have it out. I know I messed up. I want to apologize, and eat crow, and all of that. Maybe you can yell at me, if it'll help."

"At me too," Gaspard adds. "It was my fault."

Cassie sighs. "I don't want to yell at either of you."

"But aren't you upset?"

"Yeah. I was hoping that I wasn't, but I guess I am."

"So can we talk about it?"

"It's not just the shoot. It's other things too. I guess we can talk, but I don't know if it'll help. Some of it might just be because we're too different."

"You mean emotionally? Is it because of what you said about me always wanting to talk about my feelings? I'm sorry, it was wrong. I mean, I guess that's what I'm doing right now."

"It's not just that. It's because you have a college admissions coach, and you live with your two parents in a gorgeous house in the nicest neighborhood I've ever seen, and when you want to go camping in the middle of winter, your parents buy you a comically large thermos and the Boy Scouts are there to roll out the red carpet."

I blink. "The Boy Scouts? But they'll do that for anyone, you just have to sign up."

"All right, fine! They'll do that for anyone."

I glance at Gaspard. I know that he feels guilty, that he wants to stay and take some of the blame. But it's clear to me that this isn't about him, it's about me, and what *I* did. With my eyes, I try to tell him, *It should just be me and Cassie.*

"Should I go and get us some soup?" he asks. He stands up to go, and neither Cassie nor I protest. "I'll go line up by the stove, and uh, maybe have a chat with Greg. See if he knows more fun facts about World War II. Why don't you come get me when you're ready?"

He smiles tactfully and walks off.

"I shouldn't have said that," Cassie says. "Your house is great, and your parents are amazing. And I'm sure Mr. Qin is too."

"He's fine. He's good at what he does, I guess."

We both turn back to the fire, and I can see Cassie's face more clearly. Her brow is furrowed, and she has a faraway look in her eyes.

"I didn't mean for tonight to go like this. I was feeling pretty happy on the way over. I'm sorry for being grumpy about your sleeping bag."

"It's okay, don't apologize. I should have remembered."

"Can I ask you something, Felix?"

I nod.

"What do you like about me?"

It's not the question I was expecting. I'm still not quite following how everything she said connects together, what Mr. Qin and my house and the Boy Scouts have to do with it. But it's an easy question, one I've answered to myself, in my own head, dozens of times before.

"Being around you makes me happy. There are, like, a hundred reasons why. You're fun to be around. When you want to do something, you do it, even if it should be impossible. And you're also, like . . . emotionally vivid, I think. You feel things deeply, and when you express them, it's just compelling somehow. I guess that might make it hard to be you, but I find it really beautiful. I don't think that fully explains it, though. Ever since we saw each other again at the Ping-Pong tournament, I've just felt this intense pull toward you. Sorry, I know that's kind of weird. There are a lot of amazing people in the world, but I've only ever felt this with you."

After nurturing the words in my head for so long, I'm happy to finally say them out loud. I feel lighter inside, like I've finally shed a weight that I've been carrying around for months.

Cassie frowns. "But are you sure that it was me? Not just some idea of me that you had? Like, I almost beat you at Ping-Pong and then ate a bunch of hot wings, and all of a sudden I became this . . . *enigma* or something."

Now we're back at the question of how I see her. Perhaps this is what she was always getting at, back when she asked, "Is this what my life looks like to you?" I didn't want to answer, I wanted to argue with the very premise of the question. But by doing that, I closed myself off to hearing how she felt about it, to truly understanding why it bothered her in the first place.

"I think you're right. I did do that, and I never wanted to admit that there was a problem with it. I liked having this idea of you in my head as this awesome, amazing person. I was sort of hoping you'd like it. But I see why that was selfish. I need to know what it means to you when I do that."

"I don't think of myself that way, first of all," she says. "I mean, it's nice of you to say, so why not just accept it and be happy? But it bugs me. I feel like it's not true, and I didn't ask for it, and you don't want to be friends with the real me, just the idea of me that you created in your head. And to be honest, I think it became an excuse for you. It let you take—"

Suddenly Cassie lets out a mangled groan and looks down at her feet. "Maybe I shouldn't say all of this. I'm not sure there's a point."

"It's okay," I say. "It's important. Don't worry about me. If it'll help, you should say it. It sounds like something that I need to hear. Unless you want to keep it a secret."

"Okay. You're right, I think I should say this too. You're the person this is about, but you also might the only person who gets it, you know?" Cassie takes a deep breath. "I actually wrote about this, when I was supposed to be writing my college essays. I was angry, and there was this blank Google doc in front of me, and it just poured out. I wrote, Felix thinks he's making this movie about both of us, but he's not, he's taking my life and turning it into a sob story so that other people can see it and think, 'Oh, that's so sad for her, I'm glad that isn't me.'

"And then afterward, you get to take it back to your college admissions coach and write an essay about how personal and moving it was to win an award. And then if you get into Cornell or whatever school you get into, it won't be a question of going or not going, you'll just go. And I'll be the person that helped you, that gave you what you needed and had to suffer so you could succeed.

"At Van Der Donck, there are kids who seem to know exactly

what's coming," Cassie continues. "I walk into AP Chem and it kicks my absolute butt, but those kids have their summer classes and their admissions coaches and their one-on-one tutors and just tap-dance through it. Those are the kids that ended up getting into Yale and Harvard and whatever, and that's when you finally hear that all along they've been doing some secret activity like rowing a boat or sword fighting that they knew was going to be their ticket in. Good for them, it's not like they didn't work hard. I can live with the fact that they knew something I didn't.

"But you're one of those kids too, and you don't realize it. And then your secret activity isn't just a niche sport; it involves me, and taking something from me. If I think about it that way, I get really upset."

Hearing her perspective laid out like this, hearing myself described as this cold, vampiric entity—I knew it was coming, I wanted it, but it still hurts.

"Cassie," I say, my throat dry. "Do you not want to be friends with me anymore?"

"That's the thing. I *do* want to be friends. I like being around you, and I have fun when the three of us are together, but there's this other feeling now. I don't like it, and I don't like myself when I'm feeling it, but it hasn't gone away yet."

And there it is, the ugly, awful truth of what happened. That there were good feelings between us, and I broke them, and the thing between us is still broken.

"I'm sorry. I'm so, so sorry. Everything you just said about me is true. I complained so much about what happened to me in high school, without ever appreciating how lucky I was. I deserve to feel like shit about that. But that doesn't matter. I hate what I put you through. I wish I could make it up to you. I hope you believe that I care about you, Cassie, but obviously I never got to show it. So if you want me to leave you alone from now on, I will."

"I didn't say that," Cassie cuts in. "It wasn't all bad. You didn't mess up everything. I said I liked being around you—weren't you listening? I still *wanted* to do the movie. And now the movie's over, and I'm still here. Aren't I?"

I look at her. "Yeah. You're still here."

"I'm still here, in the middle of the woods with a bunch of Boy Scouts."

I laugh. "Yeah, that's true."

"I'm mad at you, Felix, and a part of me will stay mad at you for a long time. But I'm not going to drop all the good memories and remember only the one bad part. I know you pretty well by now. I know you weren't trying to hurt me on purpose. It was really nice of you to set up the camping trip."

There's a finality to this statement that lets me know that this is as far as the conversation will go tonight. It's not a full-on reconciliation, but it's not a definitive ending, either.

"Guys, come!" Gaspard comes dashing back around the campfire. "Quickly!"

"Are they almost out of soup?" Cassie asks.

"No, there's plenty. Just come see!"

We get up, and Gaspard leads us to the other end of the camp. As we reach the edge of the campfire's radius of light, he slows his steps and puts a finger to his lips.

"Shhh. Look, over by the trail," he whispers. "Do you see?"

He points at the trail that leads farther into the woods. It's dark, and my eyes are still adjusting, but I can see shapes, shadowy movement, a glint of light. And then, finally, I see it. At the same moment, Cassie gasps.

Emerging from the trees is a group of deer. Two adults, and two fawns—a family. The two younger deer dip their heads to browse for food in the grass, while the adults keep their heads lifted, ears twitching alertly for the sound of predators.

"Oh my gosh, they're gorgeous," Cassie whispers.

"Should we try to get closer?" Gaspard asks.

"No, let's just stay here. Leave Mother Nature undisturbed," she answers sagely.

As my eyes adapt, I start to make out the details of their lean, rippling bodies, their long, elegant necks, their pretty eyes and delicate heads. The fawns keep their noses to the ground and start walking toward us. The adults watch, but don't follow.

"The way they move is magical," Cassie says. "Like they're on tiptoe."

"You sure you don't wanna get closer? You could pet one of the little ones. Deer are chill, they're not gonna kick you or anything," Gaspard says.

"No, I'm happy just watching them. This is like seeing a

celebrity. You know, when you've heard about deer and seen pictures of them, but now they're up close in real life?"

The two fawns get so close that I can see their shiny black noses, the white flecks of fur around their eyes. For a few moments, we stare at each other, humanity on one side, deer on the other. The fawns tilt their heads in curiosity, shooting their tongues out to lick their lips and the tips of their noses. Then they blink, turn, and start to walk away. We watch as the family of deer moves on, back into the woods, disappearing into the darkness.

"Wow," Cassie says.

"How do you know so much about deer, Gaspard?" I ask.

He winks. "I don't. It's just intuition."

We linger at the edge of the camp, as if turning away, going back to the warmth and safety of the fire, will break the spell that's fallen over us.

"To be honest, I was pretty crushed when I realized there weren't any stars," Cassie says. "A very small part of me regretted coming at all."

"Only a small part?" Gaspard asks.

Cassie laughs. "But this was better. Way better." She looks at both of us, a wide smile spreading across her face. "This still ended up being a really great trip."

TWENTY

IN APRIL, MY PARENTS AND I TAKE A ROAD TRIP
to visit colleges. Our route takes us east along the coastline as we
hit Yale and Brown, then turns sharply northward so we can see
Harvard and MIT. At each stop, my parents load up on brochures,
ooh and aah at the stunning architecture, and gush about how
impressive and yōu xiù the tour guides are. I wonder how much
of this tour is meant to help me decide where to apply, versus just
to give them a chance to breathe in that sweet, prestigious Ivy
League air. One thing I do have to admit is that we've chosen
the perfect time for our trip. The skies are blue, and each school
is decked out in blossoms and greenery. My parents take lots and
lots of photographs, which I hope won't be used in some kind of
passive-aggressive you-failed-us slideshow when I end up going to
state school.

In the car, I message Cassie about the trip.

Cassie:

Do you look at the students and wonder, "What's so goddamn special about you?"

Everyone you see on campus looks like a normal person who put their pants on one leg at a time

But if you get to know them they probably built a rocket ship when they were ten or won the national spelling bee

I watched a documentary about spelling bees once

All I can say is if you can spell like these kids you shouldn't even have to go to college

You should just automatically get a PhD in spelling

We've settled into a rhythm of sending a few messages once per week, or twice. The mood between us is basically positive, even if we mostly talk about things of no real importance. Sometimes, though, it feels like we're just drawing out the inevitable ending. It feels wrong to ask her to hang out again, since she's got graduation parties and scholarship applications and all-state band to worry about, not to mention the looming prospect of leaving home and going to college.

The last stop of our tour is Dartmouth. After driving through miles and miles of forest, we arrive at the quaint, charming campus. With its stunning quad and almost-too-picturesque New

England architecture, it feels more like a theme park or a Potemkin village than it does a real school, with real students.

On the tour, my mom asks the tour guide, "How did you get into Dartmouth?" No euphemisms or anything, just straight and to the point. I'm standing behind her, but I try to hide my face so that no one will guess that we're related.

"Well, every year Dartmouth tries to build a well-rounded class of people from diverse backgrounds and interests," he says. "So, there's no one way to get in. With that being said, I was the valedictorian of my high school, I was a finalist for the International Science and Engineering Fair, and I was recruited for cross-country."

Psh. That's it?

My mom is so impressed that she starts clapping. Thankfully, no one else joins her.

After our tour, we go to a nearby diner for lunch. Inside is a mix of current students, locals, and families on tours like ours. The college kids stick out; they look like they've just woken up, they're wearing school sweats, and they're eating breakfast food. The perks of having already struck gold in admissions.

"You're so lucky, Felix," my mom says. "These are such beautiful schools. It's an honor just to apply to them."

I shrug. "I guess so. Didn't you get to apply to good schools in China?"

"Not like this! We never got to visit any schools, that's for sure. We couldn't even look them up on the internet."

"I just picked mine off a list, based on which names sounded good," my dad adds. "In the village, you either went to university or you didn't. No one cared about which one."

My dad grew up in the countryside. He was the youngest of five siblings, and the only one to even finish high school. I can't decide if that would be more or less pressure than being the only child.

"So was it stressful?"

"Of course," my mom says. "We all had to take the gāo kǎo. Can you imagine having your entire future resting on one exam? My mom locked me in a room so I could study. Every single night, I would cry." It sounds traumatic, but her voice is matter-of-fact.

"How could you stand that?"

"What do you mean?"

"Didn't you get depressed?"

My mom and dad exchange a look.

"Maybe we were," my mom says. "We didn't know about being depressed. My parents just said, 'Eat as much bitterness as you can, because the more you can stomach, the more of the competition you'll surpass.' You're lucky you didn't have to go through it. It's better here. You can build up yourself over time instead of only getting one shot."

"Yeah, well, it's still a lot of pressure," I say. "Studying is only one part of it. Here you have to jump through all these hoops. You have to have some kind of special talent, and you have to write an essay."

"But that stuff is fun! If I got to play Ping-Pong and make movies instead of studying eighteen hours a day, I would have been so happy," my mom says.

I shake my head, annoyed that she's making it sound so easy, and frustrated that she's probably right. Yes, it was discouraging that all my activities had to win some kind of prize to matter. But replacing all of that with a three-day megatest on everything I've learned in high school sounds much worse.

"It must have been tough, with Grandma on your back."

"She wasn't that bad. She's harsh, but it's all bark and no bite. The good thing about my family was that my sisters and I stuck together. We knew that every once in a while, we'd have to swallow a lecture, and then we'd move on."

"Sure didn't seem like it was that easy for *all* of you," I say. I'm thinking of my second aunt, and the way my grandma brought her divorce into the conversation at dinner over nothing. "You were the oldest, so you had to get tough. And sān yí was the youngest, so she had two big sisters to stick up for her. But what about èr yí?"

My mom shakes her head. "My sister might seem soft. To tell the truth, when I heard about the divorce, I thought, *Wán le, it's over for her.* But I was wrong. She's really strong. She might be the strongest out of all of us. Because she stands up for herself, but she never gets nasty, like my mom. You've seen my mom. She never knows when to stop. And she seems to always say exactly the thing that will hit you the hardest."

"Like you."

The words leap out of my mouth before I can stop them up. My dad's eyebrows shoot up in amusement, like "Whoa, kid, are you sure today is a good day to die?"

My mom looks incredulous. "Me? What did I ever do?"

"Don't you remember what happened when I quit Ping-Pong?"

My mom frowns as she tries to think back. "I remember you did it all of a sudden. It was right after a bad tournament, and you were upset. I tried to cheer you up, but you refused to keep playing."

"That's what you think happened?"

"I don't know. To be honest, I never understood why you quit. You always had fun playing it. And you were so good at it," my mom says.

"It was fun when I played for fun. But the competitions were horrible. And everyone had such high expectations for me."

"That's a compliment! It shows that they think you're good. I remember when I watched your first tournament, I thought, *Wow, my son really can do something special.*"

"Well, you never said any of that to me. All you said was that I was so weak." My stomach churns as I repeat my mom's words. I look at her face for some sign of recognition, but I can't tell if she remembers. She just looks confused.

"Well, you were. That's why you quit, right? But it's okay, you didn't like the competition. Neither did I. I got nervous watching. And I didn't like to see you get frustrated."

"But how could you just say that to me? How did you think

that I could hear something like that and be okay?"

My body tenses with anticipation. This is it, the moment I've been waiting for, the moment where I finally reveal the pain I've been holding on to for so long. I've pictured it in many ways—sometimes as an epic confrontation, sometimes as a pity party with a tearful apology. Today, though, neither of those outcomes feels right.

My mom doesn't answer. She looks at my dad like, "Do you know what he's talking about?"

"What do you mean by that?" my dad asks.

"I mean that comment stuck to me. I felt like I was missing something, and I was destined to just quit at whatever I did."

A flicker of agreement goes across my mom's face, like she really did think that about me. Then it's gone, replaced just as quickly by a look of concern. "You must have known I always believed in you. Why do you think I kept pushing you? Why do you think we hired Mr. Qin?"

I shake my head. This is a fair point, but it strikes me that my mom is avoiding the question.

"And look how well it worked out!" my mom continues. "You found your activity, and you made it stand out. Your movie was good. When I watched it, I told your father, 'I knew he could do something like this.' I was proud of you. Although you and your friend aren't very good at giving speeches."

"That's not the point, though."

My mom's brow creases. Her eyes are scanning back and forth, like she's searching through her memories and cross-checking against mine.

"Our job as parents is to make your life better," my dad says, to break the silence. "We want you to have a good home, good grades, a good activity so that you can get into college. So without Ping-Pong, we knew you had to start over. That's hard."

"But that's not how you acted. You acted like I failed you."

"No, you didn't fail anyone. But we just . . . well, it's not exactly—"

"I'm sorry," my mom says.

My dad and I stare at her.

"I was excited about Ping-Pong. When we went to that tournament, they put up that banner with the Olympic rings. I thought, *Wow, my son could make it to the Olympics, and after that he can get into any school he wants.* So when you said you were quitting, I thought you were being reckless, I couldn't believe you were giving it all up. I didn't know how to help you, either. I thought moving would be good for you, but it was the opposite. Once it was done, we couldn't take it back."

There's a pained look in her eyes. I try to see those early days in Great Neck from her perspective: the sense of accomplishment, of getting the family into a house in the suburbs, and then the gradual realization that all that work might have been a mistake.

Suddenly, I feel like my mom is the one who needs reassuring.

"It wasn't that big of a deal," I say. "You helped me a lot. And like you said, things worked out in the end. I'm . . . I'm grateful for everything. I know how lucky I am. Moving, working with Mr. Qin, all of it."

My mom looks at me, eyes glistening. "Are you mad at me?"

For a long time, I was. I was mad at her for talking to me that way, mad at myself for giving her a reason to. But now, in this moment, with the question posed to me directly, I realize that I'm not mad anymore. Maybe it was the passage of time, or maybe I found a way to forgive her. Either way, I'm ready to let it go.

"It's okay," I say. "I know you want the best for me. I always knew that. Thanks for saying it out loud."

"You're strong, Felix. I know you're not weak. It's a bad habit I have, to say things that are too dramatic. You've met my mom, you know how it is in our family. You still have to listen to your parents, but you don't have to believe everything they say."

Hearing those words, "I know you're not weak," feels surreal. For so many years, I believed that those words were a forbidden antidote, that if I could just get my mom to say them, they'd reverse all of the resentment and self-doubt that I've felt since that original comment. But now I realize that I was wrong, they were just words. The real question is something deeper, something more fundamental.

"I just wish I knew what it was all for," I say. "Why did we have to go through all of this?"

"That's what it feels like when your parents make you do

things," my mom says. "I wish there was a better way, but we haven't found it yet."

"But what am I trying to do? I know I'm supposed to get into a good college, and then get a good job or whatever, so that my kids can do even better. But what am I actually supposed to care about? What do I want out of this?"

"You just said all of it. Take care of yourself, and make sure you can take care of your kids. That's your job," my mom says.

"When we were kids, our parents and teachers told us that we were growing up in a new era. We were going to get better lives for ourselves, and we were going to help our country enter the modern age," my dad adds.

"But then you moved to a different country. So all of that's out the window now," I say.

My mom chuckles. "Well then, you're the expert. You grew up here. So what's your answer?"

The lunch rush is ending, and the diner is emptying out. The students in their green sweats saunter out of the restaurant with an air of casual eminence. By the door, the host wipes his forehead and leans against the wall.

For such a long time, I was speeding headlong toward my future, focusing too much on my destination to stop and ask myself, *What's really important to me?*

Now, looking back, there was only one time when I felt like I had an answer to that question. It was when I met a person who I care about more than pleasing my parents, more than proving to my mom that I'm not who she thinks I am. I know that now, beyond doubt, even if it took breaking everything apart to finally realize it.

But what if I realized it too late?

As the year draws to a close, time seems to accelerate. Before I know it, one month, and then another has gone by. Little by little, I come to accept a painful truth—that my time with Cassie is coming to an end, not with a bang but a whimper. Yes, we still talk, but more and more time passes between each message. Next year, even if she ends up at Stony Brook, she's going to be starting a new life. I'll be lucky to see her even once or twice. The camping trip wasn't just a time for us to finally try to talk through the problems in our friendship. It was also, in all likelihood, a goodbye. Wherever we got to, whatever final note we struck that night, is where we'll leave each other off. We both said what we needed to say, but I can't help but wish that we'd ended on a slightly better note, something that didn't leave so many loose ends, so much unresolved angst.

In English class, we read *The Great Gatsby.* In class, Ms. Esfahani asks us whether Gatsby was right or wrong to try to repeat the past.

"He built Daisy up into a perfect fantasy that no one could ever live up to," says Allie Walker. "It's just like in America, where we romanticize the Revolutionary War. You build your identity around this false narrative of yourself, and it stops you from seeing reality."

Allie is the apex predator of our class, always dropping sweet, sweet literary connections that rocket up her participation grade.

"Going off of what Allie said, I think that Daisy represents the American Dream," Elijah Goldberg adds. "Unattainable, and fundamentally childish."

"Gatsby only cared about money. He made all of his money illegally, because he had no scruples. That's a metaphor for the American Dream too," says Clara Kim.

Ms. Esfahani nods. "Tough crowd for Mr. Gatsby. Anyone care to defend him?"

Crickets. I'm not surprised; there wasn't anything in the SparkNotes about why Gatsby, a delusional and amoral representative of the hollowness of the American Dream, was actually a good guy. The top three students in the class have already used up their comments, so this next question is up for grabs.

I take a stab at it.

"I don't think Gatsby cared about money at all. For him, all he cared about was Daisy, and making money was the one way he could try to see her again. And who's to say that she wasn't the person that he thought she was? Isn't the first thing we learn about Gatsby that he has the ability to see you exactly as you want to be seen? He sees the best in people. Maybe to him, Daisy really was that perfect person. I know he made mistakes, but by today's standards, fixing some baseball games and selling some alcohol doesn't seem all that bad. Out of everyone in the book, he at least treated other people well."

Clara and Elijah are both looking at me skeptically, like I'm encroaching on their turf; Allie, unthreatened, has an expression of mild curiosity and amusement.

"Thanks for that answer, Mr. Ma," Ms. Esfahani says. "Maybe you've got the ability to see people as they'd like to be seen too. I'm sure Gatsby would appreciate your support."

A sprinkling of laughter flutters through the room, and then we're on to discussing the symbolism of the green light. Allie kicks things off with a killer comment about perspective; how the spatial qualities of green light, distant and bright and pure, make it so appealing precisely because it has not yet been reached. While Elijah and Clara fire off their remarks, I stay silent.

I want my defense of Gatsby to be true, but I know that it was wishful thinking. You don't get to chase your ideal forever. At some point, you have to reckon with all the things you did wrong, even if you did them in pursuit of your mirage. At some point, you have to stop living in the past; you have to look that beautiful memory in the eye and then let it go.

TWENTY-ONE

Gaspard:

Okay so this is going to sound weird but hear me out

Lexie wants to have another party for a bunch of her senior friends

They want to try getting drunk so they know what it's like before they go to college

She asks if we're okay to come hang out and babysit . . . lol

Hahahahaha

That is some interesting logic

Have the juniors come in to provide adult supervision

Gaspard:

"We did it for some of our senior friends last year. You do it for the karma and trust the universe to pay it back to you."

Lexie's words ^^^

> I've heard of "pay it forward" but I didn't know that we'd have to pay up front 😔

Gaspard:

Stop lying bro I know you wanna go

The thing is, he's right. I wouldn't miss it.

And so it is written that I will attend my second high school party. I'm very curious about the logistics—how is Lexie going to acquire alcohol? And how is she going to stop her parents from finding out? Or could it be that this was her parents' idea, and they're the ones providing the alcohol, so that their daughter's first experience of underage drinking will occur in a controlled environment? That would be some serious galaxy-brain parenting right there.

It's May, and the seniors' last day of classes has already happened. Now, all that's left of high school for them is the emotional whirlwind of senior prom, graduation, one last summer together. I'm touched that Gaspard and I get to be part of it.

On the night of the party, Gaspard and I pull up to Lexie's big, gaudy house again. This time, I've brought the Ferrero thirty-two-pack assorted, which has the dark chocolate noirs and white chocolate coconut Raffaellos in addition to the classic Rochers. For such an occasion, it's only right.

Lexie's wearing her brand-new NYU hoodie, and I feel the warm, happy glow of having basically finished high school emanating from her. Gaspard and I put on our fuzzy slippers and get down to the basement.

Downstairs, the party is already going; there's a music video playing, and I spot a number of flushed red faces. Most people are holding clear plastic cups full of ruby-red liquid. On the coffee table are a few bottles of wine. Damini smiles when she sees us, and her teeth are stained red.

"My two favorites are here!" she cries. She dashes up to us and gathers me and Gaspard into her arms. "Remember, dears, what happens in Lexie's basement *stays in Lexie's basement*!"

I feel a huge pressure on my back that presses me deeper into the group hug.

"Emotion. Tears. *Pain*." It's Reggie, enveloping all of three of us in a second layer of physical contact. "Wow, this feels so comfortable. Felix and Gaspard, you're both so . . . *soft*."

"Actually . . . I've . . . been . . . working . . . out—" Gaspard sputters. Reggie releases us, and Gaspard and I gasp for breath. Gaspard rubs his own stomach, looking offended that Reggie didn't notice his gains.

We play another game of The Renegades, only this time there's much more alcohol-fueled shouting and dismay. Gaspard and I are both Fifth Columnists, and we take advantage of the collective impairment by gaslighting everyone about the outcomes of previous rounds. Unfortunately, Nasr, the designated driver for the evening, is sober and sniffs us out from the way we're laughing at everyone else.

"Cast these two treacherous snakes out! Renegades, to me! The revolution will not fail!"

When the fifth and deciding mission passes, the victorious Renegades lift Nasr up into the air and parade around the room. Miraculously, no one is hurt.

All I can think about is how uncomfortable this all would have made me if it had been like this the first time I came. Instead, now that I've witnessed all these people in a much more tame setting, this second party feels somehow just as wholesome as the first.

After the game, people break off into small groups. I end up sitting on the sofa between Reggie and Nasr. They each put an arm around me and lean in close. My head tingles in expectation of a noogie.

"Felix, Felix, Felix," Reggie drawls.

"We've been thinking about you, young man," Nasr adds.

"We've been thinking about your future."

"My future?" I ask.

Reggie nods. "You see, we won't be around next year to protect you from the forces of evil."

"You'll have to fend for yourself. It's a dark and mysterious world out there. Scary indeed."

"Right. I see," I say, though not really seeing.

"But there is one thing we can offer you now," Nasr says.

"So that when you're lost and all alone, you have something to fall back on."

Nasr leans in even closer. "Can we let you in on a little secret?" he whispers.

Reggie wiggles his eyebrows. "The two of us are highly trained in certain . . . *pagan rituals*."

The two of them pause for dramatic effect. I feel the urge to burst out laughing, but I fight it back, because both of them are above six foot and look dead serious. I wonder if they plan out their routines ahead of time, or if they truly just improvise.

The two of them rise to their feet, and tell me stand in between them. Nasr produces a deck of playing cards.

"A charm of protection," he explains, as he fans out the cards.

"Take a card. Don't think too hard about it. Feel the energy and let the *card* pick *you*."

I pick a card, and then Nasr instructs me to tap on it, blow on it, to cleanse it of evil spirits.

"Now, place it over your chest."

Reggie waves his hands around his head and mouths a wordless incantation. Meanwhile Nasr circles me, chanting, "Double, double, toil and trouble; fire burn and cauldron bubble," in what sounds like a Russian accent.

Finally Reggie faces me, eyes closed, two fingers placed on his temple.

"I can feel it. Letting go of these earthly shackles, I reach out across the infinite dimensions and see that your card is the . . . six of hearts!"

He opens his eyes and looks at me expectantly. I flip the card over. It's the nine of hearts.

"Yoooooo!" Nasr cries, shaking Reggie by the shoulders. "Pretty close!"

"Closest we've ever gotten, anyways." Reggie winks.

"Just hang on to that nine of hearts, Felix. It'll protect you. Always."

Nasr and Reggie go in search of tortilla chips, leaving me alone, confused and weirdly flattered.

Just a few feet away from me, I see Lexie, sitting by herself in the corner, with a tear running down her cheek.

"Oh, um, are you okay?"

She pats the spot on the floor next to her in response. I take a seat. "Everything okay?" I ask.

"I'm fine. I'm happy to be here with my friends. But Felix, I just realized. Shin Ramyun is so *spicy*. It hurts!" She points to her abandoned bowl of noodles, sitting on a table a few feet away. "Normally I don't feel it. But tonight, I feel *everything*."

"There, there," I say, fighting not to chuckle.

"You know, you and Gaspard have the *cutest* friendship," Lexie says, fanning herself. "It's extremely endearing. Overwhelming, even. I need water. We didn't run out, did we?"

I take Lexie upstairs to the fridge so she can drink some water. Damini and Gaspard spot us on the way up and come too.

"Everything okay?" Damini asks.

"Yes. I am good. Alcohol is no big deal, right? Nothing to be scared of. I just feel tired, is all. Tired, but not in a way that requires me to rest," Lexie responds.

"She ate too much spicy ramen," I add, to clarify.

"Ah. Interesting."

Gaspard pats her on the shoulder as she drinks water.

"Felix and Gaspard are the best," Lexie says, between gulps. "Dams and I talk about your friendship a lot. Don't we?"

"You're both very wholesome," Damini agrees. "Not like our two favorite degenerates. You give me hope for the future."

Gaspard puts an arm around my neck. "We are pretty lovable together. But you've got it all wrong. Felix's heart already belongs to another."

Lexie and Damini look at each other, eyes wide. They start asking questions, their voices overlapping one another.

"Can we get a name?"

"Oh my gosh, are you *dating* someone?"

"Oh boy," I mumble. Gaspard grins at me, as if to ask, "Are you gonna tell them, or should I?"

"So there's this girl named Cassie Chow," I begin. "She lives in the city. We met at a piano competition when I was in middle school. She got first place, and I got second. And then we met again this year at a Ping-Pong tournament."

"Star-crossed lovers," Damini whispers.

"No, no, it's not like that," I say quickly. I can feel my cheeks warming at the word "lovers."

"You do kind of have a crush on her, though," Gaspard says. He's clearly enjoying watching me squirm.

"Not a crush! Well, maybe it's a nonromantic crush. A friend crush."

"You *reaaally* want to be her friend," Gaspard says. "I get it. She's a very fun person to be around."

As I relate the rest of the story—how she forgot her music folder at the tournament, how she starred in our movie—Lexie and Damini are hanging on every word. It's flattering and a little unnerving how interested they are in the details of my little life.

"So how does she make you feel?" Damini asks.

"Happy, I guess. Like, I think she's cool, and we get each other, and when we're together I wish time would stop. But also sad, because I want to be better friends with her, and I kind of messed things up, and either way we won't get to see each other anymore after this year."

"Mixed emotions!" Lexie cries. She and Damini nod along sympathetically.

"Do you guys feel that way at all, since you're leaving?" Gaspard asks.

Lexie and Damini exchange a glance.

"Kind of," Lexie offers. "There are people at school that we could have gotten to know better. Like the people that we had crushes on, but never got to date. Or even talk to."

"Yeah, but we'll probably forgot all about them, easily. There was no one who was as special as this friend of yours." Damini turns to me. "It sounds like she'll be hard to forget."

"So what does it feel like to be leaving, then?" I ask.

Damini smiles. "Feels great. I can't wait to go to college. High school was just okay, if you ask me. I'd give it three out of five stars, max, as far as how happy I was during it."

"Don't listen to her, she's just acting cool because she's drunk," Lexie says. "I'm definitely sad. Our friend group means a lot to me, and it'll probably never be the same. We'll still see each other when we're back for the holidays, but it won't feel like we're all going through the same thing together anymore. It'll never feel as all-encompassing as it does now, you know?"

"Yeah, but there'll be other things to fill the void. Maybe you'll meet people at college who are ten times cooler than your boring hometown friends. This group was just training wheels, you know?" Damini is wearing a self-satisfied smirk.

"Dams and her heart of *stone*," Lexie says, shaking her head. "She never wants to get sentimental with me. Always just plays it cool."

"It's all a front. I'm crying on the inside. All that mushy stuff you just said so eloquently, you can assume I feel it too." Damini winks.

Before we go back downstairs, Lexie insists on a group hug. "I love you all," she whispers, her breath smelling faintly of wine.

So the seniors may not be feeling quite the same way I am. But I'm still happy that I know what it's like for them to be graduating soon. It makes me feel less alone.

Back downstairs, karaoke has started. Reggie is doing "Take Me Home, Country Roads," by John Denver, but he doesn't have nearly the chops to hit the high notes. For the final chorus, Nasr turns off the light and starts to ad-lib rap flourishes in the background to hype people up.

"Country roo-OO-A-O-ods—"

"Vroom vroom!"

"Take me hooo-OO-o-o-OOme—"

"To the crib!"

"To the plaa-AA-aa-AA-aace—"

"I love that place!"

"I be-loo-OOO-ooo-OOOng!"

"Young DENVER!"

"This party is a little too ironic right now," Lexie says. "Let's bare our souls and crank up some *emotions*."

She bends over the karaoke machine and selects the next song. When it starts, the opening guitar notes sound vaguely familiar. A ripple of recognition passes through the room, and suddenly the mood changes from all-out hyped to one of quivering anticipation. Lexie takes the mic. When the lyrics start, the whole room sings along with her.

I recognize it now. It's "Mr. Brightside," by The Killers. And apparently, it's the seniors' favorite song.

They know all the words, and they even have little bits of choreography for certain lyrics. When Lexie sings, "Choking on your aaa-libiiis," everyone clutches two hands to their throat. For "Open up my eaaa-geeer eeeyes," they pull their eyelids open with a thumb and index finger. I get the sense that this isn't the first time they've sung along to this song.

For the outro, everyone links arms and cries, "I neee-veeer," toward the ceiling. Gaspard and I join in, and I feel a primal energy crackling between us, like we're prehistoric humans, howling our woes and our joys at a mysterious moon, a sky full of stars. It's a reminder that there's an animal spirit dormant inside each of us, and it awakens when the right early 2000s rock song is played at the right moment. I almost feel like Gaspard and I are graduating along with everyone else.

When the party is over, the seniors drunkenly stumble up the stairs. Reggie wraps me in a huge hug and lifts me into the air.

"Always wanted to do that," he says, winking.

"Thanks for inviting me to your parties," I say to Lexie. "You're all really nice. I'll miss you next year."

"You're a sweetheart, Felix. You're one of the good ones," Lexie says.

"Good luck with everything next year. I was kidding earlier; of

323

course I'll miss you too," Damini adds.

Gaspard and I put on our shoes. Lexie and Damini go outside to help Nasr wrangle all the drunk seniors into his Chevy Suburban, and we follow. There evidently aren't enough seats, because Gaspard and I, watching from the doorway, see a few dark silhouettes clambering into the trunk.

"How do you feel?" Gaspard asks.

"I'm okay."

"You sure?" He raises an eyebrow. "You're still thinking about her a lot, I can tell. It's okay. You can say what's on your mind, if you want."

I nod. "Talking about the seniors graduating made me think. When you leave home, and you pack up your suitcase, you take what you need, and you leave everything else behind. Well, with Cassie, I'm not going to make it into that suitcase, metaphorically speaking. I'm going to get left behind." I blink as a wave of sadness washes over me. "But it's okay, I get it. And it's fine. I guess I'm just coming to terms with it."

Gaspard puts an arm over my shoulder. "It's tough, bro. Lexie didn't hold back, talking about how it'll never be the same with her friend group. Spanish Club will never be the same, either. It'll feel empty without her. Even when she visits, she won't really be a part of it. It's a fact of life, I guess."

"It's just so hard to accept," I say, with a force that surprises me. "I feel like I barely got to know Cassie. We only spent like a

324

week or so of time together, in the same place. I was just figuring out how to be around her without making things complicated. I wanted to make up for what happened. I wish this was the beginning, not the end."

"I'm sorry, Felix. Are you still in touch at all?"

"Some. Less and less."

"That's still nice."

"It is. But it's also sad to think that one of these days I'll send her a random observation or a corny joke, and she'll say maybe 'ha ha' or something like that, and then that'll be it, our last contact. Such a letdown."

He pats me on the back. "You can't look at it like that, like it's already over. There's still time for something better than that. At the very least, you can give her a nice goodbye. Tell her what she meant to you, try to put a bow on everything. It'll feel good, I bet. Just like this party. You've got to take this thing that you're dreading, that you're sad about, and turn it into a party. You might not make it into the suitcase, but at the very least, you can be the tune she's humming as she walks out the door. Metaphorically speaking."

I smile. "Gaspard, how did you get so wise?"

"You flatter," he says, grinning widely. "I don't know, probably from reading books. And watching movies, that goes without saying. And also the internet. Duh."

Gaspard gives me a big hug, then walks down the driveway to

catch his ride. I take a deep breath of the early summer air, letting the smell of cut grass and flowers fill my nostrils, feeling the pollen settle heavily into my throat. I'm still sad, but there's a small bloom of optimism in my heart. For all of the bad memories that we've made this year, there's still time left for one last good one.

TWENTY-TWO

A FEW WEEKS AFTER THE PARTY, SENIOR PROM photos start popping up in my feed. I see a big group of seniors lined up in front of Lexie's house, wearing tuxedos and prom dresses. Reggie and Nasr tower over their dates; Lexie and Damini and the other girls line up in a row, posing with finger guns and mean mugs. One of the photos is a side-by-side of the group at the beginning of freshman year, versus now, decked out in prom regalia. In the years between the two shots, braces have been shed, hair has been cut (apparently Reggie used to have a moptop like a young Justin Bieber), and growth spurts have come in.

After experiencing all of their euphoric, nostalgic energy at the party, I feel an emptiness at their impending absence. A generation of people are out of my life, with no certainty of a reunion.

As the school year draws to a close, I start writing a letter to Cassie—sort of a continuation of the emails that I wrote while I was in China. I try to do what Gaspard suggested, tell her what she meant to me and put a nice bow on everything, but it's hard.

I keep resorting to grand, sweeping statements: that meeting her was the best thing that ever happened to me; that I'll never be the same; that I've experienced all varieties of intense emotions toward people in high school, and only one of them stands out as the best, most irreplaceable one.

In a way, it's all true. But it's not what the situation demands. These are the statements of the Felix from before, the one who gave in to big emotions and reckless, selfish yearning, the one who didn't think about how it would feel for Cassie, the person on the other side. I need to write something from the Felix of after. Something different, something that charts a new course for our friendship—or at least could have, if we'd gotten more time together.

Dear Cassie,

I think I finally understand what happened at the beginning of our friendship. I still wasn't over how hard my family's move was on me, how upset I was over the stuff that happened after we got to Great Neck. I wanted to believe that life could have been different, more fun, less painful, if we'd just stayed in Flushing. And then I met you, and it stirred up all of those feelings at once, and it made me put all of them onto you, and turn you into this deity. Getting to know you didn't feel like a normal getting-to-know-you with a friend. It felt like magic.

I know you never asked for any of that. You were right when you said that it became an excuse for me. I saw you as the person who got to live the life that I was supposed to live, not as a person who was going through her own problems. I'd hate for you to feel like your feelings don't matter to me. They do. The problem is, I think I wasn't even aware enough of my shortcomings to try to fix them. Like, looking back, it's embarrassing to me that I didn't realize how lucky and privileged I am. I wish I was more grateful. At least I understand it better now, though. I'm not sure exactly what to do about it, but I'm at least glad that I know.

To be honest, I'm really sad that you're leaving. I mean, I'm happy for you. But if I look back on our story over the last year, it's so mixed, and I'm afraid it's defined by what went wrong. When I think about that, it really bothers me. But Gaspard said that I should focus on saying goodbye—accepting that this is an ending, and turning it into a party. And I think he's right.

So if there's one more thing I can say to you, I just want to say thank you. I know that it was wrong to idealize you the way I did, and I'm sorry for the pain it caused. But even now, I'm still happy about some parts of what I felt. I still do think that you're amazing, wonderful, not normal, special, just a great, great person. Possibly my favorite person. Definitely like top three. Maybe I'm being immature and I still have some growing up to do when it comes to friendships. But also, what if this feeling is precious, and rare, and it's good to hold on to it? I guess what I'm saying is, I'm thankful that I got to meet you and feel this way about you. Maybe someday you'll meet someone and go through the same thing, and when you do, you'll see what it was like for me.

So goodbye, Cassie. I hope that things go well for you in college, and beyond. I think they will. And no matter what happens, or how much time passes, you can bet that every time I think about you, I'll be rooting for you, just hoping as hard as I can that good things happen to you. Okay, I'm going to stop writing now because I'm rambling and I might cry, haha.

Sincerely,
Felix

A few weeks into the summer, I message Cassie about hanging out one last time. For some reason, I'm not nervous at all. She says yes. We make plans to meet up in Flushing, at Ten Ren, for bubble tea.

When Cassie emerges out of the Main Street subway stop, it takes me a moment to recognize her. She's cut her hair short and dyed it a purplish-orange.

"It was supposed to be pink," she explains. "But it didn't show up quite right. My own fault. I got what I paid for."

It's our first time seeing each other since the camping trip. That, plus the hair, makes me feel like I'm meeting with a brand-new Cassie. I know the hair is just a superficial change, but it strikes me as a stark reminder that we're no longer part of each other's lives.

We weave through the crowd and into the shop, retracing our steps from that day when I brought Cassie her music folder. At the register, I put in my order, hand over my cash, and then quickly add Cassie's order (green milk tea, regular sugar, regular ice) before she can stop me. She protests, but she knows she's been outmaneuvered.

Once we get our drinks, we take our seats by the window, like we did last fall. Now, at the height of summer, the sidewalks are packed with families headed to the park, gaggles of high schoolers enjoying their vacation.

"Gaspard's friend Lexie Han dyed her hair too. Streaks of blond. I guess it's a senior thing."

"It's the season of impulse decisions." Cassie nods. "You should make sure to have some reckless ideas in your back pocket. When the time comes, I promise it'll feel amazing to cut loose."

"What did your mom say?" I ask.

Cassie grimaces. "She said that she's very proud of me for getting into college. Middle class, here I come!"

"With a full ride too."

"I'm so glad there's no debt. College is low-key a scam. So expensive, and all they really do is tell you which books to read."

"But you have to go to college."

"I know! That's what makes it such a good scam."

"Are a lot of your classmates going to Stony Brook too?"

Cassie shakes her head. "Less than you'd think. Van Der Donck is the big leagues when it comes to college apps. The average SAT score is like 1500. I feel like half of my year is going to either NYU or Cornell."

"What are you going to study?"

"I don't know. Maybe computer engineering. That way, I can make a website for the bakery. My mom always says stuff like, 'Our egg tarts are just as good as Fay Da, but Fay Da has a website!' She's always talking about how we need a website." She scratches her chin. "I do wanna try acting more, though. I still think about some scenes from the movie sometimes. How I could have done them differently. I'm not going to major in drama or anything, but I wanna try theater. I want to have the audience right in front of me. I think I'd enjoy the added pressure."

"I'm sure you'd be good at it," I say.

"Maybe. We'll see."

At each pause in the conversation, I fidget with my straw wrapper. The letter is burning a hole through the bottom of the backpack. I didn't plan out when exactly I would give it to her. Right now, the mood feels too casual to drop a bombshell like that. Plus now I'm having doubts about what I wrote—whether I overdid it with that paragraph where I thanked her, whether I struck the wrong balance of sentimentality versus contrition.

"So what do you want to do now?" Cassie asks.

"Are you down to keep hanging out?"

"Sure. I have time, I'm not in a rush to go back. Plus I came all this way."

"Let's walk around."

The moment we go outside, the hot, damp summer air wraps us up in its sticky embrace. By the time we make it back to Main Street, there's already a thin layer of sweat coating my forehead. At the entrance to the mall is a sign advertising a new arcade.

"Oh, man, I wish that had been here when we still lived here. Childhood would have absolutely ruled," I say, admiring the pictures of the arcade machines on the sign.

"Let's go in and cool off," Cassie says.

The AC inside the arcade is on full blast, to the point where after a few minutes, I start to shiver. It's dark; the only lighting comes from the arcade machines and a few strips of purple neon on the ceiling.

By the entrance, there's a big crowd formed around a Dance Dance Revolution machine. The two people playing both look like ordinary Flushing teenagers—a tall, painfully thin boy with a short ponytail, and a slightly older-looking girl wearing athletic leggings and fingerless gloves, like she's here to work out. But once the music starts, everything changes.

"Holy crap, they're like professionals," I whisper. The two of them are both leaning back and gripping the metal railing, moving their feet with inhuman speed and accuracy. The arrows telling them where to step are racing up the screen faster than the brain should be able to process, and yet as we watch, every step is either "Great" or "Perfect."

"There are so many different ways to dedicate your life," Cassie marvels. "Once you find your thing, there's no limit to how much time you can spend getting good at it."

Deeper inside the arcade, we each sit down behind the wheel of a racing game, for one last head-to-head competition.

"Are you good at these driving games?" I ask as I test out the steering wheel and tap on the foot pedal.

"I'm not telling you. Never reveal your strength to your enemy before the battle begins. Pretty sure that's in *The Art of War*."

After we're done, we head back out into the heat and walk toward the Flushing Community Center.

"Are you going to keep dyeing your hair in college?" I ask.

Cassie chuckles. "Funny you should ask. This was definitely meant to be a one-time thing. But I was thinking, having this hair is going to change what kind of first impression I make. I feel like people will think of me as that edgy girl who dyes her hair. A rebel. After that, it would be kind of a letdown to go back to normal."

"Can't go disappointing your fans like that."

At the community center, we go looking for Coach Fang so that Cassie can say hi to him one last time. But when we go into the basement, he isn't there.

"He went to visit his daughter's family in New Jersey this weekend," Assistant Coach Gao explains. "They just had their first child. Coach Fang is a grandfather now."

"Wow! Well, that's too bad, this was probably my best chance to see him," Cassie says, looking momentarily disappointed. But then she smiles. "It's great to hear that he got to reach that milestone, though. It probably means a lot to him to be a grandparent."

"I'll tell him you stopped by. I remember you. You and Felix played against each other last year. It was a good match."

When we get back outside, I start to feel sad. I know that the afternoon is almost over, that I have to say goodbye soon.

"Hey, is your old house close to here?" Cassie asks.

"Not really. It's by the park."

"Wanna stop by?"

"You sure? It's kind of far."

"Yeah, why not? I still have time. And I'm having fun."

"Yeah, me too. All right, let's go. I don't think I've been back at all since we moved."

We walk down Main Street, away from the crowds of restaurant-goers and grocery shoppers. It's a route that I must have walked hundreds of times with my parents, but I'm surprised at how unfamiliar it feels. I hardly recognize any of the businesses; maybe they've changed, or maybe I didn't pay enough attention when I was here before.

The walk is shorter than I remembered. Cassie and I cut through the park and emerge in a neighborhood of compact townhouses.

"It's this one," I say. We stop in front of my old house. It's strange—over the last few years, there have been plenty of times when I ached to be back here, like it held some secret missing piece that we'd mistakenly left behind. Now that I'm here, it looks smaller and shorter than I remember. You could lean over the rail of the second-floor balcony and practically high-five someone standing at the front door.

"So this is where it all began," Cassie says. "It's nice that you grew up so close to that big park."

"Yeah, we used to walk on this one trail through the woods every weekend. Our old grocery store is just down the street too. If you go up a few more blocks, there's a big Hindu temple, with a food court in the basement."

"No kidding."

Someone else's car is parked in the driveway, and seeing it there gives me a feeling of unease. It's weird to think that there's a new family that calls this place home, that they're inside at this very moment, living in our old rooms.

"Let's walk away before they notice us," I say. "They'll get creeped out if they catch us staring."

We turn away and start to walk back the way we came.

"I'm glad I got to see it," Cassie says. "This is where the legendary piano prodigy Felix Ma got his start."

"It's weird being back. I guess I always think of that house as this perfect, golden place, where I was safe. But then in person it's just a house, and it's kind of small too. It doesn't feel like it belongs to me anymore."

"It's still a part of you." Cassie smiles. "Just not the most important part."

When we reach the park again, we linger by the entrance of the trail that I mentioned, but we don't go in. With nothing else to do, we start to head back toward downtown.

Now it's really almost over. My mind walks on far ahead of us, and I picture the crowds on the sidewalk, the shoppers coming in and out of the stores, the green railing at the subway entrance where we'll say goodbye. The final grains of sand are trickling out of the hourglass.

The return journey on Main Street is much too short. By the time we reach the arcade, I find myself thinking that we couldn't possibly have arrived back so quickly, that we must have been speed walking without my noticing. I want to stop in my tracks, cry out, "Wait, this isn't right, I'm not ready!"

"Well, I guess this is it," Cassie says. We're on the corner of Roosevelt Avenue and Main Street, and the subway station is right below our feet.

"Uh, one sec," I say. I take off my backpack and fumble with the zipper. "I have something for you. I wrote you a letter."

She raises an eyebrow, and a small, ironic smile dances across her face. "A letter? But I'm right here. We can just talk. Unless you're going to read it to me?"

My courage falters a little. I definitely didn't plan on reading my own words aloud. "Well, it's more of a goodbye letter. Something to mark this day, you know? Maybe something you can remember me by, I guess."

I pull out the letter and extend it to Cassie, unsure what comes next. She studies the envelope, smiling at the cursive Cassie written on the back, brushing her fingers over the piece of tape I used to secure the flap because the adhesive was too old and dried to stick. The roar of an arriving subway train fills my ears, drowning out all other noise.

Finally she holds the envelope back out to me.

"Keep it, Felix," she says.

"Keep it?" I blink. "Aren't you going to open it?"

"Yes, of course I am. Eventually. But not yet. So I'm asking you to keep it. For now."

"For now," I repeat. My body feels weightless, like I might start levitating. I'm not sure what's going on, but I don't feel afraid.

"You know what's funny, Felix? I've lost people in my life. People that really, really mattered. But for some reason, I'm not worried about losing you. I mean, think about it. What were the odds that we'd ever meet at all? One in ten thousand? A million? But we did. We saw each other at the piano competition, and then literally a week later we saw each other at the Met. And then we met again at the Ping-Pong tournament. I mean at some point, even a cynic like me has to admit that the universe is clearly pulling us together."

She remembers running into me at the Met. A dam breaks inside my chest, and all of a sudden I feel happiness rocketing like a blown-out oil well.

"My point is, I want that letter. I'm just asking you to hold on to it for me. Give it to me when I see you again. I'm one hundred and fifty percent sure that I will."

I swallow a lump in my throat, nod, and put the letter away.

"Not to one-up you or anything, but I have something for you too. And you have to accept it, because if you tell me to hold off, then I'll accuse you of plagiarism." She winks. Out of her bag, she pulls out a beat-up old Ping-Pong paddle, with a red ribbon tied around the grip. So she had her own gift prepared too. Gaspard isn't the only one who likes a send-off.

"You remember how I got the Mandate of Heaven, right? I had to beat the old man in the basement with the chalkboard. 'For whomsoever shall defeat the holder of the Mandate of Heaven shall thereby come into its possession.' Those are the rules. Well, Felix, I gave you my best shot, but for once in your life, you managed to come up clutch against me. That means this paddle rightfully belongs to you."

She hands me the paddle, and I turn it over in my hands. The rubber is coming off, and on the wood underneath, Cassie has

339

written her name in blue ink, with the number one. Next to it is a blank spot with a number two, where I'm meant to write my name.

Yeah, she outdid me. Of course she did. This is Cassandra mother-freaking Chow, for crying out loud. Did I expect anything less?

"This was a good gift," I say.

"Yeah, I know. Good speech too, right?"

I look at her again, and this time it hits me that she's about to go. All that's left until then is the goodbye. I can feel the lines of my face wavering, threatening to come undone.

"Good luck with everything next year," I say, my voice cracking a little. "Not that you need it. I'll just be sad that you're not here. Not sad, exactly. I mean, I'll . . . miss you. Yeah, I'll miss you."

"All right, all right, bring it in," Cassie says.

She pulls me in for a hug, and I want to memorize it, take all of the sensations of this moment and fold them away, to take out when I need them again. If only.

In just a few minutes, she'll head down underground, and I'll watch her black-and-orange hair disappear down the stairway. The arc of my life will bend away from hers, and time will go on and on, as time does. Eventually, perhaps, our paths across Planet Earth will point back toward each other, and the distance will close, until we're together again. No, not perhaps. They *will*. I know they will.

But for now, we're both still here. There's no distance between us. That euphoric state that I always seem to be trying to reach when I'm with her—for once, I'm in it, and I think she is too. You don't get a moment like this every day. Maybe you only get a couple per lifetime. So the only thing left to do is to burrow deep into the moment, inhabit it, stretch it out, make it last as long as it can.

So I do.

ACKNOWLEDGMENTS

THANKS TO PATRICE CALDWELL, SARAH GER-ton, and the rest of the team at New Leaf Literary for your guidance and expertise. Many thanks to my editor, Jen Ung, for all of the great feedback and encouragement. Working with you always helps me bring the story that's in my head out onto the page, and for that I'm grateful.

Thanks to Leslie Teng for being my first and kindest reader. You always help me find confidence and excitement in my work. And thanks to my friends Bharat Chandar and Michelle Zhao for reading early versions of this book and giving helpful suggestions.

Thanks to my parents for raising me, buying me books, and helping me out with the Mandarin in this text.

Thanks to Catherine and Richard for taking care of me on weekend trips to Plainview. Mr. Teng, your consulting company was the inspiration for the college coach in this book, but of course, you provide much more thoughtful and empathetic counsel than Mr. Qin does.

For the rest of the team at Quill Tree Books and HarperCollins Children's: Kathy Lam and Joel Tippie, thank you for turning my Google Docs into beautifully designed physical objects. Special thanks to Jacqueline Li for the cover art! I love all of the little details and Easter eggs you put in. Thanks to Shona McCarthy and Laaren Brown for finding all my typos and fixing all my commas. Thanks also to Sean Cavanagh, Suzanne Murphy, Jean McGinley, Lisa Calcasola, Patty Rosati, Kelly Haberstroh, Kerry Moynagh, Tara Feehan, and Laura Raps.

And finally, thank you, dear reader, for reading this book!